PRAISE FOR JAMES NEWMAN!

"A beautifully written adult story of murder and a boy. Grimly true-to-life, evocative and compelling. I love it!"
—Piers Anthony, author of *On a Pale Horse*

"James Newman has written a smashing dark debut that kept me turning pages right through to the end."
—Ed Gorman, author of *Black River Falls*

"Most dark fiction comes across like empty chocolates—you take a bite in eager anticipation and then find out there's no filling. But James Newman is a literary confectioner of near-legendary generosity."
—Peter Crowther, author of *The Longest Single Note*

THAT NIGHT

I never even told my brother, Dan, about my Secret Place. I don't know why. I'm sure my big brother would have understood, would have shared fond memories with me of his own Secret Places when he was my age . . . yet the Old Shack and the Well were the only things in the world not even *Dan* knew about me. And that made my Secret Place all the more special.

A single room. One filthy, moth-eaten mattress. And lots of mosquitoes. They were all you'd find inside my Secret Place. But I didn't mind. I never stayed more than a couple of hours. I think I feared if my Old Shack got too familiar it might lose its special magic.

It never did. It never lost its magic.

After the night of August 5, 1977, however, it sure as hell lost its appeal.

Forever.

MIDNIGHT RAIN

JAMES NEWMAN

LEISURE BOOKS   NEW YORK CITY

To Glenda: I love you.
And to Jenny O., who never let me quit.

LEISURE BOOKS ®

August 2004

Published by

Dorchester Publishing Co., Inc.
200 Madison Avenue
New York, NY 10016

ISBN 0-8439-5389-6

The name "Leisure Books" and the stylized "L" with design are trademarks of Dorchester Publishing Co., Inc.

Printed in the United States of America.

Visit us on the web at www.dorchesterpub.com.

ACKNOWLEDGMENTS

The author would like to thank the following very special people for their infallible support and encouragement: Mom, Dad, Teresa, Kim Levi, Joseph Guice, Jeff Corriher, Kevin Storch, Paul Miller and Earthling Publications, Andy Monge, Donn Gash, M. J. Euringer, Mark Sieber, James Futch, and Brian Keene.

Also, "Newt"—who may have been the very first fan.

MIDNIGHT RAIN

Prologue

Do you remember the exact moment at which your childhood ended?

I do.

For most of us, it is impossible to pinpoint that single *instant* when we became adults. We treasure the memories both perfect and bittersweet, reminisce on old friends and days gone by. We can't remember how it all ended—despite an infallible belief, once upon a time, that it never *could* end—but it did. Eventually.

We hold on to the memories leading up to that point as best we can. We pray they will never fade, because when they do the magic is gone. That's when we grow old.

Or go mad.

This is the way *my* childhood ended. . . .

Not when I got my driver's license. Or the first time I tried marijuana.

Nor did it end with that initial teenage taste of sex—awkward groping up at Storch's Rim, my home-town's rendezvous point for young lovers with raging hormones and an indifference toward patrolling lawmen.

The day the North Carolina school system deemed me an adult with a fancy certificate and a clammy handshake from Principal Colin Maxwell meant little in regards to the death of *my* boyhood.

It was nothing so prosaic as all that, in a town called Midnight.

It happened on August 5, 1977. One month after my twelfth birthday.

What I saw that night changed me, forever altered the way I look at other people and the masks they sometimes wear.

Do you remember the exact moment at which your childhood ended?

I do. . . .

That was the night I witnessed the murder of a young lady named Cassandra Belle Rourke.

August 5

Chapter One

I remember wondering several times if it would ever stop raining, during those two dark weeks in '77.

Even when the booming thunder grew silent for a while, when the lightning did not illuminate my hometown every few seconds like brief glimpses of daylight after dusk, all my old haunts around Midnight, North Carolina, seemed doomed to bask in that gray autumn chill forever.

It just kept *raining*.

The storm seemed destined to never end, as if one day my town might drown beneath it all, float belly-up and drift off to some other place far away. . . .

After what happened, I almost wished it would.

"Danny. Hey, Dan, man . . . you awake?"

The sounds of blankets rustling, a bedspring squeaking. A groan from my big brother.

I shook him again, whispered his name with a tad more urgency. Part of me envied Dan as I watched him come to, coveted his ability to doze without images of death and violence filling his dreams. It didn't seem fair.

Of course, he hadn't seen the things I'd seen. He hadn't witnessed what I witnessed.

"D-Dan, wake up," I said. My lower lip trembled as I tried my best not to cry.

I shook him again.

"Um-merzgrhl," said Dan.

"Wake up. Please?"

I used to think Dan could sleep through a nuclear war (getting him awake was "like tryin' to shake the brown off shit," Mom used to say, and that wasn't too far from the truth). There were times when I carried on lengthy conversations with him only to discover later that he'd been half-conscious the entire time and remembered not a word of them.

Finally he opened one eye, squinted up at me. "Kyle? What's going on?"

"I'm scared." It was all I could think of to say at first. My voice was thick with oncoming tears, my head filled with the lingering crimson images of the awful things I had seen earlier that night.

Dan yawned, sat up, squinted at the clock on his nightstand. "Jeez, man. It's two-thirty in the morning. You know I got that thing tomorrow."

"I know," I said. I sniffled, let out a frightened little moan in the darkness, and plopped down on the bed beside him. "I'm sorry."

A flicker of lightning outside Dan's window suddenly lit up the room, and my big brother resembled something malevolent looming before me. He was a black shape in the night for those next few seconds, a tall silhouette with its hand on my knee . . . but then the thunder that followed was weak, distant, and he was just my brother again.

Dan yawned again. He tossed the covers from

atop his body and scooted closer toward me. "What's the matter, bro? You in some kind of trouble?"

Tears gathered in the corners of my eyes. *Oh, Dan . . . if you only knew. . . .*

"Didn't ride your bike through old Ms. Mertzer's flowerbed again, did you?"

"Huh-uh."

"Samantha Barrett caught you peeking through her bedroom window! I knew you'd get busted one day, loverboy."

"No," I said, through clenched teeth. "It wasn't anything like that, Dan. It wasn't anything like that at all."

Dan said, "Turn on the light, Kyle. Tell me what's going on."

For another minute or two I just sat there. I didn't ever want to leave my brother's side. But then he nudged me, and I staggered over to turn on the light. Any other time I got a chuckle out of that face-plate on Dan's light switch—a cartoon drawing of a well-hung pervert opening his trench-coat, the switch his vulgar knob exposed for all to see—but this time I just stared at it blankly before returning to sit beside Dan on the bed.

"Aghh, God." My brother pretended to shriek in agony when the lights came on.

In a daze I glanced around his room, at all those trophies from his high school basketball team, at his movie posters (his favorites at the time: *Rocky, Jaws,* and *Kentucky Fried Movie*) and pin-ups of rock stars like Led Zeppelin and Aerosmith. My teary gaze lingered longest on the Farrah Fawcett centerfold above his stereo. Farrah wore a pink one-piece bathing suit in that glossy photograph. Her lips were pursed and she stared at the camera with a hungry expression I would recognize years later as "bedroom eyes." The picture was signed, but a crooked DISCO

SUCKS bumper sticker covered the "Stu" to whom it had been personalized (Dan had purchased the poster at a yard sale for a nickel). The closer I came to puberty the more infatuated I became with that picture, with Farrah's supple curves and hints of exposed woman-flesh, but this time I stared right through the model. She might as well have been dead and blue up there.

Dead and blue . . .

Outside, the autumn rain continued as if it might never cease.

"Shit," Dan said, rubbing gritty sleep from his eyes. "Eight o'clock's gonna come real early." He yawned again, loud, took a second to scratch his crotch before staring at me with one eyebrow cocked. "So what's the matter, little bro? You have a nightmare or something?"

Dan was eighteen years old, a recent graduate of Gerald R. Stokely High. God only knows why I turned out the runt and he had always been the gangly basketball player type, but my big brother stood six-foot-three at last count, and Mom often said he was gonna keep growing till his head burst right through the ceiling. He had our father's deep blue eyes—the only visible trait from Dad that I can claim as well—and a head of sandy-blond hair he wore in one of those "bowl-cut" styles.

Dan had been pondering a career in gynecology. Gynecology or politics, he hadn't decided which. It was the sort of thing folks liked to tease him about ("one wrong move and you're in deep shit either way," his friend Chris said one night and, although I didn't get it then, I giggled like it was the funniest thing I ever heard), but Dan never joked about his future. In less than seven hours on the night in question he was scheduled to board a plane headed to

Tallahassee, Florida, where he would spend the next four years as a student of Florida State University. I don't think I have to tell you my thoughts on *that* matter. The whole town seemed to idolize my big brother, the way he'd earned that basketball scholarship with little effort. He had become a sort of local hero. I, however, could not get past my own selfish desire to keep him in Midnight forever. I honestly felt, as the moment of Dan's departure grew closer, that my life would end the second he left me behind.

"Is something wrong, Kyle?" he asked me again. "What's up?"

I could hold it in no longer. The dam inside of me broke at last, and a flood of tears began streaming down my face like the rain at my brother's bedroom window.

"Hey . . . Kyle . . . ?"

Dan had been sleeping in his Fruit-of-the-Looms and that baggy orange tank top with the big green 12 on it from his varsity basketball team. When he put his arm around me I couldn't help but notice a musky odor about him beneath his sweaty sleep-smell and faint aroma of aftershave. It was a smell I would later in life recognize as the salty scent of sex.

"D-Dan," I said, watching my hands fidget in my lap like pale creatures with minds of their own. "If I t-tell you something . . . do you p-promise not to tell anybody?"

"Sure, man." He grinned, rubbed the top of my head with mock-roughness. "Unless, of course, you're gonna confess you're a fag. Then I'll have to tell the world."

Normally I would have giggled high and loud at that. I'm sure I would have frogged my big brother on the arm, called him "butt-wad" or "ass-lick." But Dan realized I was in no mood for jokes the second the words were out of his mouth. His smile faded and his brow furrowed as he waited for me to tell my story.

"You gotta promise, Dan," I whispered. "Swear it . . . you can't tell *anybody*."

"Okay, I promise! Cross my heart and all that jive! Jeez, man—what *is* it?"

At last I told him, all rapid-fire words running together because otherwise I feared I might never get it out:"*LastnightaftertheAppleGalaIsawagirlgetmurdered*."

For those next seconds the only sound between us was the muffled drone of the rain upon our roof. A quiet but steadily building soundtrack for my own personal horror movie just beginning.

Finally, Dan said, "You're not kidding around, are you, Kyle? Good God. You're serious."

"I'm serious."

"Does anyone else know about this?"

I shook my head.

"Not even Mom?"

"Especially not Mom."

"Who was it?" Dan asked.

"What?"

He bit at his thumbnail, spat a pale sliver of it across the room, but never took his eyes off me. "The . . . girl. Who was she?"

I wiped at my dripping nose with the collar of my Spider-Man pajamas. "I don't know. She . . . looked kinda familiar, I guess. But I'm not sure. Her face . . . oh, God, Danny . . . her f-face. It was . . . a-all *messed up*."

I stared down at my feet, studied my big toe poking through a hole in my left sock. For some reason I suddenly found it hard to make eye contact with Dan. As if *I* had done something wrong. Even Farrah glared down at me accusingly from her place upon the wall, and I wished she would stop.

"We gotta tell somebody," Dan said.

I quickly looked back up at him. *"We?"*

"Sure. You don't think you're gonna be alone in this, do you? I'm with ya, little bro. All the way."

"No," I said. "That's why I made you promise. I can't tell *anyone*."

"First thing in the morning, we'll talk to Sheriff Baker. I'll go with you, tell him what you saw. My plane doesn't leave till ten. The sheriff can—"

"No, Danny! No! You don't understand!"

My brother flinched beneath my harsh tone. "Shh. Okay. Easy. Why don't you tell me exactly what happened. . . ."

"He was *there*, Dan," I whispered. "The sheriff was *there*."

Dan went pale. My big brother—my rock, my role model, my portrait of strength when I had nowhere else to turn—looked like he'd been punched in the face.

"Sheriff Baker killed that girl. He *murdered* her. I saw it with my own two eyes."

Chapter Two

Midnight, North Carolina, held its Annual Apple Gala every year during the first weekend in August. It was such an exciting time for the whole town, I remember, and each festival seemed infinitely better than the last. It hardly mattered that, as adolescence dawned, I outgrew the Free Fire Engine Rides, the Dunk-Your-Teachers Booth ("All Proceeds Go To United Way!"), and the one-time allure of the Miniature Petting Zoo sponsored by the Futch Bros. Dairy outside of town. Although I eventually reached an age at which I considered myself far too "cool" to enjoy the silly antics of the Gala's clowns and the cheap noisemakers those grease-painted jesters tossed to the masses of fun-drunk children, that point was moot. Everyone, of all ages, loved Midnight's Annual Apple Gala. Vendors hawked delicious cotton candy, caramel apples, and fat funnel cakes throughout the two-day affair. All along the sidewalks of Main Street aspiring artists hawked their homemade crafts, competing nonstop with dozens of other amateur dollmakers, caricaturists, and whittlers for the dollars of the masses. I often reminisce on those spectacular days, and I can hear the innocent laughter of children beneath the wackier, louder chuckling of the dancing clowns (local retirees like Greta Morgan, Hap Somerside and Marvin Creedle, folks who dressed up every year "just for the kiddies" and seemed to have the time of their lives just playing young again). I can still hear the phantom tones of the Gerald R. Stokely High School Band, with their off-key renditions of songs I did not know (the theme from *Star Wars* excepted, of course) but which somehow seemed familiar. And of course the smells . . . oh, the smells! *Autumn* smells, I have always thought of them since. Those mouth-watering aromas seemed to linger about Midnight for several weeks after the Gala's conclusion, and to this day they conjure images in my head of tiny hands sticky with cotton candy, paper nacho boats steaming with mounds of hot yellow cheese, and humongous apples impaled upon Popsicle sticks dripping with sticky strands of caramel.

My God, what a grand time we all had! Midnight's Annual Apple Gala was the dying summer's grand finale, its glorious *swansong* if you will, as well as our town's boisterous welcome to the autumn that took its place.

They were the greatest days of my childhood, those annual celebrations. Such perfect memories.

Once upon a time.

On the night of August 5, 1977, I rode with my big brother to the Apple Gala, as was tradition every year. This time, however, Dan informed me—with a sly wink and a suggestive waggling of his tongue— that I should make myself scarce after the Gala.

Seems he and Julie, the girl he'd been dating for a couple of years, planned to pay one last visit up to Storch's Rim before he left for college. I took his hint, could even appreciate Dan's motives in some way I was as yet unable to comprehend. Of course, I especially didn't mind the whole plan since Dan loaded up my Schwinn bicycle in the back of his pick-up, assuring me that if I promised not to tell Mom I could ride home by myself after the Gala. How I used to cherish that spectacular sense of freedom I felt when secretly cruising through Midnight on my bike late at night. Dan insisted I return home by ten o'clock, though, a stipulation he sternly imposed with one long, skinny finger in my face. He rarely talked down to me, but when he really meant something—God, that was when he looked most like our father.

He was my hero, my idol. If I grew up to be half as cool as my big brother, I used to think, I'd make it all right in the world.

So we shook on it. Dan gave my wrist a minor Indian burn "to consummate the deal" and we swore Mom would never know a thing. This covered Dan's "scorin' some poontang," he said, as well as my "gallyvantin' through the woods like some kinda little monkey." As long as I promised to be home by ten, everything would be kosher.

Kosher. Dan used to say that a lot, and I never knew what the hell it meant.

In any event, I knew I had to stick by my word. God forbid Mom ever found out her youngest son had ventured through the Snake River Woods alone. Or that Dan had allowed me to do so.

She would undoubtedly kill us both. Slowly.

With our mother, that was only *slightly* an exaggeration.

* * *

There's something I should tell you about Darlene Mackey. I'm not ashamed of it, though in those days you would have been hard-pressed to get me to talk about it at all.

My mother was an alcoholic, a die-hard alcoholic who would continue to be such until the day she died. It was that very disease that killed her, in fact. Don't get me wrong—I loved my mother. I know she did the best she could under the circumstances, raising my brother and me all by herself. She worked long, hard hours in the local woodworking plant to support her family. But nothing had been quite the same in the Mackey household since the day that man in Dad's division showed up decorated with all his fancy stripes and medals to tell Mom her husband was dead. I think after my father died she built a frigid wall around her heart so nothing could get in or out. And she turned to the bottle to help her deal with it all.

Neither Dan nor I ever said anything to Mom about her problem. Perhaps we should have tried during some rare moment when she was sober, but we knew it would only start another fight. If Mom was happy, see, *everyone* was happy. If she was pissed, she could be the nastiest person you ever met. Her disease seemed to hang over our odd little trio like some invisible veil, slowly smothering the family but never quite killing us all the way. We could see it, we could smell it, and God knows we felt it all over us like walking through spiderwebs in the forest. But there wasn't a damned thing we could do about it.

If I may digress for a moment, I remember an incident several months before the Apple Gala when Mom was at her worst. . . .

I'd gotten up to grab a snack in the middle of the night. Some milk and cookies, maybe a Twinkie. I made my way down the hall, turned the corner, but froze when I entered the living room.

Mom sat in Dad's old armchair in the center of the room, her mousy brown hair for once not tied into a neat little bun but flowing to her shoulders like muddy rapids. Her baggy pink nightgown seemed to swallow her whole. Her cheeks had that ruddy pink glow they always got when she'd been drinking. Lightning flickered beyond the big bay window on the far side of our living room every few seconds, casting a strobe-light effect upon her statuesque form.

She was so, so . . . *still*.

The rain started then, a heavy downpour that pelted the roof like scampering feet, and I squinted in the darkness to see that Mom held a photograph of my father. She gripped its shiny gold frame in one hand so tightly her knuckles seemed to glow bone-white in the flashes of angry lightning outside. In her other hand she held a bottle of Wild Turkey.

"Help you with something, Kyle?" she said suddenly, and my heart skipped a beat. Her tone wasn't angry, just cold. But she didn't even turn around. As if she had eyes in the back of her head.

"I couldn't sleep," I replied. "Thought I'd, um, grab a bite to eat."

She said nothing for the next few minutes. Just kept staring at that picture of Dad as if in some spooky trance, a photograph I still have of him today: standing in front of a plane in Saigon, looking so regal in his finely pressed fatigues . . . Sergeant First-Class Daniel Emmett Mackey, Sr., decorated war hero, posthumous recipient of the Purple Heart as well as Bronze and Silver Stars. . . .

God, how we missed him. My father had been killed by a sniper's bullet on the other side of the world when I was five years old. They said he died instantly, didn't suffer at all, but that hardly helped us cope with such a loss. As time passed my memories of Dad grew foggy, yet not a day went by when I didn't wish he were around to do with me all the things fathers do with their sons.

Mom turned toward me, took another swig from her bottle. I felt naked beneath her glassy-eyed gaze.

"Where's your brother?" she asked me, her voice flat and lifeless.

"He's in bed, Mom."

She laughed. A low, almost masculine laugh. I stared down at my feet, wondered what was so funny. But now I know. Nothing. It was the liquor, laughing. Laughing at my family, mocking my mother's addiction through its slack-jawed, slurry-voiced slave.

"Mom—"

"Go get him, Kyle. My precious Kyle." She stared at me sweetly, but something about her expression made me feel dirty. It reminded me of the look a ravenous wolf might give a sheep strayed from its flock, seconds before said wolf begins to feast.

"Dan's asleep, Mom. Apparently he got in pretty late."

"Apparently," Mom mocked me. But her voice remained so calm, which made her words all the more chilling. "Go get your brother, Kyle. Wake him up. Now."

With that she turned her back to me again, and resumed her dark ménage a trois with the liquor and Dad's old photograph. End of discussion.

What else could I do? I sighed, staggered down the hallway, dreading what I knew was about to ensue. My heart raced. I felt like such a traitor. It took me several minutes to wake Dan, but finally he sort of sleepwalked out of bed in a pair of yellow boxers and a ratty old Alfred E. Newman ("WHAT, ME WORRY?") T-shirt. He cursed as he followed me, when one of his shins barked against the edge of his bedroom doorway.

I would have preferred to be anywhere on Earth than in the Mackey house that evening. I don't know what got Mom started in the first place. I suppose she'd had a nightmare about Dad, probably rolled over to find that picture of him which looked so much like her firstborn son staring at her from her nightstand. This would have been only a matter of days after all the news programs announced how President Carter had pardoned ten thousand Vietnam draft evaders, and I guess that got Mom brooding on the injustice of it all. Dan tried to talk sensibly with her while she swung her arms and drank from her bottle and swore at him through a spray of spittle that she knew he was "gonna run off to die just like his father" and how did he think his "precious Julie" would like that? It broke my heart. The whole thing ended with Mom ripping Dan's shirt, trying to kick him in the balls while she swung at him and wailed, "You don't care about me or your brother! You're gonna leave us just like that sorry son-of-a-bitch!" until she finally grew too tired to continue.

Dan caught her arms and with my help carefully laid her on the couch to sleep it off. Within a matter of seconds she was out like nothing had ever happened.

Dan looked at me, sighed.

"You okay, little bro?" he asked me.

"I'm fine," I said. "You're the one I'm worried about."

"It's cool," he assured me with a sick little laugh. "I'm used to it, ya know?"

And that we were. So used to it.

To say the very least.

* * *

The Snake River Woods—so called because they ran perpendicular to a winding stream on the northern edge of our county named, you guessed it, Snake River—cut through the middle of Midnight, bisecting the town almost perfectly into two halves. On one side lay the town's business district, home to establishments like the Big Pig Grocery, Jack's Hardware, Corriher Guns n' Ammo, and the offices of the *Midnight Sun*; on the other sat Midnight's residential area, where our middle-class homes were nestled in a comfortable sort of juxtaposition that never felt too crowded despite the county's growing population.

The Snake River Woods was one of my favorite places to go in the whole world, my own private domain where I could be alone, I could explore, I could do all the things boys do without adult eyes always watching like something might get broken.

My favorite thing of all was the Old Shack. And the Well.

That's how I saw them in my mind: not just any old shack, not just any well . . . but *the Old Shack*. And *the Well*.

This was my secret place. My *Secret Place*. All boys have a Secret Place, I believe, and the Old Shack was mine.

It sat, far as I knew, smack dab in the middle of the Snake River Woods. My estimate might have been off several hundred yards, of course, but for my purposes the Well and the Old Shack were the perfect landmarks for the halfway point between the business district of Midnight and my home at 2217 Old Fort Road on the opposite side of the forest.

The Old Shack was little more than four slanted walls, a rotting wooden floor, and a battered tin roof. No door. Inside lay a mildewed mattress that had once been white but had long ago gone a sickly yellow-gray. I often wondered if someone used to live there, if he or she had lain upon that mattress as the sounds of the forest lulled him or her to sleep. As improbable as such a thing seemed to me I suppose at one time *someone* had called my Old Shack home. A crotchety old hermit, perhaps. A family of hippies who had turned their backs on the Establishment to live amongst nature, but then abandoned that idea when the Age of Aquarius met its demise. Better yet, I often imagined that my Old Shack might have once been a refuge for runaway slaves in the 1800s, a way station on the Underground Railroad, and such possibilities made me all the more proud of my Secret Place, as if by frequenting the site I somehow became a part of history.

The Well sat eight or nine feet from the eastern wall of my Old Shack. It was an ancient, craggy thing made of fat brown rocks like those bordering the Snake River on the other side of town. It stood even with my belt line in those days, and was about half as wide as my closet back home. Thick moss as soft as a kitten's fur covered most of it (not to mention a plump gray hornet's nest on the side facing my neighborhood); no rope, no bucket, no fancy little roof like one might imagine if one ponders the aesthetics of wells for any length of time. Far as I knew, the thing went all the way to the center of the Earth. Sometimes I would imagine the Morlocks from H. G. Wells's *The Time Machine* living and hunting and doing dark Morlock things down there. I envisioned them looking up at me as I peered down at them, seeing me where I could not see them. It gave me delightful chills, that scenario, the same kind I used to get reading comics like *The Witching Hour* or watching Darren McGavin stalk the night as Kolchak.

I never even told Dan about my Secret Place. I don't know why. I'm sure my big brother would have understood, would have shared fond memories with me of his own Secret Places when he was my age . . . yet the Old Shack and the Well were the only things in the world not even *Dan* knew about me. And that made my Secret Place all the more special.

A single room. One filthy, moth-eaten mattress. And lots of mosquitoes. They were all you'd find inside my Secret Place. But I didn't mind. I never stayed more than a couple of hours. I think I feared if my Old Shack got too familiar it might lose its special magic.

It never did. It never lost its magic.

After the night of August 5, 1977, however, it sure as hell lost its appeal.

Forever.

Chapter Three

Mom never bought us a pet—"nasty things," she called them, especially dogs. Cats were out of the question too because she was allergic to them. I did buy a goldfish once with some birthday money my great aunt Florence sent me (I named him "Pop-Eye," not in honor of any spinach-eating cartoon sailor but because of the animal's huge, buggy eyes, which made old Pop-Eye appear as if he were in a constant state of fishy surprise); that lone pet died mere days after I brought him home, however, when I failed to heed Dan's warnings about overfeeding my aquatic friend with the fragile belly.

Pop-Eye looked famished, had been my argument.

And that was the extent of my childhood experience with pets.

So . . . since we couldn't have pets, I often treated my *bike* like one, weird as that sounds. I always thought bicycles were better than dogs, in fact, because you can ride bikes! I loved mine. I talked to him, treated him like a beloved member of my fam-

ily. I even named him. I called my bicycle Burner.
God only knows how I came up with that. I suppose I
envisioned the bright blue bike as some mighty
rocket from an Isaac Asimov novel, flaring out the
back as it took off faster than light.

Burner was a 1975 Schwinn Scrambler that Mom
had given me for my tenth birthday. He sported a
larger gear than the more streamlined Stingray model
idolized by most kids my age, as well as a razor
fender, a high-flanged front hub, and original BMX-
style handlebars with those hard rubber grips that
made you feel like more than just a kid on a bicycle.
They made you feel like an *adventurer,* a rugged ex-
plorer whose hometown was an uncharted land of
delicious danger just waiting to be conquered.

Burner was fast, too—did I mention that? Oh, yes.
Back then I was quite sure he might have been the
fastest bike ever built. I can't begin to tell you how
many scraped knees and bloody elbows were the results of our adventures around my hometown. Once
I even broke my collarbone over on Orosel Avenue,
when I decided to brave what us kids called Evel
Knievel Hill, but that never stopped me from hopping right back on Burner and doing it all over again.

I never regretted a single moment I shared with my
best friend, even when our adventures resulted in
numerous stitches or the loss of precious lifeblood.

Battle scars, I thought of the many injuries I ob-
tained atop mighty Burner. And that made it all okay.

After the Gala I rode Burner out of Midnight's business district, past the new Kmart Plaza on Harris
Boulevard, down the alley between the Midnight
Drug & Sundry and Hank's Hobby Shop, until I found
our trail. It began behind the vacant lot of an abandoned feed store, a tin building with a rotten loading

dock out front speckled with broken glass and soggy cigarette butts. Burner and I didn't create the trail we used to get to my Old Shack—it had been there as long as I could remember—but we helped keep it a trail. I often imagined that some giant snail had once crawled up from the bowels of the Earth to visit Midnight, but the founders of our town shot at the poor creature simply because they did not understand it. Where our trail began was where the pitiful behemoth had dragged itself into the Snake River Woods to nurse its wounds; where the trail stopped was where it had lain down to die. A crazy story, I know, but it was fun.

As I always did, at the point where the forest swallowed up our path completely, I hopped off Burner and proceeded to walk him the rest of the way. By the time I reached the edge of that grove in the middle of the woods where the Well and the Old Shack sat like old friends awaiting my return, a soft rain had begun to fall on Midnight. My clothes grew damp as Burner and I walked, and my hair soon lay plastered to my skull as if a schoolyard bully had spilled something there during one mean, messy prank.

I picked up my pace.

Finally the Old Shack was upon me, a squat black shape in the darkness that at first resembled a tired old beast stopped in the clearing to catch its breath.

"Here we are," I said to Burner, stopping within a hundred yards or so of the Well. I patted the seat of my beloved bicycle, admired the way his slick blue body glistened in the night's falling rain.

But then, I slowed as I drew closer. As I noticed something about my Secret Place.

Something *wrong*.

I frowned, leaned Burner up against a massive oak

tree to our left. I knelt down beside my bike as if Burner might protect me.

There were lights on in there, inside my Old Shack. Flickering lights, as if from candles or kerosene lanterns.

Someone was inside.

"What the hell?" I whispered.

Never before had I encountered another person intruding upon my Secret Place. It was the first time, in fact, that I had seen *any* sign of civilization this deep in the Snake River Woods, with the exception of an occasional private plane coming in for a landing at the Midnight Independent Hangar. Not only was I *angered* by this invasion of my territory . . .

. . . I knew, immediately, that something *was not right* here.

"Stay here, Burner," I said, as if he might defy the laws of physics to leave me there alone. I suppose I wanted to imagine my bike as a living companion, because somehow that made me feel better about the developments at hand.

Above the whisper of the midnight rain through the trees and the chorus of crickets chirping around me, I could hear at least two different voices coming from inside my Old Shack. . . .

Mumbling, conspiratorial tones. An angry curse every few seconds.

Under that, music. Motown. Tinny, as if on a cheap radio.

Slowly I made my way to the Well, leaving Burner propped against the oak tree behind me. I approached the Old Shack at an angle from which I could see in at least one of its dusty yellow windows, and each step seemed to take hours. I flinched at the horrid crunching of leaves beneath my feet—a sound so terribly loud, so obvious. I knew the intruders inside were bound to hear me.

Finally I reached the Well, knelt down behind it. The rain pattered down inside there like tiny hands clapping against its stone walls. Like ghostly children trying to escape its cold black depths. I held my breath, squinted through the closest window of my Old Shack to see what was afoot. . . .

The blurry tops of two heads were all I could see at first. Two men? Maybe. Until I ventured closer, though, I could not make out their features through that filthy glass. The window was covered with a dusty film, thin gray curtains of cobwebs above a silver-black carpet of dead flies, rat turds, and cricket carcasses.

"What kinda goddamn mess you got us into, Henry?" I heard one of the men say, a deep voice with a gruff Southern accent that sounded very familiar.

I didn't move. I didn't breathe.

"Jesus H. Christ." Deep, basso.

I knew that voice! But from where?

I still didn't move. I still didn't breathe. I listened. Waited.

"I said I was sorry, Dad," came the reply at last. This voice was higher-pitched than the first, whiny. It sounded like a teenager.

"You're *sorry*. I suppose you think that makes everything okay? You fucked up, Henry, and *I'm the one who has to fix this shit!*"

"I know, Dad." The younger voice again. "I wish I could take it back."

That did it. I *had* to see more. Curiosity killed the cat, as the saying goes, but some would argue that inquisitive ol' feline retired from this world so satisfied. . . .

"What a fuckin' mess," said the man inside as I moved closer to the cabin. A cough. "My God."

As I drew closer to my Old Shack, I recognized the Marvin Gaye song playing on the radio inside, a soulful melody so ominously out of place here. Marvin was singing about lovin' and kissin' and sexual healin'.

But then his song went silent in midverse.

"For Chrissake, turn off that nigger shit. I can't even hear myself think."

Several long, quiet minutes passed, ticking by with each clamorous beat of my heart. The shrill chirping of crickets and the steady hiss of the rain around me seemed deafening now, yet neither could drown out the sounds of heavy footsteps on the Old Shack's wooden floor, or the intermittent thumps and scrapes against its interior walls. Every few seconds I heard a labored grunt, as if the two men were moving stuff around in there.

At last I took another cautious step forward, and I could feel the vibrations of their movements beneath my feet, through the muddy ground.

My heartbeat grew more frantic with every passing minute. My brow was slick with sweat.

"This is bad, Henry," came the deeper voice again. "You've really outdone yourself this time."

"I know, Dad." The younger man sounded like he might start crying. "I didn't mean for this to happen."

"We'll have to burn her clothes. Everything. Clean all this shit up till there ain't even a pussy hair left."

That cinched it. No way could I leave without knowing who they were. What they were doing in there. But even at a distance of just several feet from the cabin, I was too short to view more than the tops of the two men's heads through the windows.

Still moving as tentatively as my Great Snail might have once moved, I sneaked around toward the rear of my Old Shack and began searching for something to stand on so I could see inside the filthy windows. In the thick black shadows behind the Old Shack lay several plastic milk crates ... an ancient toilet, cracked and yellow ... a couple of busted Mason jars ... and an old red dog food bowl (BOO, read the name on the side) filled with dead brown pine needles floating in stagnant green water. But then, farther back, I spotted exactly what I needed. A small homemade table constructed from what looked like a tree-stump base and a flat cross-section of a larger stump for its surface. Perfect. If I dragged it over to one of the windows—without making too much noise in the process, of course—I could climb atop it for a perfect view inside my Old Shack.

I grunted as I sat the table upright, bit my tongue so hard I tasted blood. Beneath the scarce light of the night's yellow half-moon I winced at the sight of thousands of earthworms and centipedes and what we used to call gray "roly-poly bugs" churning in the soft ground where the table had lain for years. I tried not to think about black widows and the sorts of places they liked to hide.

I wiped my hands on my shorts, carried the thing with great effort to the side of my Old Shack, careful not to drag it through the leaves.

Several more hoarse curses drifted out the Old Shack and into the woods. The continuous din of heavy footsteps inside kept a sort of counter-rhythm to the furious beat of my heart. I flinched when something slammed into the wall closest to me so hard the whole cabin seemed to shake.

Slowly I crawled atop my makeshift stool, making

sure I was properly balanced before trusting the stump-table with all my weight.

I ran one hand through my rain-damp hair, leaned forward to peer through the window. . . .

And I gasped.

Though I had expected to recognize the men inside, suspected that what they were doing was something far more sinister than playing a friendly game of poker, my jaw dropped as I stared through the spider-web pattern of cracks in that dirty window. . . .

I could see everything now. Much more than I really wanted.

The two men in my Old Shack I did know. They were local men.

Sheriff Burt Baker. And his son, Henry.

I recognized Henry from the Big Pig Grocery on Brady Boulevard, where he worked part time as a bagboy. He looked about twenty years old, give or take, and I suppose the girls his age might have considered him handsome if a tad awkward. His lips were full, red, almost feminine. He had been trying to grow a mustache, apparently, but had experienced scant luck with it so far. He wore his dark brown hair just shy of his shoulders, like Vinnie Barbarino on *Welcome Back, Kotter*. Henry suffered from a slight case of Tourette's Syndrome, I noticed as I stood there watching the men, and though I did not know the name of his affliction at the time, I did recognize that his nervous tics—a twitchy clenching and unclenching of his fists every few minutes followed by a quick upward jerk of his head—weren't normal. By no means was his problem severe, yet he could not have hidden his occasional fidgeting even if he tried.

On the night this all happened, Henry Baker wore

a faded Bruce Springsteen *Born to Run* T-shirt, jeans so tight they looked painful, and a pair of powdery-looking latex gloves.

They both wore gloves, I noticed, as the two men in my Old Shack went about their morbid business. . . .

Sheriff Burt Baker was a tall, stocky man in his mid-forties, a fellow whose khaki uniform never seemed to fit quite right, especially around his gut. His hair was short, black, always looked as if weeks had passed since he last washed it. Though he was Caucasian, far as I knew, his skin was so dark I often wondered if the sheriff's family tree might have branched off at some point from Native American lineage. Baker's cheeks were pock-marked with bad acne scars, his lips were large and almost pouty-looking, and as crude as this may sound, I must admit I considered the sheriff to be one of the most unattractive folks I'd ever met. This opinion grew tenfold, of course, when I saw what ugly things he and his son were up to inside my Old Shack. . . .

They were hard at work moving the body of a young woman. A girl. She could have been no older than fifteen or sixteen, at most. I figured she might have been pretty by the dim light of a kerosene lantern in the middle of the room, her hair long and straight and blond, her figure trim . . . but I couldn't be sure.

Because her face had been battered beyond recognition.

My stomach churned as I gazed upon her ruined features, a pulpy mess of swollen flesh and crimson smears and awful purple bruises. That poor, poor girl. Her breasts were small, nipples very pink against her pale skin, and I saw faint purple bruises around her areoles, along her neck and collarbone, even on the inside of her thighs like dark blotchy fingerprints.

Although I had done nothing wrong here, I felt a sudden pang of gut-wrenching shame. And something else. At the sight of the naked girl I felt a mysterious growing warmth below my belt that I could not explain. It made me sick. And ashamed.

My God, what had they done *to her?*

The sheriff held the dead girl by her arms, Henry by her legs. Her head rolled limply to one side as they propped her up in one corner of the room next to a small battery-powered radio with a bent antenna. In the same corner sat a single kerosene lantern and a scuffed leather jacket I assumed belonged to Henry. Beside the jacket lay a pile of what must have been the dead girl's clothes: a pink skirt with lavender piping, orange blouse, a pair of Keds, panties and a small lace bra. The panties, I noticed, were ripped down one side.

The dead girl's eyes were closed, but I couldn't help noticing how her mouth fell open as the two men plopped her down. Just enough to give me a glimpse of her perfect white teeth and too pink tongue. When they let her go and she hit the floor, her body made a low farting sound.

I covered my mouth with one hand, swallowed back the bitter taste of bile rising in the back of my throat.

Henry Baker stepped away from the body, grimacing. "Aghh, Jesus—"

"It happens," the sheriff grunted, without batting an eye. "Don't worry about it."

For the first time, I noticed the hot-pink scratches that ran from just under Henry Baker's left eye down to his jaw line. Three long, nasty gashes like claw marks from one very pissed-off cat. I touched my own cheek when I saw them, made a low hissing noise through my teeth.

She hadn't gone down without a fight.

The sheriff cleared his throat, made a sound like hawking up phlegm though he never expelled it from his mouth. "Son of a bitch. Did you ever fuck up this time, Henry . . ."

Henry turned to look at his father, but when he found himself facing the dead girl again his gaze quickly averted to his shoes.

Sheriff Baker's hands went to his hips as he stared at his son accusingly. I knew that pose well—it was the sheriff's authoritarian pose, the one he took when watching out-of-town drunks do their clumsy walks along the white line, the getting-down-to-business stance he assumed while standing over the loser of a scuffle down at Lou's Tavern. It was the posture of a well-respected man, Polk County's elected keeper of the peace.

"Please just tell me you didn't take her to the Gala," he said. His voice sounded as if he were in pain. "Tell me nobody saw you two together."

"Just that black guy, with the wagon," Henry said.

"What black guy?"

"One they call Rooster."

"You talkin' about that retard, walks around collectin' cans?"

"Yeah."

"Shit!" Sheriff Baker's hands balled into fists. He covered his mouth with one, gnashed his teeth, looked as if the world had just dropped out from under him. "Goddammit, Henry!"

"It's okay, Dad. He ain't gonna say anything. It was dark. I don't know if he even saw us. You know that nigger's always in his own little world anyway." Henry risked a self-conscious giggle at that, but then covered his mouth as if to force it back in should his quip rekindle the flames of his father's rage.

The sheriff pointed one fat finger at his son, looked like he might scold the boy some more, but didn't. He arched his back till his bones popped like kernels of popcorn, shook his head slowly before eyeing the long furrows in Henry's raw red cheek. A cruel smile crept through his stern expression.

"Got you good, didn't she?"

Henry's hand went to his wounded face. He winced.

The sheriff's chuckle was so deep it was nearly inaudible.

Suddenly lightning lit up the forest, and for a moment everything around me seemed basked in daylight. Thunder rumbled a few seconds later like the sonic boom of an invisible airplane hitting Mach 1 above the woods, and the rain began to pick up, harder. I flinched beneath Mother Nature's fury, tensed as I saw the two men inside do the same.

The sheriff turned toward the window through which I peered, his cold blue eyes narrowed.

I froze, my teeth clenched like those of a stray dog kicked in the ribs. My heart slammed in my chest. The scent of ozone tickled my nostrils, making me want to sneeze. For a second I could have sworn Sheriff Baker looked right at me. Right *through* me. His bad complexion appeared rougher than ever during that moment, the way the light struck those old acne scars on his cheeks and the shadows of his surroundings danced about his pitted flesh. His face resembled something carved from thick red clay with a blunt tool, all blotchy and coarse and hard.

Finally he turned back to his son, and I could breathe again.

"Didn't you learn your lesson the last time?" The sheriff's voice cracked a bit, as if he were so disappointed in this child he had raised to do the right thing. "I mean, after what happened . . . for Chrissake, you'd think . . ."

He trailed off, shaking his head.

Henry said nothing, just kept staring at the floor. He gave a little shrug. His right hand clenched and unclenched three times fast within its rubber glove. Then his left, once.

"You're absolutely *positive* no one saw you two together?" his father asked him.

"Swear to God."

"Just the nigger?"

"Just the nigger."

"Where's the Ford?"

"What?"

"Your fuckin' truck, Henry! We ain't got all night."

"That vacant lot across from the ABC Store," Henry replied, sounding fatigued. He followed this with some unintelligible mumble.

Sheriff Baker stood there scratching at his bumpy brown chin for the next few minutes, thinking over every detail of his scheme.

The rain tapped hard at the shack's cheap tin roof like someone dropping ten-penny nails from the heavens. I strained to listen to the goings-on inside my Old Shack, but the rain began to fall harder. Louder.

"We're gonna fix this, Henry," said Sheriff Baker. "We're gonna fix this, and it's gonna be okay."

Henry watched his father move across the room. Tears glistened in his eyes. But he said nothing.

"I got an idea. I think it'll work. But we gotta move

fast. Come on. Grab her legs again. We're gonna take her to my patrol car."

On weak knees, Henry moved to obey.

They hefted the body between them.

And that's when it happened, as if on cue.

That's when the dead girl came alive.

Chapter Four

She sat up with a blood-curdling shriek so horrendous I not only heard it, I felt it in my bones as well. It was the most terrible thing I had ever heard, the scream of every victim in every horror movie I ever watched with Dan at the Lansdale Drive-In on Forster Boulevard. The girl's arms flailed about, groping for nothing and everything at once as she shot to her feet and flew across the room, heading for the door, her limbs jerking madly and her naked breasts jiggling and her hellish wail never abating, while Burt and Henry Baker stood frozen in shock. I suppose it would have been quite comical had the situation been different, those two evil men in my Old Shack looking like they had dropped huge brown loads in their pants. Henry backed away from the screaming dead girl in short, stiff little steps until he slammed against the far wall of the shed with a pained grunt. He babbled something that sounded like "OhmyGodohJesusshe'sstilla-fuckin'-*live*," and I saw a dark wet patch in the crotch of the teenager's jeans that had not been there seconds before.

"Fuck me!" Sheriff Baker spat, whirling toward the girl. *"FUCK!"*

And then, before I realized what was happening, she was in the sheriff's burly arms. God, how fast he moved for such a big man. He jerked the girl up like a lifeguard grasping hold of a drowning victim, as if he only meant to help her, and he whispered something to her as he moved, something like "no, no, come here, honey, don't fight it now, it's gonna be okay." She fought bravely, her bruise-mottled legs kicking and thrashing in the air as he hoisted her several feet off the ground, her arms slapping at him even though she could not see him behind her with her dirty blond hair in her eyes, and all the while that horrible shriek continued.

"Fuckin'-A, Henry!" Sheriff Baker barked between labored breaths as he fought to keep the girl in his arms. "I thought you said she was fuckin' *dead!*"

I could barely hear Henry's replies beneath the girl's banshee screams, his hissing spit-wet stammer: "I th-thought she was. . . . J-Jesus, Daddy . . . I thought she *wasssz*. . . ."

As fast as it all began, it was over. Suddenly *over*, just like that . . . as if the girl had never gotten up at all from her place in the Old Shack's corner. I barely noticed my clothes dampening with every passing second, never noticed the rain growing stronger all around me or the constant strobe-flicker of the lightning looming so close, as Sheriff Baker gave his son a disgusted look, a cock-eyed expression that seemed to say *if you want something done right you might as well do it yourself* . . . and then he gripped the screeching girl's head between his huge hands and jerked it violently to one side, back toward him and all the way up to his left. I will never forget the sickening *CRACK!* that seemed to fill the woods when he broke her neck—I could feel it in my teeth! One second that poor girl was alive, screaming and twitching like a marionette on some insane puppeteer's invisible strings . . . and then she was *gone*. Her body went limp again, a stream of bright yellow piss ran down the inside of one naked leg, and her eyes went empty as her life was taken—sweet Christ, it had been *stolen*—by the sheriff of our town. By Sheriff Burt Baker.

My knees didn't go weak; they instantly seemed to not exist. Vomit rushed up the back of my throat and maybe a little even escaped from between my lips as my legs did their own thing below, falling out from under me like two weak little twigs unable to hold my weight. I stumbled backwards, sliding on the rain-slick face of that stump-table beneath me. I heard myself, an almost disembodied sound that seemed to come from someone else, gasping "Ohhh!" as my makeshift ladder was thrown off balance, and with the center of gravity—*me*—no longer where it should have been, the table tipped over onto the ground, taking me with it. *Nonono nononoNO*, is all I remember going through my head—a hundred, a million times—as I seemed to fall forever away from the window. I watched it recede from my desperately clutching fingertips as if the shed were moving instead of me, before my ass finally hit a patch of wet leaves and the bottom of the table thumped up hard—so horribly *loud*—against the wall of the Old Shack.

A muddy earthworm smell assaulted my nostrils. I gagged, coughed. Cold drops of rain struck me in the face as I struggled to get up.

"What the fuck was that?"

Sheriff Baker. He had heard me.

"Holy shit, Henry! Somebody's out there!"

The air grew thick with not only the crackling ozone smell of lightning, with the earthy smell of rain and mud, but also the sweaty stench of my own terror.

"Goddammit, boy, don't just sit there! *Go!*"

"OhJesusohJesusohJesus," I whispered again and again as I got up, and I could hear Henry Baker stammering the same thing inside.

I tried to get up. I tried to run. I could already hear their boots inside, heading for the door, Sheriff Baker's heavier footsteps a split second behind those of his son as they tossed the girl's body aside and commenced the chase.

I stumbled, fell, slipped again and again in the wet leaves, sliding every which way. The midnight rain began to fall harder than ever.

"Oh, God," I whispered. And it was real. I was *praying*. "Oh, God . . . don't let them get me. . . ."

And at last I was up, up . . . on my feet . . . running to beat the devil as the rain pelted down on me in great dime-sized drops, slashing through the overhead canopy of trees and upon my flesh like hail. . . .

"Who is that?" I heard the sheriff cry out behind me. He might have been mere inches from grabbing my shoulder with one of those massive, murderous hands. "*Hey!* You! Who the fuck is that?"

I did not turn back. I just kept running . . . running . . . toward my house on the other side of the Snake River Woods . . . through the rain . . . in the opposite direction from which I had come . . . my breath exploding out of me in labored bursts . . . fleeing through the storm like an escaped convict on the lam from a pack of bloodthirsty dogs . . . wondering if the sheriff already had his gun out, if a bullet would pierce my skull any second . . . wondering if I would be dead before my face struck the cold, muddy ground. . . .

"Come back here!" the sheriff bellowed again through the darkness, and I prayed he would not recognize me in the dark. In the rain. His voice echoed through the forest, through the night, so loud and so *close*.

"We can talk about this, hear? Nobody's gonna hurt you, son! Come on back!"

I imagined him lumbering after me in the darkness, arms outstretched and eyes wild like Christopher Lee's in *The Curse of Frankenstein*.

"You! Get back here!"

"Screw *you*," I whispered, and I ran harder than ever. Not slowing down for anything. I barely felt the whip-crack pain of branches and dead autumn leaves against my arms and legs, ignored the rain lashing my face like the sting of a hundred angry, frigid-bodied bees as I burst haphazardly through the forest, seeing only the lights of Midnight's residential district ahead like a glowing oasis on the horizon . . . like a promise of sanctuary. . . .

I just kept running . . . until my whole body ached. . . .

Running like hell . . . for my life.

Chapter Five

How I got to sleep that night I will never know—after I saw what I saw—but I did doze off eventually, after lying in the darkness, trembling, waiting to hear Dan pull up in our driveway for what felt like an eternity.

It felt as if only several minutes passed between the time I last remembered staring at my alarm clock in the darkness, praying for sleep, and a hellish nightmare woke me all but kicking and screaming, slick all over with a stinking sheen of sweat that made my skin feel slimy like the walls of the old Well.

The nightmare began innocently enough, as most do. Walking through the woods, I made my way toward my Secret Place. In the distance I could hear the laughter of children, murmurous crowd noise. The occasional *whirr-pop* of a cheap noisemaker. The *whistle-hiss-BAM* of fireworks soaring then exploding over my town like so many battling starships. Gala noises.

As I approached the clearing in the middle of the forest, it became obvious right away that something was not right there. An eerie blue glow enveloped my Secret Place, an uncanny luminescence emanating not from the moon but as if from some supernatural force. The Well and the Old Shack appeared oddly translucent, as if displaced from reality. Ghosts of inanimate objects.

And then came the sounds from inside the Well as my dream-self stood there wide-eyed . . . a sudden din from down there in the darkness that chilled my very soul.

At first, it sounded as if some poor forest animal had fallen into the Well and couldn't climb back up. Scuffling noises and soft splashing sounds bounced against the chamber's hard rock walls, echoed throughout the forest clearing.

I moved closer to the Well, not wanting to do so but finding that I couldn't help myself.

"Help me," came the nightmare voice, and to this day I can still hear her haunting cry from inside that subterranean chamber. It was a voice so innocent and sweet yet possessed of an underlying darkness at the same time. It seemed to be not one voice, but many. A feminine inflection was the most evident, yet voices of every varying pitch and tone cried out from the depths of her watery grave as well, as if all the world's injustices had personified themselves through one dead girl, and now they spoke to me from the bottom of an old well in Midnight, North Carolina.

"Help me," she said again. *"Kyle . . ."*

I shook my head back and forth several times fast. This couldn't be happening.

"Help me. Please. It's so dark. . . ."

"Shut up," said my dream-self. I covered my ears. "You're not real. You're dead."

And that's when she came up.

I sensed her approach, could feel her floating to the top of the Well. Like a rush of displaced air, I anticipated her silent ascent before she materialized before me. But I didn't step back.

Now the dead girl—all pale and bloated, yet still pretty in some demonic way, like the stench of something rotten might also smell strangely sweet, though you can't put your finger on how—rose to greet me as if on invisible wings.

"Help me, Kyle," she wept. *"You must."*

She kissed me, and her breath smelled like mud and earthworms, blood and sweat and sex all at the same time.

I screamed. I ran. I ran as if my life once again depended on it.

"Please, Kyle," I heard her phantom many-voice moan behind me, and with it came the spider touch of an elongated bone-finger stroking the nape of my neck. *"Don't leave. I'll show you things . . . down here . . . please. . . ."*

"NononoGod*no*," I babbled, never looking back.

I knew if I looked back the phantom-girl would be floating along behind me. Just inches away.

I could never outrun her.

"Leave me alone!" I cried.

And then I collided with Sheriff Burt Baker, who waited for me on the edge of the Snake River Woods.

He grabbed me by my collar, pulled me close, and a fat pink earthworm fell from between his puffy brown lips into the carpet of leaves at our feet.

"We'll have to burn her clothes," he said. *"Everything. Clean all this shit up till there ain't even a pussy hair left."*

August 6

Chapter Six

BODY OF LOCAL GIRL FOUND, the headline blared from the front page of the *Midnight Sun* the next morning. I don't think I had ever seen a bigger, bolder caption in my hometown's newspaper. At least, not since the powers-that-be had announced the end of the Vietnam War.

I saw it as I sat down beside my mother for a bowl of Raisin Bran and a glass of Minute Maid orange juice. My heart leapt into my throat, though for Mom's benefit I tried to act more interested in my breakfast than this news of which I was already far too aware. Mom watched me with sleepy disinterest as I began to eat, sipping loudly at her coffee all the while (MOMS ARE MADE FOR LOVIN', read the slogan on the side of her mug), but after several minutes of awkward silence she gestured toward the newspaper article before me.

"They found her last night, washed up on the banks of Snake River," she said. "Midnight's first murder in over fifty years."

Mom was always one of those folks who insisted on being the first to tell any kind of news (good or bad, but of course the latter is so much more fun), as if this somehow made her feel special. I always let her have her way.

"Really." I shifted in my seat, pulled the paper closer to my bowl.

"Mm-hmm. Last one was back in the Twenties, I think. A moonshine deal gone bad, something like that."

"Wow," I replied, for lack of anything better to say. But my tone was deadpan. I wondered if my own family had been involved in the mess of which Mom spoke, decided I wouldn't bet against it. Her folks always did love a good stiff drink.

I let my spoon slide down into my bowl of cereal, lost it, but didn't care. I blocked my mother's voice out as best I could then, and my heart raced for the next few minutes as I read that article on the front page of the *Midnight Sun*:

BODY OF LOCAL GIRL FOUND
FOUL PLAY CONFIRMED, SHERIFF PROMISES
QUICK ARREST

Polk County Sheriff Burt Baker made a tragic discovery early this morning during a random patrol. Upon investigation, a body found on the northern edge of Midnight's Snake River was revealed to be that of Cassandra Belle Rourke, 16.

While the exact cause of Ms. Rourke's death has yet to be determined, it is obvious that the young lady was sexually assaulted, Sheriff Baker told the *Midnight Sun*.

"Cassie" Rourke worked part time at Annie's

Country Diner on Main Street. She is survived by her parents and one brother.

"(An arrest) is inevitable," Sheriff Baker said. "The department already has several good leads (and) ... this heinous act will not go unpunished."

I let the paper fall to the table, slumped back in my chair. My Raisin Bran didn't look so edible anymore. And not just because it had gone soggy in its bowl. I felt sick. Sick from what I had seen the night before. Sick of Sheriff Baker and his lies.

Outside the window above the kitchen sink, a fat robin chirped merrily from its place in Mom's birdfeeder. The rain had slacked off a bit since the night before, but a soft mist continued to fall upon Midnight like a thin gray blanket of melancholia following one girl's tragic death. Despite the weather, that damn robin chirped on and on as if everything was hunky-dory in its world.

"I've heard she was quite a little slut," Mom said, her voice so low and matter-of-fact I almost did not hear her.

"What?"

"The Rourke girl. They say she was really easy." She gave a little sniffle, looked down her nose at the newspaper before me. "That's what I heard, anyway."

I swallowed a lump in my throat. " 'Easy?' "

She gave an exaggerated sigh, as if I had solicited her crude commentary to begin with but my questions had become tedious and disrespectful. "Far be it from me to speak ill of the dead, Kyle, but word is she got around. She was a loosie-goosie, if you will. I don't know. I'm just telling you what I've heard. Eileen Sealy says she'd been sniffing around her boy, Paul, since he taught her class in Vacation Bible School last summer. And he'll be thirty next month!"

I frowned. I didn't know what Mom meant, then again I did. Somehow. I felt dirty, certainly did not wish to continue such a conversation with my mother.

For that matter, I no longer wanted to talk to her at all. I stood, preparing to leave the kitchen.

As much as I loved my mother, sometimes she could be my least favorite person in the world.

"Something wrong, Kyle?" Mom asked as she poured herself a generous shot of brandy from a bottle beside the refrigerator. She topped it off with more coffee, took a hearty swig and smiled sweetly at me. "You barely touched your breakfast."

"I'm fine," I said. I wanted to take that damn bottle of hers and chuck it out the window. Preferably at the gay little songbird perched there. "I'm just not hungry."

"Suit yourself." Again Mom sipped at her mug. Some of it dribbled down her chin, but she must not have noticed. She didn't wipe it off.

My chair scraped loudly against the linoleum when I pushed it back under the table.

Mom winced as if I had just shattered the morning's tranquility with an ear-piercing scream. But I ignored her.

I staggered into the bathroom across the hall.

"Oh, Kyle? Will you wake Dan, please?" she called out to me. I could barely understand her as she asked in the middle of a loud yawn, but I caught the gist of it. "He's gonna have to hurry if he doesn't wanna miss his flight. . . ."

"Whatever," I groaned.

"Kyle!" Mom called.

"Yes!" I shouted back, with all the twelve-year-old fury I could muster. "I heard you the first time!"

Into Dan's room I went, moving like a zombie.

I stood over my big brother, watched him snore for a minute or so. His mouth was open, his lips spit-wet. His nostrils flared.

"Dan," I said. "Time to get up."

I fought back tears as I stared down at him.

"Dan."

I had never felt so helpless in my life.

"Dan. Wake up. Come on."

I cursed myself. Cursed my yellow-bellied way of avoiding this whole matter.

I knew damn well Dan had overslept. Mom didn't have to tell me. It was I, after all, who had switched the time on my brother's alarm clock from seven A.M. to seven P.M. shortly before I drifted off to sleep beside him in the wee hours of the morning after telling him my story.

I did not want to go see Deputy Linder, report what I witnessed out there in the Snake River Woods, yet I had known Dan would make me no matter how strongly I objected. He would take me to the Sheriff's Department himself, and he would make me tell Deputy Mike what I had seen.

I had fixed that problem, though.

This way my brother would barely have enough time to throw on his clothes, load everything into his truck, and still catch his plane to Florida.

I should have been smiling. But I wasn't.

I felt so low, as if I had betrayed my whole family. Myself. That poor girl in the woods.

I realized too late that I had made the wrong decision.

I ran from Dan's room then, leaned over the toilet,

and puked up everything I had eaten in the last twelve hours or so.

I wiped my mouth, grimaced.

I heard Mom turn on her radio in the kitchen, the one atop the refrigerator. A few seconds later she started singing along with it. Something about cats in cradles and silver spoons.

I leaned over the toilet again, started dry-heaving. Slammed the bathroom door to muffle Mom's off-key crooning about Little Boy Blue and the man in the frigging moon.

"What the hell am I gonna do now?" I wept.

The only answer was my own anguished cry, echoing inside the toilet bowl before me.

Chapter Seven

Sunday, August 6, 1977, proved to be one of the worst days of my life. As if I have to tell you.

I idolized my big brother, all but worshipped him . . . and he left me behind like an unpleasant memory.

By the time Dan fully awoke and stumbled out of bed he didn't even have time to take a shower. He threw his bags in the back of his pick-up before running all over the house, swearing up and down that he *knew* he was forgetting something and holy shit his plane left in *forty-five minutes* and what happened to that goddamn alarm 'cause he was *sure* he'd set it for seven-thirty!

"Where did you learn such terrible language, Danny?" Mom asked him from her place upon the couch. "Christ. You sound so uncivilized. Perhaps if you hadn't stayed out all night with that *Julie* girl . . ."

A year and a half they'd been dating, and still she was "that *Julie* girl" to Mom. Sure, I had experienced my own occasional pangs of jealousy, since Dan started spending most of his time with Julie. But I was twelve. And I liked my brother's girlfriend, for the most part. The same could not be said for our mother.

"I just hope you were safe," Mom mumbled in a condescending, sing-songy tone, but Dan did not respond even if he did hear her.

Several years would pass till I knew what Mom meant by that. At the time I assumed she meant Dan and Julie should always wear their seatbelts, or perhaps keep in mind the old "stop-drop-and-roll" rule if they ever caught on fire.

I kept my mouth shut throughout the chaos. Stayed out of the way and prayed those final forty-five minutes with my big brother could just stretch out into forever. I did not help Dan carry his things to his pick-up, though I could tell he needed me. I just sat there wishing I could stop time, like the guy with his magic stopwatch on that old *Twilight Zone* episode.

Mom drove Dan's truck to the airport in Asheville. For years our mother had expertly driven under the influence without weaving all over the road or running into telephone poles. It was a hell of a talent, let me tell you—if such a "skill" were something to boast about—yet it terrified me to no end each time I rode with her in Dan's Ford F100 or her own station wagon. I'd heard stories of Mom's cousin Tony, who had been in prison ever since he killed a young lady on his way home from a bar in Weaverville shortly after I was born. Surely it was just a matter of time, I feared, until my mother suffered the same sad fate. . . .

I sat between Mom and Dan for the ride, gazing up at my big brother as he stared out his rain-streaked window, nervously tapping his fingers on his knees in some offbeat rhythm only he could appreciate. He reminded me of a scared little boy, sitting there in his maroon FSU cap and his new denim jacket that was a size too large for his skinny frame. At some point Mom turned on the radio, and for the last few miles of our trip Leo Sayer crooned "When I Need You" from the truck's speakers. It sounded like shit. Not only because the song was disgustingly sappy and Mom's humming along made it even more horrendous, but also because one of the pick-up's speakers had been blown a few months back when Dan drove to Charlotte with a bunch of friends to see a Kiss concert. I hardly paid attention to the music, though. I sank in my seat, nearly started crying when I saw the airport on the horizon, the planes coming and going like massive silver birds roaring over our heads, the control tower in the center of it all overlooking the chaos like a proud parent supervising the chores of its offspring.

It wouldn't be long, I knew. Dan would soon be gone.

I clenched my fists. I hated them all. The pilots, up there in their cockpits. The shaky old man in the short-term parking booth who gave Mom a ticket before waving us through the gate. The long-legged flight attendant standing outside the main entrance, puffing on a Virginia Slim in the early-morning drizzle.

My mother.

My big brother, for leaving me.

After checking Dan's bags, then braving a veritable labyrinth of moving sidewalks and too-slow escalators and hundreds of bustling strangers, we reached the correct terminal with just five minutes to spare. A skinny stewardess with big boobs but too-thick glasses and a high-pitched, squeaky voice was announcing that all remaining passengers of Flight 237 to Tallahassee, Florida, should now board.

I noticed she smiled at Dan when we walked up. He smiled back, and her cheeks turned bright pink as she returned her microphone to its cradle.

Before I forgot, I made sure to place her on my ever-growing shit list as well.

Dan hefted his carry-on bags, staggered beneath their weight. He glanced out the huge plate-glass window, over the busy tarmac below, and I couldn't help but notice the lost-little-boy expression that loomed upon his normally strong, worry-free face.

He looked back toward us, winked at me and mussed up my hair. "I guess this is it."

Mom started crying. She pulled Dan into her arms, hugged him so tight I heard him gasp for breath.

"You take care of yourself, baby," she sobbed. "I'll never forgive you if you run off and get yourself hurt."

"Oh, Mom," Dan said. He peered over Mom's shoulder at me, rolled his eyes. "You guys don't have anything to worry about. I'll be fine."

"You better be."

He started to move my way several times, but Mom kept pulling Dan back to her. Squeezing him. Sobbing softly.

"You're not gonna make a scene, are you, Mom?"

Mom let him go. Shook her head. Found a Kleenex in her pocketbook, dabbed at her runny mascara.

"No," she said. "N-no. But I could give a damn what anyone thinks. My son's going away to college. Folks can turn their heads if they don't like it."

She blew into her tissue long and loud, crumpled it up and shoved it back in her purse. All the while she glared at a Japanese family who were seeing off their own loved ones several feet away, as if she suspected those folks, specifically, of begrudging her time with her son.

Dan turned to me.

"Sport," he said.

"Dan," I said.

"You take care of Mom, okay?"

"I will," I said.

"You're the man of the house now. You know that, right?"

I nodded, wiped my eyes with the back of one hand when a tear tickled its way down my cheek. My bottom lip quivered as if it might leave my face and take flight outside with the planes at any moment.

"I'll be back before you know it," Dan said. "You'll see. Thanksgiving break's only a couple months away. Then there's Christmas and New Year's!"

I nodded again, could feel my face scrunching up against my will. Any second I knew I would start bawling like a baby. Perhaps Dan should quit stalling, I thought, just get on the damn plane and skip the sorrowful good-byes. Otherwise it wouldn't be Mom making a scene.

"I love you two," Dan said. "Very much."

A squeal of feedback over the P.A. system interrupted us then, and the stewardess said, "Last call, please. All passengers of Flight 237 to Tallahassee, Florida, should board at this time. Repeat. Last call. All passengers of Flight 237, please board at this time."

"I'd better go," Dan said.

And suddenly I was all over him. I leapt upon my big brother like a wild animal, held him so tightly I thought for a second I heard his bones creaking and popping in my grip. He let out a moan, dropped his bags, and I buried my face in his neck when he lifted me off the ground. Dan smelled of Brut aftershave, and at that moment I considered it the greatest smell in the world.

"I love you, Dan," I cried. "I wish you didn't have to go."

"I love you too, little bro," he said. "But you know I have to."

He tickled me in the ribs, and I giggled. It felt good. Damn good. I giggled again, and Dan laughed with me.

"Remember, tiger . . . take care of Mom for me."

"I will," I said.

"Not an easy job."

"I know."

His voice dropped to a whisper. "And do the right thing, Kyle. Please."

My breath caught in my throat. I said nothing.

"You know what I'm talking about?"

Still, I said nothing. I looked off toward that Japanese family, suddenly very interested in their tearful embraces and heartfelt *sayonara*s. I smirked, wondered how their loss could ever compare to mine.

Dan set me down, leaned into me. "Go see Deputy Linder. Today."

"Maybe," I said.

"Don't put it off. You know it's the right thing to do."

I could not meet his eyes.

"Tell Deputy Linder what you saw. Swear to God, if I hadn't overslept I would have gone with you . . . but that stupid alarm . . ."

I'm sure my face turned sunburn-red. But if Dan noticed he didn't bring it up.

"Make them pay for what they did, Kyle. Don't let Henry Baker get away with this a second time."

I frowned, wondering what he'd meant by that. . . .

"I'll see ya, little bro." Dan stepped back, adjusted

his Seminoles cap. He picked up his bags again. Winked at me one last time. "Make me proud, okay?"

And at last he was on his way. He waved at us.

"B-bye, Dan," I said, biting at my lower lip nearly hard enough to draw blood.

While I *did* cry, when all was said and done, I was able to hold off until Mom and I got back in Dan's truck. Then we both started bawling like bratty toddlers pitching tantrums when they don't get their way.

We wept all the way home. Even when Mom took me to Mr. Smiley's Ice Cream Hut for a triple-scoop chocolate sugar cone—like she did when I was younger, after visits to the dentist or other arduous tasks through which I behaved like a perfect gentleman—it didn't help at all. In fact, I only took several half-hearted licks off the thing before I threw it out into the rain.

Of course, Mom treated herself to a reward of her own. She stopped at the ABC store on Fifth Avenue, and I stayed in the truck while she went in to purchase a bottle of Johnnie Walker Black. She smiled so contentedly when she came back out, that wrinkled brown bag protected in the crook of her arm like a beloved prize, and for some reason that made me feel ten times worse.

Meanwhile, the chill autumn rain kept falling. On and on and on.

First thing I did when we got home was sprawl out on Dan's bed, listening to his *Led Zeppelin 4* album over and over while I stared at a map of the United States in one of my big brother's old textbooks, trying to figure out exactly how far Tallahassee, Florida, was from Midnight, North Carolina.

Three hundred forty-eight miles, as the crow flies.

It didn't seem that far, on paper. Only a little over three inches.

Outside, the rain continued. Usually I associated the sound of a nocturnal storm with such tranquility, the voice of the night itself whispering me to sleep. Its pitter-patter upon the roof might have been the silken footsteps of angels mere feet above my head. Yet it had become, in the space of the last day or so, a very ominous sound.

Before long, sleep overtook me like a villain that had pursued me relentlessly since the night of the Apple Gala. I fell beneath it. Hard.

I slept all day, though it felt like only a few minutes. I didn't stir until nearly eight hours later, when Dan's clock radio suddenly blared the Eagles's "Hotel California" loud enough to wake Old Man Gash over at the junkyard on the other side of Midnight. My heart raced as I came to. My brain felt foggy. I tried to remember where I was, the time of day, but to no avail. After separating myself from the sticky puddle of drool that had leaked from my mouth onto the sleeve of Dan's favorite record, I rolled over to squint at the time. *7:45*. I would have been unsure whether the numbers displayed there reflected A.M. or P.M. had it not been for the gathering darkness outside Dan's bedroom window . . . and I remembered how *I* was responsible for the alarm going off twelve hours later than Dan had set it to wake him.

Thunder boomed outside, vibrating the entire house.

I rolled over, slammed one hand down atop the radio. The Eagles shut up. The rock n' roll stations had all been running that song in the ground for well over a year, and I failed to comprehend why everyone loved it so. All that crap about dark feasts and stabbing at beasts with steely knives and never checking out. I found the tune to be quite depressing, creepy.

It was one of Mom's favorite songs ever. Go figure.

Everything felt oddly dreamlike as I rubbed my eyes and gazed around Dan's room. Even with my big brother's belongings filling up the space—his books, his basketball trophies, his posters, and the various model cars he had once enjoyed working on for so many long hours—Dan's domain appeared so empty. *Hollow.* Like this wasn't really his room at all, but a cheap Hollywood soundstage set up to resemble my absent brother's sleeping quarters. Everything appeared mutated, too, not quite right, all stippled with the blotchy shadows of the foliage outside Dan's window, painted with the wormy gray streaks of the autumn storm batting at the glass like a noisy burglar.

Dan's Led Zeppelin album had long since stopped playing, and only the muffled *shish-kthump-shish-kthump* of the player's needle scratching against the LP's label kept me company. It was a lonely, ominous sound, rhythmic but strangely menacing above the constant white-noise hiss of the rain.

I rose from the bed, turned off Dan's stereo. For the millionth time since I'd watched him board his plane that morning, I reminded myself that my big brother wasn't *dead*. He was coming back, and soon. Thanksgiving would be here in just a few short months, and Dan would be home for four whole days that weekend!

That didn't make me feel any better, though. At all.

I sighed.

From her place upon the wall, Farrah Fawcett seemed to mock me.

I showed her my middle finger before leaving the room, slamming the door behind me.

Chapter Eight

Perhaps it was everything that had transpired over the last twenty-four hours, the constant worrying over what I planned to do about the crimes I had witnessed in my Old Shack on top of fretting endlessly that I might never see my brother again . . . so much going through my head, so many conflicting emotions and anxieties the likes of which most twelve-year-olds are never forced to suffer. . . .

Strangely enough, I hadn't thought about Burner once. Not since the last time I had seen him, out at my Secret Place.

Before I left Dan's room that evening and retired to my own bed, I'd taken a minute to check on Mom. She was passed out on the living room sofa in only a pair of baggy sweatpants and a lacy bra the color of cantaloupes gone bad. That bottle of Johnnie Walker Black she had purchased earlier lay empty on the floor beside her. I shook my head, covered her with a ratty old afghan we kept draped across the back of the couch. I kicked her bottle across the room before turning off the television, ignoring the three talking heads waxing melodramatic despondency over "this horrendous murder in Midnight" ("more on that later, Jim, for now here's Ted Roker with your WHLP weather report . . . for goodness sake, Ted, how long can it *possibly* keep raining?").

At last I collapsed upon my own bed, drained.

I had just closed my eyes when I suddenly sat up, one word on my lips: *"Burner!"*

My heart skipped a beat. The temperature in my bedroom seemed to drop thirty or forty degrees. Lightning flickered outside my window, and thunder crashed like the voice of God reprimanding the town for its sins.

"Oh, no . . ."

I stared into the darkness of my room, breathing heavily. For a second or two I almost slapped myself. I couldn't believe I hadn't thought of it before. . . .

"Burner . . ."

The night after the Gala, when I fled from Sheriff Baker and his son through the Snake River Woods, fearing what they might do if they caught up with me . . . I had left my bicycle behind. I had abandoned my best friend like an empty promise.

Burner was still out there, I realized. He sat on the other side of the Old Shack, propped up against that oak tree in the forest between my Secret Place and Midnight's business district. Waiting for me to come back for him.

"Holy shit," I said, and my voice seemed unnaturally loud in the silence of my bedroom.

Darth Vader stared down at me from my *Star Wars* poster upon the wall like the awful repercussions of my careless mistake personified and standing before me in the night.

I couldn't believe it. How could I have been so *stupid?*

I fell out of my bed then stood, and my legs felt like Silly Putty as I made my way to the closet where my shoes and jacket waited.

Once upon a time, I had loved the night, cherished that strange but wonderful blue-black period between sunset and dawn. The world seemed so much larger when we were children, and in my mind Polk County, North Carolina, might have encompassed the entire globe during those hours when the sun ducked behind the Blue Ridge Mountains as if it had better things to do than hang around. I used to love to sneak out of my bedroom window after dusk to ride Burner through Midnight's dark streets and alleyways, weaving in and out of the beams of my hometown's streetlights as if basking in their glow for even a second might shatter my bliss completely.

I was the King of Midnight, back then.

Of course, after the god-awful things I had seen in the Snake River Woods, my love affair with the night had become a thing of the past. In the space of just several days my hometown had become a ravenous beast waiting to swallow me whole as I ventured through its massive black belly.

For the umpteenth time since I realized I had left my bicycle behind, I asked myself: *How could I have been so stupid?*

With nothing but an old scuffed pair of tennis shoes and a cheap windbreaker covering my Spider-Man pajamas, I ventured out into the vast ebony maze that was Midnight approaching its namesake, preparing to bring Burner home. The rain had slacked off, at least temporarily, though a faint mist kept my clothes damp throughout my quest. I couldn't stop shivering, no matter how hard I tried.

Before long, as I walked through my back-yard . . . through the knee-high grass Mom had begged Dan to mow for over a month, but he never got around to it . . . past the rusty swing-set I hadn't touched for years and around the corner of my family's small storage shed, which almost resembled a miniature Old Shack in the far corner of our property . . . as I cut across the widow Mertzer's lawn next door and at last entered the Snake River Woods. . . .

I began to pray.

It wasn't something I did often, pray. I could count on both hands the times my family had attended church since Dad passed away, and I would probably have several fingers left over when I was done. But that certainly did not mean I no longer believed in God. Over the leaves crunching beneath my feet, over the somehow tangible silence that blanketed my hometown, I spoke aloud to the Big Man Upstairs without shame or inhibition. A sense of peace seemed to envelop me, like a shield protecting me from the horrors I had seen the night before, and several times I even closed my eyes as I walked so I could focus fully on the things I needed to say. . . .

This was important. I felt I had to get it right the first time.

"God?" I said aloud, my voice as deeply sincere as any twelve-year-old boy's can be. "This is Kyle. Kyle Mackey? You know . . . I live at 2217 Old Fort Road? My brother's name is Dan, and my mother's Darlene Mackey? Dan just left for college, which really suck—er, stinks. I'm sure gonna miss him. You might remember my Dad too. Sergeant Daniel Mackey, Sr.?

He died when I was five. He's up there with You now, I guess. Would You tell him I said hello, please?"

I bit my lip, fought back the stinging tears that last part brought to my eyes.

"Anyway . . . if You do remember me, God, I need Your help. I need it bad. I know we haven't talked in a while. I guess the last time we spoke was around the time Mom wanted me to pray for her to get that raise at the juice factory. She didn't get it, but You know that. I guess that was a crappy thing to pray for anyway. Aw, man . . . umm . . . where was I?"

I shook my head, felt like slapping myself for veering off on this unrelated tangent. Then, as I continued my prayer, I began to search for my Old Shack in the darkness up ahead, wanting to get this over with as soon as possible. . . .

"I guess I just wanna ask You to watch out for me, God. That's all. If You can find the time, I mean. Please take care of Dan, too, while he's down there in Florida. And watch out for Mom. I guess she needs it most of all. You know all she ever does is drink, and one of these days I'm scared it's gonna kill her. My mother can be really difficult sometimes, God, but I do love her."

At last I could see them up ahead, in my tear-fogged vision. My Old Shack. And the Well. I stopped walking, just stood there and stared at them for several long, unnerving minutes, chewing vigorously at my nails as I did so. Where my Secret Place had once felt like an old friend, the sight of it now made my bowels lurch. I shuddered. I didn't want to go any closer.

Please, God, I finished my prayer, but this time I spoke to Him in my head. *Please just look out for us all, okay? Help me figure out the right thing to do. I know Dan's right. I can't let them get away with what they did. But I'm scared, God. Really scared. . . .*

My prayer trailed off at last as I passed the Old Shack. I could *feel* the evil that had transpired there the night before, like something rotten that has been thrown out but continues to taint the air with its lingering stench. That whole grove in the middle of the Snake River Woods seemed . . . *contaminated*, somehow, a hateful, alien place where I could not believe I had once spent so many wonderful hours.

I made the mistake of looking back once, and when I did a frigid rash of goose bumps broke out all over my body. My teeth began to chatter. The darkness beyond the Old Shack's doorway was a thicker, blacker, more terrible darkness than any I had ever seen. It seemed to plead with me, inviting me to reclaim my territory and cherish my Secret Place the way I had cherished it before the Gala.

I shook my head, walked on past it. *No way, Jose.*

The night beyond that open doorway seemed to shift, move. Pulse.

I picked up my pace, glanced over my shoulder every few seconds as I hurried toward the copse of trees about a hundred yards to the east of my Old Shack, where I knew I had left my bicycle. I squinted through the blackness for that familiar glisten of Burner's bright blue body in the night, but I saw nothing yet. The moon, smothered as it was behind the gathered thunderclouds above, barely offered enough light for me to see more than seven or eight feet ahead of myself.

There. I spotted it, then. That massive oak tree I had propped Burner against that night. I breathed a sigh of relief, so ready to retrieve my bike and hurry home, never to return to that hideous site I had once loved more than any other place in the world. . . .

I rounded the tree. Smiled.

Gasped.

Suddenly lost my smile.

Burner wasn't there.

"I . . . I—" I could only stammer uncontrollably as I walked all the way around the tree. Then again. Then a third time. I *knew* this was the right tree. It had to be. Just in case, though, my eyes flitted nervously about the immediate area. Searching . . . searching . . .

My bicycle was not there.

"Oh, God . . . p-p-please, n-no," I stammered.

Only a slight disturbance in the soft black mud and dead leaves at the base of the tree proved Burner had ever been there at all.

Someone had picked him up, carried him off.

The night seemed to close in on me. I could hear the blood rushing through my head. My feet felt heavy, my brain weightless and fuzzy. . . .

I took off then, running for home as fast as my weak, trembling legs would carry me. Otherwise, I knew I would faint right there on the cold forest floor. Vulnerable and alone.

Somewhere to my left an owl mocked my fear as I ran. A screech owl. The sound it made was not unlike Cassie Rourke's wail of terror just before Sheriff Baker killed her in my Old Shack.

Salty sweat dripped down my forehead and into my eyes despite the chill rain falling upon me.

This couldn't be happening. It couldn't. I wanted to knock out my own teeth for being so damned irresponsible. I might as well have signed my name in the dirt at the foot of the Old Shack's doorway so Sheriff Baker would know exactly where to find me. I should have pinned a note to that tree, giving him and his son my home phone number and street address.

What the hell was I supposed to do now?

At last I burst from the Snake River Woods, but then amidst my disorienting fear I realized I had exited the forest a block or so down from my own house.

The streetlights resembled the eyes of demons watching my every move. Midnight had never seemed so menacing. The distance to my house never seemed so long.

A car passed me on Old Fort Road when I came within just a few hundred feet from home. A big blue Dodge Charger, all sleek and mean and shark-like in the night. Its windows were down. The Doobie Brothers were singing "Jesus Is Just Alright" on the radio.

Someone laughed inside there. A girl, it sounded like.

Off to my right, a leftover Gala streamer scuttled down the cold gray sidewalk like a brightly colored snake stalking the night.

I shuddered.

I was still trembling all over a few minutes later, when I finally sneaked back through my bedroom window and slid into a bed that seemed so lumpy and uncomfortable.

I wondered if I would ever sleep again.

Later, as I lay in the darkness not daring to close my eyes, I heard the high-pitched warble of a police siren peaking and fading somewhere across town. I wondered if it was *him*. Out there doing his thing, roaming my town under the guise of upholding the law. I wondered if Burner was imprisoned even now in the trunk of his patrol car, if the murderous bastard cruised the streets of Midnight in search of the child to whom that bright blue Schwinn belonged. . . .

What next?

I couldn't stop shaking. I pulled the covers over my head and curled into a fetal position.

I wondered how long I had left to live. And what it would feel like to die.

Chapter Nine

During the days following Dan's departure (not to mention the abduction of my beloved bicycle), I struggled with indecision. With guilt. With trying to determine how—*if*—I should do the right thing. My every waking hour, it seemed, I saw the dead girl beckoning to me from beyond the grave. Everywhere I turned, something lurked to remind me of the injustice of it all—whether it was the follow-up articles each morning in the *Midnight Sun* covering the investigation into the murder of Cassandra Belle Rourke, or just seeing Sheriff Burt Baker cruising down Main Street in his patrol car without a care in the world despite the vile things he had done in my Old Shack.

The nightmares continued, too. Once I dreamed I was stuck down in the Well. Faces swam out of the black, taunting me. Skeletal hands tore at my clothes. Cassie Belle Rourke's pale visage leered at me, weeping *"Why, Kyle, why?"* beneath the distorted echo-strains of "Hotel California" as performed by the

71

Gerald R. Stokely High School Band. Baker's scowling face insisted we had to clean everything up till there wasn't even a pussy hair left. Henry Baker tried to convince me, as his hands twitched spastically and his head jerked up and down every few seconds, that he thought all along she was dead, that she hadn't been moving so what else was he supposed to think? Dan was there, cocking an eyebrow at me, ordering me to "do the right thing." Of course, Mom showed up once or twice as well, drunkenly scolding me for going out to that "nasty old cabin" in the first place. I was grounded from *ever* having a decent night's sleep again, said my wild-eyed dream mother, and I believed every word she said.

I knew I had to do something. Soon.

It was up to me. Only me.

Yet I was so afraid. I heard suspicious noises outside my bedroom every night. On those rare occasions when I left my house during the next few days, I studied my fellow townsfolk with wary scrutiny and paranoid distrust. Every time I heard the crunch of gravel beneath tires in our driveway I would tremble uncontrollably, knowing the end had come for me, only to discover that the car pulling into our property was merely some lost driver turning around on our dead-end street and not the murderous law-enforcement officer who haunted my nightmares.

Simply put, I was a nervous wreck. I could not ignore the fact that someone—*the sheriff? his son?*—had found Burner after I had foolishly left him behind. When the nightmares were over and the light of day bled through my bedroom windows to push back the shadows and chase away my nightmares, I knew there were no such things as ghosts. I knew no tortured soul beseeched me from beyond the grave to avenge its untimely death. Yet there did exist a very real terror, living in Midnight. Someone was out there—waiting, watching, aware that I knew the Bakers' dirty secret—and that *someone* was a creature of flesh and blood.

He had Burner.

He knew where to find me, anytime he wanted.

Everything I had been taught about policemen, the trust we place in them and how it's their undying duty to shelter us from harm . . . had all been a terrible lie. The man who had sworn to protect and serve my county—my *world,* as far as I was concerned at the ripe old age of twelve—had spit in the face of every person who had voted for him, who looked up to him, who counted on him to take care of us all and keep the bad guys behind bars where they belonged. My belief system regarding good and evil, crime and punishment, the role of the law and those who enforce it, had been irrevocably shattered. Not to mention my budding outlook on the way things work when you grow up. My faith in adults in general. Since the night I witnessed Sheriff Burt Baker's heinous crime, I no longer respected my elders as I had been taught to do since a very young age. I could not trust them. I feared them.

I knew I did not ever want to *be* one of them.

I felt betrayed. So alone.

Yet at the same time I felt like the traitor.

Guilt filled my soul like acid burning me up from the inside out as I waited, doing nothing, but I asked myself time and again what *could* I do?

I was a child with few friends and even fewer relatives to whom I could turn. Most folks in town knew of my mother's little "problem." I saw the holier-than-thou expressions on the faces of my neighbors, could not ignore the way they looked down their noses at my family as if we were just a step above poor white trash. Sure, Dan had been a local basketball hero, everyone knew and loved my big brother, but I doubt more than a handful of Midnight's citizens even knew my name. Long past were the days when folks greeted me with patronizing sympathy in their eyes, as they had shortly after Dad died in Vietnam. Most of the townsfolk probably recognized me as nothing more than "the son of that alcoholic lady" where they had once so valiantly insisted we shouldn't hesitate to call "if we ever needed anything."

I did briefly consider taking my story to Father McKinney, at the First Lutheran Church of Midnight over on Craig Street. My family had worshipped there occasionally when I was four or five. Perhaps he could set my mind at ease. Problem was, Father McKinney was somewhere in the vicinity of eighty years old, and I'd heard he was going senile. He would recall very little of what I told him. I feared he might get my story all mixed up, and subsequently Dr. Brent Barker, Midnight's resident veterinarian, would be arrested for cold-blooded murder.

Dan had been right. My only option was to go to Deputy Linder. Not only was he one of the nicest men in town (memories of visits from Deputy Mike to check on our family after Dad passed away filled my mind as I conjured my plan of action), he was second-in-command to Sheriff Baker himself. He would know what to do. He would take my statement, investigate my accusations, and Cassie Rourke's murder would be avenged.

Yet I couldn't do it. Not yet. I wanted to do it, knew I *needed* to do it, but I couldn't.

Just another day or two, that's all, I kept telling myself. *Just a few more days and I'll go. . . .*

Who could I trust? Who should I fear? The questions plagued me night and day. And kept me from doing the right thing.

My big brother was the only person in whom I could confide, at this point. The only soul I knew I could trust unconditionally.

And he was gone.

So I waited.

August 7

Chapter Ten

Two nights after Sheriff Baker killed her in the Snake River Woods, the dead girl was on television.

"Taken Too Soon: Portrait of a Midnight Angel," the show was called. It came on right after the Channel 5 Six o'Clock News, and lasted just under twenty minutes.

They sure hadn't wasted any time in throwing it all together. In theory, it sounds like a respectable thing to do, that "Exclusive Report, In Memoriam," but ultimately the show ranked just a step above tabloid sensationalism. A desperate grasp for small-town ratings disguised as sugar-sweet sentimentality. Not to mention the long string of "sponsors" that received free advertising and priceless PR potential by lending their names to the list of companies the program had been "brought to you by" (Futch Bros. Dairy, Wilkinson Auto, and Bradley Heating & Air-Conditioning were just a few).

The program began with a choppily edited look at Cassandra Belle Rourke's short life, showing a montage of still shots from her childhood set to a song that sounded just enough *un*like Elton John's "Tiny Dancer" to avoid accusations of copyright infringement. Following that were interviews with the decedent's friends and classmates at Gerald R. Stokely High School. Several misty-eyed teachers discussed the kinds of grades Cassie Rourke had made ("mostly B's and C's, but she always tried so hard, which made Cassie anything *but* average"). So many "best friends" came out of the woodwork for the show to declare how terribly they would miss Cassie Rourke I couldn't help wondering if it was possible for someone to be so universally adored. The dead girl's parents were interviewed as well, and through everything else *they* were the ones with whom I truly sympathized. Their emotions were real. Too real. A mother who couldn't stop shaking, whose features were red and swollen from days of constant crying. A little brother, who proudly displayed for the camera the ugliest teddy bear I had ever seen, boasting that his big sister had given it to him "just before she went to Heaven." Cassie Rourke's father spoke briefly, but I do not remember what he said. Here stood a man who was not so much in mourning as drooling at the prospect of revenge. As crude as such a thing may sound on my part, considering everything Mr. Clinton Rourke had been through, there was something about that burly, balding man with his thick Southern accent and his crooked, too-sharp teeth that I did not trust. Beneath his stunned, watery gaze, there seemed to lurk something mean. Something gruffer and more cruelly vindictive than grief.

Finally, I could watch no more. I left the room about the time Sheriff Baker's fat, ugly face filled the screen. He vowed to catch "the animal who could do something like this to one of Midnight's innocents," claimed he would "spare no expense" in hunting down the culprit and punishing him to the fullest extent of the law. It was his "personal duty."

The whole thing sickened me. I could watch no more.

Just before I turned my back on the television to head for my bedroom, Mom started sobbing, blabbering about how god-awful she would feel if she ever lost Danny or me. I could barely understand her, though, through her river of tears and snot.

Even after I slammed my bedroom door and turned on my radio to drown out the sound of it all, I could still hear Mom in there. Making comments every few minutes over the sound of the TV as if providing her own compulsory two cents to Cassandra Belle Rourke's short legacy. Honking crudely into her Kleenex like something from the wilds of Africa trumpeting its grief into the night.

I shook my head, rolled my eyes. Grimaced and barely refrained from throwing my radio across the room when Steely Dan's "Reelin' in the Years" segued into the opening chords of "Hotel California."

For a while I tried reading a Batman comic Dan had bought me a couple weeks before (Issue #258: "Threat of the Two-Headed Coin!"), but before long I gave it up. The evil scarred half of Batman's nemesis Two-Face reminded me too much of Sheriff Burt Baker's ugly, pitted features.

I decided to lie there for a while and listen to the midnight rain. Perhaps it would lull me to sleep.

I was wrong.

I covered my head with my pillow, curled up in a fetal position upon my bed, and lay like that for at least an hour.

Dark questions plagued my mind. I tried to ignore them, because I knew the answers were moot.

James Newman

A girl had died. An innocent had been murdered.

Yet the more I thought about it, the more I wanted to scream out to Cassandra Belle Rourke, wherever she might be. . . .

You seemed like such a good girl . . . what were you doing out there in the Snake River Woods with Henry Baker in the first place?

August 8

Chapter Eleven

I used to love horror movies. The nights I rode with Dan to the Lansdale Royal Drive-In on Forster Boulevard to partake of such breathtaking B-movie fare as *The Bat People*, *Beware the Blob*, and *The Incredible Melting Man* were some of the best times of my life. Nothing compared to those hot summer nights spent hanging out with my brother in his pick-up, dwarfed by the flickering horrors upon that massive drive-in screen as we chowed down on a bucket of popcorn almost as tall as me. More often than not the soundtracks to the many movies Dan and I watched at the Lansdale were distorted through the drive-in's tinny speakers—bulky gray things resembling battered robot heads that never wanted to hang quite right on the windows of Dan's Ford and always seemed to short out several times during the movie—but none of that mattered to me. I loved every gloriously tacky second of it.

What incredible, magical times those were. The

Lansdale Royal Drive-In, when I was a kid, might have been heaven on Earth. . . .

Yet things change. *People* change. If monuments that have stood for centuries can eventually erode and crumble, then humans must be the most fragile, malleable creatures ever to exist. We try to believe otherwise, but we are at the mercy of our merciless environs.

My point?

Literally overnight, my love for horror movies ceased as if it had never been at all.

After what had happened out at my Secret Place, I was perhaps the only twelve-year-old boy in America no longer infatuated with celluloid monsters and madmen and things that go bump in the night. Three days after the Gala I ripped down from my closet door that oversized poster of Lon Chaney, Jr., stalking the night as *The Wolf Man*, not stopping to think for a second about how desperately I had pleaded with Mom to buy it for me for my tenth birthday. I retired my old dog-eared copies of *Famous Monsters of Filmland* to the space beneath my bed, never to open them again. I had seen enough death, enough suffering during the ten minutes or so I had stared through that filthy, fly-specked window of my Old Shack, I decided that I no longer wanted to see the same things simulated in magazines or pictures or upon the Lansdale's weathered screen. Though I knew by the age of seven or eight that such visions were nothing more than Hollywood special effects, harmless concoctions of latex and corn syrup and fake blood, I never again wanted to perceive even a cheesy facsimile of man's inhumanity to man.

During the second week of August 1977, the Lansdale Royal Drive-In began hosting a Terrifying Trio of

Fearsome Flicks For the Luridly Low Price of One Dollar. Three movies for a dollar was unheard of, even in those days. Any other time I would not have missed such a momentous event for the world. Even without Dan around to smuggle me through the theater's gates, I would have gladly sacrificed all comprehension of the films' already illogical plots to view the marathon from atop the old water tower on Cardinal Street. I had done so once or twice before, and it was the next best thing to being parked right there beneath the big screen as long as I brought along a blanket and a thermos full of hot cocoa to push away the night's chill.

The movies on tap that week were *The Hills Have Eyes* (a brand new film I should have been dying to see, as the trailers on TV appeared oh-so-deliciously terrifying), *Day of the Animals,* and *The Creeping Flesh*. These were the sort of trashy, low-budget flicks I would have insisted were the greatest ever made, no matter what the critics believed, and I'm sure Dan would have agreed.

As I said, though, things had changed. *I* had changed.

The Lansdale Royal Drive-In hosted its horror-movie festival, with that Terrifying Trio of Fearsome Flicks For the Luridly Low Price of One Dollar, but the whole thing passed for me. A sappy romantic comedy might as well have graced the screen that week, or some yawn-inducing documentary about the mating habits of salmon. Much to my mother's surprise I never even considered attending the Lansdale's latest monster-fest ("I'm so proud of you, Kyle, that you've finally outgrown such silliness," Mom said at some point, but I pretended I didn't hear her), and soon *The Hills Have Eyes* and *Day of the Animals* and

The Creeping Flesh were replaced with two new movies advertised on that grand billboard looking out over Forster Boulevard.

I did not miss them at all.

Once I would have given up every precious plaything I owned before I'd miss such a lineup. But I had seen enough terror, enough death, to last me the rest of my life.

The first evening *The Hills Have Eyes* and its B-movie brethren came to my hometown (with little fanfare, where I was concerned), I turned in shortly after dark. I strongly suspect I set a new world record on the night in question, as no child could ever have willingly gone to bed so early during those last carefree days of August. It would have seemed like a waste of perfectly good summer!

I had a reason for retiring by seven-thirty that night, however.

The next day I planned to visit the Midnight Public Library the second it opened its doors.

It was time, I had decided, to play Sherlock Holmes.

Chapter Twelve

Something had come to me the morning after I discovered Burner was missing. It was one of those things that picks at the back of your brain, nags at you until you're forced to acknowledge it or else it'll drive you crazy.

That night. In the Snake River Woods. Something Sheriff Baker said to his son.

Once it finally rose out of the muddy quagmire of my subconscious, it wouldn't let me go. . . .

"Didn't you learn your lesson the last time?" Baker had asked Henry.

And I couldn't help wondering what that meant.

My curiosity grew overwhelming . . . especially when I remembered Dan had said something very similar to me at the airport.

"Make them pay for what they did," my big brother told me. "Don't let Henry get away with this a second time."

A *second* time . . .

Had Henry done this before? Had there been an-other girl, *before* Cassie Belle Rourke?

God, how I missed Burner that morning, as I headed to the library on foot. I restricted my trek across town to Midnight's side roads and back alleys, creeping through backyards and vacant lots like a man on the run from the law.

I felt so alone, like a social pariah without a friend in the world. As if *I* had done something wrong.

Despite having always been an avid reader and lover of books, I had visited the Midnight Public Library only once or twice during the previous year. It had changed quite a bit since the last time I'd been there. The whole site had been remodeled the previous summer, and for a few minutes I couldn't even find the new entrance to that white-brick building on Hyatt Street.

I came face-to-face with the sole reason why I no longer patronized the place on a regular basis the second I walked through those fancy new automatic doors and into the library's warm confines.

Her name was Constance Schifford.

We all called her Miss Shit-Bird.

Behind her back, of course.

Crabby old Mrs. Schifford was the Midnight Public Library's head librarian, had been for as long as I could remember. She was also one of the meanest creatures to ever walk God's Earth. I am only slightly exaggerating when I say that Constance Schifford was more disagreeable than a rabid Tasmanian Devil with a rusty knife up its butt and something in its eye.

The librarian's face reminded me of the gnarled wood of an ancient, weatherworn tree. Her hair was always pulled into a tight ball atop her skull the color of cobwebs and dust. Her hands were clawlike, covered in blotchy brown liver spots. I remember when I was much younger I always had feared she would grab me with those hands and I would waste away to something gaunt and satanic just like her. Miss Shit-Bird always wore long, dark dresses—navy blue, black, storm-cloud gray—as if her perpetually antagonistic mood would never allow her to wear anything but the most depressing, funereal colors.

Mrs. Schifford had despised me since one evening the previous autumn, when a boy named Teddy Worsham and I had disrupted the otherwise immaculate tranquility of her library. Our fifth-grade teacher had assigned us all a project in which we were to research a specific animal in teams of two. Teddy and I had chosen the Great White Shark. Problem was, on that windy October day we weren't digging through the library's card catalog for information on man-eating marine life, as our mothers had dropped us off to do. At some point we had stumbled across a tome of such greater interest we lost track of not only time, but our own civilized behavior as well.

That oh-so-fascinating book that stole our pre-adolescent attention for so many minutes (and simultaneously sealed our fates as patrons of the Midnight Public Library for the remainder of that year) was called *The Joy of Sex*. My God, how Teddy Worsham and I giggled and poked at one another like fools there in our dark corner of the library, as we rifled through that how-to manual on making love. We laughed so hysterically we nearly cried at the explicit pictures inside. Teddy even tore several out of the book, swore he was going to tease all the girls at school with them. I begged for him to stop as he constructed himself a pair of paper glasses out of two large, stiff-nippled breasts, then proceeded to model them for me like some midget professor with sex on the brain instead of quantum physics.

Unfortunately, Teddy had chosen to don his new double-D spectacles just as old Constance Shit-Bird rounded the corner and walked up to our hiding place.

I saw her first. I gasped. Time seemed to stand still. Teddy's makeshift glasses slipped off his nose, drifted to the floor like an autumn leaf falling to the ground in the dead of night.

God, how tall and menacing old Miss Shit-Bird appeared during that moment. All we could do was admit we were busted, pray she would spare our lives and please not eat our souls. Teddy's chubby hands trembled as he passed her the crumpled pages he had torn from the book, but even with so many stiff, veiny appendages and hairy pink places exposed in those explicit diagrams from *The Joy of Sex,* the librarian never blushed or batted an eye.

Mom had grounded me for a few days after the incident. I wasn't allowed to hang around Teddy anymore (after we finished our ill-prepared project on the Great White Shark, of course). And old Miss Shit-Bird had hated me ever since.

"Kyle Mackey," she said to me that day I came looking for information on Henry Baker and the sins of his own sordid past. Her voice reminded me of something crawled from the grave to terrorize the living. "To what do we owe this dubious pleasure?"

I swallowed, approached her desk slowly. Like one might approach a pissed-off cobra, if one were stupid enough to do such a thing.

"Umm . . . hi," I said, and no matter how hard I tried, I could not look into her piercing, ocean-blue eyes. I feared I might fall in. I would drown.

She cleared her throat, pursed her lips tighter than

ever, and looked me up and down. Behind her, on the wall, a poster exclaimed in bright red letters **SHHH! LIBRARIES ARE <u>QUIET</u> PLACES!** Beneath those words a fat brown owl stood on a colorful stack of books, holding one wing up to its beak in the universal gesture of *shush*ing.

"How are you today, Mrs. Schifford?" I asked, as sweetly as I knew how.

"I am splendid, thank you," the librarian replied. I could tell she would rather step on me, squash me like a pesky insect crawling across the library's recently vacuumed floors, than speak to me with any semblance of civility. "Is there something I can help you with? Or are you here to cause more trouble?"

"N-no. Not at all, Mrs. Schifford. I just—"

"If there is something you *need*, spit it out," she said. "I have many things to do today. A number of *hoodlums* nearly destroyed the children's section this morning, and there's no telling how long it's going to take to put everything back in its place."

I couldn't help noticing the way she stressed the part about "hoodlums," as if describing pint-sized literature vandals no less iniquitous than myself.

That did it. I had always been taught to respect my elders, but *this* was just unfair. Something snapped in me. I had paid for the sins I committed with Teddy Worsham—I had taken the grounding Mom gave me like a man, had stayed away from the library for the rest of that year as commanded—yet old Miss Shit-Bird didn't ever want to let it go.

I refused to take any more.

"Look, Mrs. Schifford," I said. "How come every time I come in here you look at me like I'm a piece of dog crap you just stepped in?"

The old woman's jaw dropped. Her eyes grew as wide as Teddy Worsham's bulging boob spectacles.

"I don't think I heard you correctly, young man."

"You heard me," I said. "It's not fair."

"Why, I *never*—"

"And you probably never will with that attitude, lady." That sly little quip I had learned from Dan, when he bumped into some fat lady once at the new Kmart across town and she'd rudely berated him even after he apologized.

I grinned at old Miss Shit-Bird.

"I . . . I . . . you—" She couldn't believe it. Never before had anyone dared speak to Constance Schifford in such a manner.

I hoped I didn't give her a heart attack. I needed her, to help me find the information I had come for.

"I said I was sorry, Mrs. Schifford, for what I did that time with Teddy," I said, one hand splayed out on the desk before us in a placating gesture. "I paid for the book. I have just as much right to come here as anyone else. I've grown up a lot since I did that."

Truth be told, it hadn't even been a year since what happened, but when you're young, always anticipating your next birthday as if it is some monumental occasion, the difference between eleven and twelve years old might as well encompass millennia.

"I can't believe what I'm hearing," the librarian rasped.

"I know you don't like me," I said, "but all I ask is that you do your job and help me find what I'm looking for."

Mrs. Schifford's bony hands went to her hips. "You have quite the mouth on you, Kyle Mackey."

"I take after my big brother."

Her eyes grew watery. Her mouth worked soundlessly. She looked like a dying fish.

"Please, Mrs. Schifford," I said. "I'm not here to

94

cause trouble. I just need to know where you keep all the old newspapers, stuff like that."

After what felt like forever, old Miss Shit-Bird cleared her throat and looked down her nose at me. "Archived newspapers, you said?"

"That's right. Like old issues of the *Midnight Sun*."

"Follow me."

It couldn't believe it. It had worked!

Mrs. Schifford walked quickly around the desk then led me through the library to the rear of the building. Her black dress swished audibly around her legs as she gestured toward a dimly lit room marked NORTH CAROLINA GENEALOGY.

"Do you know how to use our microfiche machines?" she asked me.

"Yes, ma'am, I do."

"Very well."

I genuinely meant it when I said, "Thank you so much for your help, Mrs. Schifford."

But the librarian was already gone. She had sauntered off to pick her dentures with the bones of small children or whatever it was she enjoyed doing in her spare time.

Meanwhile, I was alone with Midnight's past.

The room was smaller than I expected. A long, rectangular painting of a lighthouse above roiling ocean waves hung slightly left of center along the back wall (THE OUTER BANKS, read the small brass plaque set in its wooden frame). A row of black file cabinets took up the wall to my left, and opposite those sat a wide shelf filled with various hefty tomes documenting North Carolina history. Beside the bookshelf a trio of oak desks was topped with three bulky black microfiche machines.

**20 MINUTE LIMIT—PLEASE RESPECT OTH-
ERS WAITING TO USE MICROFICHE VIEWERS**,
read a sign on the wall behind the desks. It was the
color of dried blood, shaped like a stop sign. An additional notice, written in black marker on a piece of
notebook paper, was taped to the bottom of that sign:
PLEASE PUT FILM BACK WHERE IT BELONGS!

The work of Old Miss Shit-Bird, I assumed.

Outside the rain began to pick up again, tapping at
the roof of the library like Mother Nature herself
wishing to come in from the chill to read a good
book. Thunder rumbled in the distance like an idle
threat.

I moved toward the closest desk, ready to begin
my search. I still wasn't sure what I needed to look
for, specifically, but I planned to do my best. I took
off my jacket, plopped down before a microfiche
machine. My chair made a soft farting noise. I wondered if old Miss Shit-Bird knew about the graffiti
etched into my cubicle. I hoped she didn't try to
blame me for it. SUPPERTRAMP, read someone's mis-
spelled ink-pen ode to his or her favorite band, and
some other bored music aficionado had carved SUX
below that with a sharp object.

I switched desks, turned on the viewer to my right.

My best bet, I guessed, would be to start with information pertaining to Sheriff Baker's induction into
office. Obviously the local newspapers would have
covered such a story, and this might serve as my most
reliable starting point from which to branch off toward other things I needed to know. . . .

The library's microfiche files were categorized by
publication, one periodical in each of the five file
cabinets against the wall opposite the viewers. Available for perusal were not only archived issues of the

Midnight Sun, but also the *Asheville Citizen-Times,* the *Hendersonville Times-News,* the *Charlotte Observer,* and even the *New York Times.* I moved quickly to the *Midnight Sun* cabinet, squatted down, and read the dates on each drawer starting from the bottom. The oldest files were stored farthest down—those went all the way back to the Jan. 4, 1888 edition of the *Midnight Sun*—and each higher drawer contained, in chronological order, every subsequent issue leading up to the present. They were segregated in groups of about thirty years each.

Burt Baker had been sheriff for just over two years, I mentally calculated, which meant he'd been elected in November 1975.

I opened the top drawer. The microfiche film was stored in red and blue boxes about twice the size of a cigarette pack. The labels on the top edge of each box were typed, faded and peeling but still legible.

After only a few seconds of digging through them, I found the box I needed: "Midnight Sun"/Nov. 1, 1975—Jan. 1, 1976.

I took the box to the microfiche viewer. Opened it. Out fell a fat gray spool of film. I loaded the film into the machine, and then scrolled to the November 9, 1975, issue. That would have been the one published the morning after Election Day. On its front page was a lengthy story about how President Ford had named George Bush as the new head of the CIA. On page two were articles about the civil war in Lebanon as well as a brief piece about a new software company starting up in Seattle, an outfit co-founded by a Harvard dropout named Bill Gates.

Finally, in the Local News section, I found what I was looking for. It had been given equal space on page three with an article praising the Girl Scouts of

Midnight, who had apparently raised $1000 selling cookies the previous summer. The Scouts planned to donate the money to a local children's hospital during the upcoming Thanksgiving holiday with a little help from the Channel 5 News Team and local celebrity Mickey Marvin, of the Oakland Raiders.

I frowned, adjusted the focus on the viewer.

And there he was. That son-of-a-bitch.

Burt Baker, I mean. Not Mickey Marvin.

His hair was slightly longer in that grainy black-and-white photograph than it had been the last time I saw him. He wore a white cowboy hat, blue jeans, and a bulky flannel shirt. He appeared to be a few pounds lighter back then. He smiled for the camera, waving to the fine citizens who had elected him Sheriff of Polk County.

I adjusted the focus on the viewer again, started nibbling at my fingernails as I read about how Burt Baker had deceived us all. . . .

POLK COUNTY ELECTS NEW SHERIFF

Polk County voters delivered a strong turnout to the polls Tuesday to elect a new sheriff for the first time in nearly thirty years.

Republican Burt L. Baker tallied 8323 votes in Tuesday's election, or 59 percent of the total. Democrat Fred K. Irvine received 5666 votes, or 41 percent.

Baker, 42, expressed gratitude Tuesday night to Polk County voters. He also thanked former sheriff Irvine, 74, though he insisted, "(We) must strive to move forward, instead of living in the past."

Burt Baker, a widower, moved to Midnight two

years ago with his son, Henry. He is a former Deputy Sheriff of Gaston County, North Carolina, and a member of the Midnight Masons (Lodge #133).

Baker will be sworn into office on January 1.

I sighed, leaned back in my chair. A brief tide of sadness washed over me as I read about former sheriff Freddy "Tex" Irvine and his loss to Burt Baker. Baker had won that year's election based on a sleazy campaign consisting primarily of constant jabs at Irvine's age, a far-from-subtle "out-with-the-old-in-with-the-new/you-can't-teach-an-old-dog-new-tricks" mentality. I had been nine years old when Irvine last served as Sheriff of Polk County, but I remembered him well. He was a good man, an older fellow I always thought looked like a real cowboy. A true John Wayne type. Sheriff Irvine's grandson, Jimmy, had been my next-door neighbor for several years, and Jimmy and I had been treated often to rides in the sheriff's patrol car, wailing sirens and flashing lights and all.

I rolled my eyes, realizing I had digressed from the task at hand. I shifted uncomfortably in my chair, cursed myself for getting off track before reading the article again. . . .

This time I focused on the brief biographical bit about Baker at the end. Burt Baker was a former Deputy Sheriff of Gaston County, North Carolina, it said. That was just outside of Charlotte, I was pretty sure. I had been to Charlotte a few times in the past to visit my aunt Jen, and the more I thought about it, I was quite certain Gastonia sat within a few miles of what us North Carolinians call the "Queen City."

This led me off on a new search. I removed that piece of film from the microfiche machine and carefully stuffed it back in its box before moving across the room to the file cabinet containing archived editions of the *Charlotte Observer.* After finding a range of dates I assumed would contain the information I needed, I grabbed several boxes from the top drawer of that cabinet, starting with four or five spools of film all cataloging issues within about three years before Burt Baker had been elected Sheriff of Polk County, when he and Henry lived in Gastonia.

It took several tries, sure—not to mention over an hour of constant scrolling and skimming, removing one spool of film then threading the next one into the machine, repeating the tedious process again and again as I searched for Baker's name in the news—but I eventually found everything I needed within a box labeled "Charlotte Observer"/April 1, 1973—June 1, 1973.

It happened on May 27, 1973. I gasped when I saw it, although I wasn't all that surprised:

LOCAL TEENAGER SOUGHT FOR QUESTIONING
ACCUSED OF RAPE

Police are searching for Henry Ronald Baker, 17, for questioning in the alleged rape of a 14-year-old neighbor.

Baker was last seen Saturday night at Gilby's Steak House on Tenth Street, where he is employed part time. He is the son of Gaston County Deputy Sheriff Burt Baker.

The Gastonia Police Department requests anyone with information leading to Henry Baker's whereabouts call 1-704-555-4645 as soon as possible.

I just sat there for the next minute or so, nodding. I popped my knuckles, and the sound was very loud in the Midnight Public Library's NC Genealogy room.

This confirmed what I knew all along, what Baker had mentioned that night in my Old Shack and what my brother had alluded to at the airport. . . .

He had done it before. Henry Baker had a *history* of messing with underage girls.

I had to know more. I started scrolling again . . . skipping useless crap about how Richard Nixon accepted "full responsibility but not blame" for Watergate and about the launch of America's first space station, *Skylab*, and details of the massive food drive the Gaston County 4-H Club planned to sponsor the following summer. . . .

What I did not expect was for Henry's story to turn out like it did.

The sheriff's son was in the news yet again in an issue of the *Charlotte Observer* published two days after the previous article I had read. My jaw dropped when I learned what he had done this time, though, as it was an act so uncharacteristic of the Henry Baker I knew, it seemed like fiction at first:

RAPE SUSPECT SURRENDERS TO POLICE

Monday afternoon Gastonia Police Chief Scott Thompson arrested Henry Baker, 17, for the rape of a local girl.

Gastonia Police have been searching for Baker since Saturday night, after the alleged victim filed a complaint with the Gaston County Magistrate's Office.

Chief Thompson said Henry Baker was arrested without incident, though the young man "denies any wrong-doing." Meanwhile, Judge Gordon Hurkee denied public defender Victoria Lawson's request for bail yesterday.

Baker is the son of Gaston County Deputy Sheriff Burt Baker.

At first I could only sit there and stare at the screen, confused. But then I started nodding. And I kept nodding like that, dumbly, for the next two or three minutes. . . .

As perplexing as it all was, it made so much sense at the same time. I could feel the gaps filling themselves in the more I read, could almost *see* the story playing itself out in my head like one long, disquieting movie. Although every detail was not yet lain out before me, and most of the jigsaw puzzle facts were still spread about waiting for me to bring them together, I knew what had happened in Gastonia a little over four years ago as clearly as I knew I had two arms and legs.

I knew because I knew *them*. Burt Baker and his son.

Henry had raped another girl. And he had run away. That much was clear from the first newspaper. Yet another fact became obvious to me as I pieced it all together. . . .

After Henry ran, and the cops began their search for him, Deputy Sheriff Burt Baker had faced embarrassment the likes of which he had never known. Perhaps dear old Dad's job had been in danger because of his son's crime.

Burt Baker couldn't have that, of course. He *wouldn't* have that. The scandal was too much for him to bear.

"Cut your losses and do the right thing," I imagined

him telling Henry, days after the troubled teen forced himself upon a neighbor who was still more child than woman. I envisioned the sheriff's thick black eyebrows furrowing, spittle escaping from his fat brown lips as he gnashed his teeth and demanded not because it was the right thing to do but to save his own sorry ass, "By God, boy, you will do as I say, or I will carry you back to Chief Thompson myself!"

Once Henry did that—once he turned himself in and the powers-that-be punished him for his crimes—Burt Baker's reputation would be saved. Bad memories eventually fade, after all. Humans favor resolution. Once the rapist was behind bars, Gaston County could forget what had happened. And Burt Baker could go on with his life.

For once, he had been unable to protect his delinquent son. So he'd been forced to do the most important thing. Look out for Number One.

I couldn't find out fast enough how the whole thing had ended. I cursed as I realized I had come to the end of that last spool of film. I jerked it out of the machine, and my hands shook as I replaced it with the next spool on the desk beside me. I dropped the new one twice before I finally got it threaded into the microfiche viewer. . . .

This time I skimmed over catalogued issues of the *Charlotte Observer* published from June to August, 1973 . . . searching carefully for key words like "Gastonia," "Deputy," "rape," and "Baker."

Finally, there it was, a brief article on page three of the July 12 edition of the *Charlotte Observer*, approximately six weeks after Henry Baker had turned himself in. I started biting my nails again as I read it, and my heart slammed in my chest like some dark creature fighting to free itself from a prison of flesh and bone.

CASE DISMISSED AGAINST GASTONIA TEEN
CHARGED WITH RAPE

Henry Baker, the 17-year-old son of Gaston County Deputy Sheriff Burt Baker, is a free man as of yesterday morning.

The young lady who previously accused Baker of rape recanted her story on the witness stand mere minutes after Baker's trial began. Judge Gordon Hurkee then granted public defender Victoria Lawson's immediate request for a dismissal of all charges *in toto*.

Henry Baker's only statement to the *Charlotte Observer* was "I knew the truth would come out. (This is) the best birthday present a guy could ever have."

The temperature in the room felt as if it had risen a thousand degrees. My forehead grew slick with sweat.

That couldn't be right.

"No," I said aloud. My voice was hoarse. "Impossible . . ."

I read the article again. Then a third time.

"He can't . . . no . . . he couldn't have gotten away with it. . . ."

But he had. And I knew how.

My stomach roiled. I wanted to slam my fist through the screen of that microfiche viewer.

The article told me nothing and everything at once. . . .

After all that had happened, after Henry Baker came so close to having to pay for his sins, his father had pulled his skinny ass out of the fire once again.

Burt Baker had forced the poor girl to recant her

story. He had threatened her, had warned her not to testify against Henry. Or else.

And she had taken it all back. Like one big, dirty lie meant to destroy an innocent young man's future.

I idly scrolled through the rest of that piece of film, not wanting to read any more. My hands shook, and the words upon the viewer screen blurred like fading memories beneath the tears in my eyes.

And then I saw it. In an issue published one week after Henry's exoneration.

He had not gotten away with his crimes after all, it seemed.

My stomach roiled as I read it. I felt strangely hollow inside. Perhaps I should have been pleased in some sick, vindictive way, but at that point I no longer knew *what* to feel about the whole godforsaken thing:

LOCAL YOUTHS ARRESTED FOR ATTACK ON MINOR
VICTIM IN STABLE CONDITION

Last night Gastonia Police arrested three local teenagers after a younger man was attacked in Bergen Park.

According to Police Chief Scott Thompson, the suspects—Chad Simple, 20; Greg Gonce, 20; and Malcolm Stahl, 19—face various charges including aggravated assault on a minor and assault with a deadly weapon.

Shortly after 10 P.M. Monday evening, 17-year-old Henry Baker was admitted to Gaston County Memorial Hospital with a number of severe injuries. According to Dr. Gil Halford, Baker is now in stable condition, though "psychologically he may never be the same."

According to one officer who asked to remain anonymous, police have closed Bergen Park to the public until further notice as they search for a (unspecified, at press time) dismembered part of the victim's anatomy.

I realized my mouth had been hanging open as I read. I closed it, but otherwise I did not move for several long minutes.

The rain droned on outside. Like a whispered taunt from some invisible tormentor.

"Holy shit," I said.

Finally I took a deep breath, turned off the microfiche machine.

I cupped my testicles through my jeans. Wondered if I would ever sleep again without one hand covering my penis.

My brain throbbed as I tried to process everything I had learned in the last couple hours. . . .

Henry hadn't raped Cassandra Belle Rourke that night in my Old Shack after all. Such a thing might not have even been possible, if my assumptions were correct regarding what had happened in Gastonia. He had hurt Cassandra Rourke, yes. He had beaten her until she could barely stand. But he had not raped her. If those young men had mutilated him to an extreme at which the *Charlotte Observer* insinuated, Henry would never force himself upon a woman again. He would never make love to a woman.

They had disfigured him. Taught him a grisly lesson.

I shuddered, wanted to let out a sick chuckle as I thought about that, but at the same time I wanted to run and hide from what I knew, leaving it behind like something I could just drop off in the nearest muddy gutter.

I almost felt sorry for Henry Baker.

Almost.

Four years ago the sheriff's son *had* paid for his crimes, contrary to what I had believed mere minutes before. Henry Baker got what was coming to him, and brutal as his punishment had been, I could not deny that he deserved it.

For some reason, though, I did not feel better about any of this at all.

"Good-bye, Mrs. Schifford," I said a few minutes later, throwing up my hand. My voice cracked when I said it. My hand shook like the pale appendage of something twice as ancient as Old Miss Shit-Bird, and I quickly shoved it into my pocket so she would not notice as I passed by her desk.

Mrs. Schifford said nothing. She glanced up at me and her eyes narrowed suspiciously, but after a couple seconds she went back to whatever she had been doing.

It was the last time I would see Miss Shit-Bird for many years—that final image of her standing so straight and proper, meticulously stacking those GET YOUR OWN LIBRARY CARD TODAY pamphlets on one side of her desk with a look on her face like she'd just smelled the king of all farts. The old lady retired not long after that, and a younger, friendlier librarian took her place.

August 9

Chapter Thirteen

On Wednesday, August 9, I realized I had no choice but to act immediately.

I *had* to do something.

That was the day Sheriff Burt Baker arrested an innocent man for the murder of Cassandra Belle Rourke.

I rose from bed that morning with a terrible headache, and I remember wondering if this was how Mom felt the mornings after her binges. How could such throbbing pain be worth something Dan assured me didn't even taste that good?

I stepped into the bathroom across the hall to grab some aspirin before going to find Mom on the other side of the house. I started my search in the kitchen, but it was empty. Where the room should have been filled with the delicious aromas of eggs, bacon, and toast, only a pungent fermented smell permeated the air. The bittersweet stench of fruit gone bad.

I shook my head, disgusted. Once again, my

mother had "tied one on" the night before, and it was up to me to work out all the knots.

"Son-of-a-bitch," I said under my breath, before moving toward the living room.

It was already seven-forty, which meant Mom should have been out of bed. Her shift at the woodworking factory began at eight, and even on a day when traffic was sparse the drive took her about twenty-five minutes. That was *all* we needed, her getting fired. We could lose everything we had.

"Mom!" I shouted through the silent house. "You're gonna be late for work!"

Finally I found her. On the sofa in the living room, watching television. She was still wearing her nightgown. It was thin, and I could see her tiny brown nipples through the flimsy material. I swallowed, quickly looked away to the lamp stand beside her. It was coated with a gray sheen of dust, yet the fat bottle of vodka atop it was shiny and new. The bottle almost looked pretty next to every other ratty old thing in our middle-class home, like some expensive new knick-knack amidst a world of junky clutter.

"Is all that shouting really necessary, Kyle?" Mom asked me, her moist gaze never leaving the television. "Jesus. Wake the dead, why don'tcha?"

I could smell her from where I stood, an odor stronger even than that of her liquor. I was used to it, though. The sour stench of her addiction. It had been seeping through her pores for years, festering in her breath until it had become a part of her, just like my mother's bright blue eyes and the way she licked her lips when she was nervous.

I said nothing to Mom, just stepped farther into the room so I could see the TV. It was turned to Channel 5, the WHLP Morning News from Tryon.

"Looks like they found him," Mom said. "Should've known Burt Baker would get his man before long."

I yawned. Didn't have a clue what she was talking about. But then I froze. My mouth hung open as I watched. As I listened. I forgot all about Mom being late for work.

"No," I said to the television, beneath my breath. "That can't be . . . he—"

"Bastard's gonna fry," said Mom. "At least, we can all hope."

On our battered old Zenith a man with perfect white teeth and immaculately combed blond hair offered me a smile so laughably fake, so condescending, for a second or two I thought he looked plastic. All the color must have drained from my face as I listened to what he was saying, as guilt ate at my soul like something with a multitude of hungry, razor-edged mouths. . . .

Especially when the suspect's mug shot flashed upon the screen. When those sad, sad eyes stared across the living room into mine.

"Shortly after six this morning," announced the anchorman over the grainy photograph, "Sheriff Burt Baker arrested thirty-year-old Calvin Tremaine Mooney for the murder of Cassandra Rourke, the young lady whose body was found in Midnight's Snake River this past weekend. Further details are currently unavailable, but rest assured, the Channel 5 News crew will keep viewers updated as we know more ourselves."

I covered my mouth with one trembling hand, made a pained whimpering sound in the back of my throat.

"Back to you now, Freddy, with this week in sports."

I turned away from the television to stare through

James Newman

my mother while a guy who couldn't have been more than a year or two older than Dan rambled on about football or baseball or some such trivial nonsense.

"I always knew that guy was weird," Mom said. Her hand went to her chest, a moment of sheer melodrama. "Isn't that scary, Kyle? You pass someone on the street every day, but you never know what's lurking just beneath the surface."

I did not reply. I shook my head as I staggered out of the living room and down the hallway.

I didn't bother turning on the light as I entered Dan's bedroom. I collapsed on his bed, feeling both physically and mentally drained.

With these latest developments it became clear to me that the whole terrible situation had changed drastically. My dilemma was no longer as simple as it should have been the night I witnessed the murder, and now it was not only Cassie Belle Rourke's blood that stained my hands, should I shirk my responsibilities once again. . . .

Calvin Tremaine Mooney was a skinny black man who had walked the streets of Midnight for as long as I could remember. Everywhere he went he towed a squeaky red Radio Flyer wagon behind him, a wagon filled with soda cans and bottles he had scavenged from all over town. That was how he earned his meager living, apparently, returning those cans and bottles for their nickel and dime deposits.

The kids all called Calvin "Rooster" because the way he'd flap his arms and make high-pitched squawking noises when he got excited. He probably weighed a hundred pounds soaking wet. His mouth always hung open slightly, as if he were constantly planning to say something but couldn't remember what it was. His teeth were horselike, crooked and discolored. Along his left temple and half of his

114

cheek he sported a birthmark, a thin pinkish stain I'd always thought resembled a shriveled worm trapped just beneath his flesh.

Loath as I am to admit it, being black in a small Southern town circa 1977 was only one of several unfair strikes against someone like Calvin Mooney. I had seen the way Midnight's upper-middle-class white folks—ladies and gentlemen who would otherwise argue that such prejudiced behavior was far beneath them—looked down their noses at Rooster, the way they watched him with expressions of self-righteous distaste as he shambled about town. I had heard carloads of teenagers yell cruel epithets his way as they raced down Whitman Boulevard in their parents' shiny sports cars, had seen beer bottles hurled from such vehicles nearly hit Calvin when he bent to replace an errant can that had clattered from the glittery aluminum mountain atop his wagon.

I cursed Sheriff Burt Baker when I heard the news of Calvin Mooney's arrest. I wished I could get my hands around his fat fucking neck.

Despite that nagging, instinctual sense of self-preservation which had thus far kept me doing the right thing, there was no way I could allow an innocent man to take the blame for what Baker had done.

It was too late for Cassie Belle Rourke. But not for Calvin Mooney.

I knew what I had to do.

Chapter Fourteen

There was just one thing I had to do before I paid my long-overdue visit to Deputy Mike Linder.

I had to be *sure*. . . .

As soon as Mom left for work, I went to the phone in the kitchen. I stood before it, swallowed. Cleared my throat. Wiped my clammy palms on my shirt.

I stared at the phone for several long minutes as if it might bite me should I step too near.

For as far back as I could remember a list of emergency numbers had been taped on the wall above the telephone, to the right of our refrigerator. That bright white piece of notebook paper always stood out in stark contrast to the ugly melon color of our kitchen wallpaper even after the paper started to turn a dusty-yellow, but I can't recall ever needing to use the list before the day I visited Deputy Linder. Just a few of the numbers there, all of them written in Mom's barely legible scrawl, were contact info for the Midnight Fire Department, our family doctor, and the Polk County Sheriff's Department.

I sighed, picked up the phone. Squinted to read Mom's hastily scribbled number for the Sheriff's Department. Dialed it.

It rang. And rang. And rang again. My heart slammed in my chest while I waited for someone to pick up.

"Polk County Sheriff's Department," said a deep male voice, halfway through the fourth ring. "May I help you?"

"I—" My breath caught in my throat. I couldn't speak.

"Hello?"

"I . . . h-hello?"

"Hello. Polk County Sheriff's Department. How can I be of service?"

"Could you, um . . ."

"Yes?"

"C-could you p-please t-tell me if Sheriff B-Baker is available, please?" I whispered into the phone. I cringed. My voice sounded so high-pitched and squeaky.

"No, I'm sorry, he's not," came the reply. "May I take a message, or perhaps if this is an emergency I could be of—"

That was all I needed to know.

No Sheriff Baker.

I hung up.

I threw on my jacket and hurried out of the house, not even bothering to lock the front door behind me.

It was now or never, I knew.

I was ready as I'd ever be. . . .

Chapter Fifteen

It seemed as if years had passed since the last time I'd seen the sun. Ever since the night of the Apple Gala I had become increasingly convinced that the pall of gloomy weather hanging over Midnight might never go away. The storm faded to a faint drizzle as I made my way through town, down New Fort Road toward Main Street, but it did not dissipate entirely. A thick blue-black promise of more hard rain loomed upon the horizon like an ugly bruise on the sky, and thunder rumbled beyond the Blue Ridge Mountains like a dirty secret. The streets and sidewalks were littered with soggy leaves and dead pine needles stuck to the ground like rust-colored insects flattened by the storm.

Occasionally I would spot a fat brown earthworm in my path, trying to find its way home, and with a boy's unending infatuation for all things slimy and oozing I would cup my wriggling discovery in one palm, moving him off the cement where he might burrow down into the earth to venture homeward instead of awaiting squishy death beneath the feet of

118

passers-by. Perhaps I merely delayed the inevitable, walking slower and slower the closer I came to the Sheriff's Department, though I tried to tell myself I was brave, that nothing could stop me from doing what was right. I missed Burner more than ever as I dodged dozens of mud puddles or accidentally stepped through them when I failed to pay attention to where I was going, splashing muddy water over the legs of my jeans in the process. Normally I would have ridden right through those miniature ponds without a second thought—Burner and I would have intentionally hit every one, in fact, as if it were some sort of messy game. But times, they were a-changin'. And they had been ever since the night of August 5.

Everything looked so gray, so dreary, in my town. As if the whole place were drowning beneath a thick, watery fog of wrongness.

The offices of the Polk County Sheriff's Department were located at 327 North Main Street, in a nondescript brick building sandwiched between the offices of the *Midnight Sun* and a vacant establishment that had once been a pool hall called Happy Jack's. In front of the Sheriff's Department was a tall silver flagpole. A U.S. flag clinked and clanked upon it in the day's cool breeze, and I noticed the flag flew at half-staff, presumably in memory of Cassandra Belle Rourke. The giant gold badge painted on the office's plate-glass window was the only hint as to what went on inside there; otherwise the Sheriff's Department might have been just another Mom & Pop's diner or arts-and-crafts store at first glance.

My heart started thudding in my chest like a jackhammer when I saw it looming so close before me. . . .

I didn't want to go in there. Never in my life had I *not* wanted to do something so badly.

But I knew I had no choice.

I shrugged off my windbreaker when I came within a hundred feet or so of the building, took a deep breath as I tied it around my waist.

For a full five minutes I must have stood there. Not moving. Just staring at the offices of the Sheriff's Department.

Somewhere in my peripheral vision an old blue-haired lady pulled her Cadillac alongside the curb, got out, and waited while her poodle left a tiny pile of turds at the base of the flagpole. She might have said something to me, but I wasn't sure. On the other side of the street, four burly rednecks conversed loudly as they entered Annie's Country Diner (FREE O.J. WITH LARGE BISCUITS-N-GRAVY PLATTER, read the sign in the window, above a smaller pink banner: WE MISS YOU, CASSIE). One of them said something about a "crazy sonuvabitch," and "huntin' season," but that was all I could make out.

The blood rushing through my head as well as my own nervous respiration had grown nearly deafening during those last few seconds.

I blocked everything else out, then. I stared at the offices of the Polk County Sheriff's Department up ahead. Swallowed nervously. Took a few steps forward. The only thing upon which I could focus, during those last few seconds before I entered the building, were the bold white letters painted beneath that badge on the window:

POLK COUNTY SHERIFF'S DEPARTMENT
BURT L. BAKER, SHERIFF

I wanted to run. I wanted to hide. I wanted to trade places with that old lady's poodle on its too-tight leash.

120

I wanted to be anywhere but here.
But I knew I had to do this. Before it was too late.
So I opened the door and went inside.

The interior of the Sheriff's Department was nothing like what I expected. Thanks to TV shows like *Columbo* and *Dragnet*, movies like *Serpico* and (Dan's favorite) *Dirty Harry*, my twelve-year-old brain had envisioned a room bustling with mad activity. Chaos. Stern-faced boys in blue escorting tattooed scumbags and scantily clad hookers to the dingy jailhouse at the back of the building. Baggy-eyed detectives with five o'clock shadows sipping from cups of hot black coffee. The smell of blotter ink, cheap cigars, and gun oil. Not to mention phones—a shrill chorus of telephones constantly ringing ringing ringing.

On the contrary, when I entered that one-room building and the little bell over the door announced my arrival (far louder than I would have preferred), the first thing I noticed was the almost haunting quiet of the place. It didn't seem right.

Outside, I heard the *swoosh* of a car driving through a puddle. The loud fart of a diesel engine passing then fading in the distance. Through the building's thin walls I could faintly hear Stevie Wonder singing "Sir Duke" on a radio, sounded like it was coming from the newspaper place next door.

My guts roiled as I looked around the place. I wondered if I really could go through with this.

Two identical desks sat side by side in the center of the room, neither covered with more than a modicum of paperwork. A bank of puke-green file cabinets lined the wall beyond the desks. At the rear of the room another door led to an area designated AU-THORIZED PERSONNEL ONLY. To the right of that door a microwave and a coffee machine sat atop two more battered file cabinets. The microwave hummed softly.

The smell of beef stew filled the room.

I stood there for several long minutes, wondering what I should do. Wondering what came next.

A toilet flushed. The door at the back of the room squeaked open.

A man in a khaki uniform came through, wiping his hands on his pants.

My breath caught in my throat. My heart skipped a beat.

The microwave *ding*ed.

The man in the sheriff's uniform glanced first toward the microwave, then at me. Our eyes met.

A phone on one of the desks rang.

MIKE W. LINDER, DEPUTY SHERIFF, read the nameplate atop that desk.

I began to breathe again. My heartbeat slowly returned to normal.

Deputy Mike Linder threw up his big right hand. "Well, look what the cat dragged in! Mr. Kyle Mackey!"

The phone rang again.

I returned the man's smile, but shyly stared at my shoes. Wondered what to do next.

"Be with ya in a second, 'kay?" Mike said.

I nodded.

Mike Linder and my father had been old high-school buddies. He and his wife, Terri, used to bring my family warm meals after Dad's funeral, but they stopped coming around following a nasty scene Mom had made one evening when I was eight or nine years old. Deputy Mike had dropped by to check on us, and once again my mother had been drunk out of her gourd. She answered the door in only her bra and a denim skirt, a bottle of Jim Beam gripped tightly in her hand like some copper-bodied parasite affixed to her palm. As soon as she opened the door, she asked Mike what the fuck he wanted. He barely had time to say anything before she accused him of looking down on our family. She informed him that we did not want his "charity." Then she threw herself upon him, started smothering him with vulgar wet kisses.

Mike apologized that day after shoving Mom off him, and when he saw me peeking around the corner, he waved at me. The smile on his face, however, was very sad. He sniffled once, softly, before stepping off our doorstep for the last time.

Linder was a big man, but he possessed one of the kindest, gentlest faces I ever saw. His brown hair was peppered with early streaks of gray. He volunteered a lot as a Salvation Army Santa Claus around the Christmas season, and he was perfect for it. His bright blue eyes seemed to sparkle with kindness. A number of faintly visible freckles dotted his fat cheeks, a trait that made him appear ten years younger than his thirty-some-odd years.

"Okay," Mike said, into the phone. "Love you too. No, I won't forget. Bye."

I cleared my throat, shifted my weight from one foot to the other as I waited.

"Sorry about that," Mike said, hanging up the phone at last. His voice was deep but not intimidating. "Wife checking in. Both the girls have been sick. Doc Laymon's gonna write 'em a prescription for me to pick up on the way home. How are things with you, buddy?"

That was the thing I liked most about Mike Linder. He always spoke to me as if I were his equal, not just another dumb kid. He made me feel like a real person, in spite of my family's predicament.

Still, I popped my knuckles nervously, fidgeted beneath Mike's gaze. For some reason I could not make eye contact with the deputy, as if I had come here to confess my own crimes.

"Earth to Kyle," Deputy Linder said with a chuckle, startling me from my inner torment. "Hello, hello?"

I laughed uneasily. "Um, s-sorry. H-how are you, Mike?"

He gestured toward the microwave at the back of the room. "Do you mind? I was about to grab some lunch."

"Um, yeah," I said. "Of course. G-go ahead."

"Been one of those days, lemme tell ya. I don't gobble it down now, I'll never get the chance."

"Yeah," I said. "I do . . . um . . . I hear things have been really, um, busy around here."

"You can say that again. Been nonstop all morning after . . . well, you know." He glanced toward the jailhouse at the back of the building, beyond that AU-THORIZED PERSONNEL ONLY door. Shook his head.

I wondered if Calvin Mooney was back there behind bars even now, wrongly imprisoned at the hands of a murderer with a badge while I delayed justice because of my own paranoid sense of self-preservation. Perhaps he heard every word we said. I wondered if Burner was back there as well. Waiting for his best friend to come bail him out.

Mike opened the microwave, pulled out his bowl of beef stew. "So I understand Dan left for Florida a few days ago."

"Yeah," I mumbled, not wanting to talk about that at all.

"Good for him. He's gonna go far, that kid. Won't be long till he's fielding offers from the NBA, you wait and see."

"Probably."

"Guess you're the man of the house now, huh?"

"I guess."

"Gonna miss him?"

My reply was barely a whisper: "If you only knew . . ."

"I was always crazy about my big brother when I was your age. Worshipped the guy. He works in the White House now, writing speeches for President Carter. Can you believe that?"

Then Mike forgot all about Dan in Florida and coveted government jobs and how much we both missed our brothers as he turned back toward me and carried his dinner to his desk. He sat, pulled from his desk drawer a small baggie containing a fork, a napkin, and several salt and pepper packets, and began to eat.

He spoke to me between loud, smacking bites: "So what's up, Kyle? What brings you to the offices of Midnight's finest?"

I pointed to a metal chair in front of his desk. "May I?"

"Mmm." He swallowed, took another big bite of beef stew. "Please. Sit."

I sat.

"Not hungry, are you?"

"No," I replied, though the way he chowed down so voraciously I wouldn't have expected him to offer me any of his lunch even if I had accepted his offer. "Thanks."

"So what's up, little buddy?" Deputy Linder asked me, his mouth full. "Somethin' wrong, or did you just drop by to say 'hi'?"

For the next minute or so I stared at a picture on Mike's desk, unable to find my voice. It was a framed photograph of Mike's twin daughters, Staci and Traci, a snapshot the family had taken during a trip to Disney World, judging from the majestic castle in the sunny background and the beaming, tuxedoed rodent who stood between the Linder twins.

Perhaps it was everything on my mind of late . . . but those girls looked so much like Cassandra Belle Rourke at that moment, with their long blond hair and innocent teenage smiles, I wanted to run screaming from the room. Mickey Mouse resembled something sinister embracing the girls, a malevolent creature with obscene intentions despite the very friendly expression upon his mammoth black and white head.

"Kyle? You okay?"

I looked up, and Deputy Linder's face seemed to glow with compassion. His fork was still in his hand, but he had stopped eating.

"What's the matter? Has something happened?"

"I . . . I . . ."

"What is it, Kyle?"

"I . . . I n-need to tell you, Mike—"

I heard the front door of the building open behind me then, but I didn't turn around. The words I had prepared to say to Deputy Linder caught in my throat. *Shit.* After all this, someone had interrupted us? How long would it take for me to build up the nerve again to tell Mike what I knew? *Could* I do it? Or would this be Calvin Mooney's only chance at freedom?

Mike looked past me, over my shoulder, and greeted the person who had entered with an upward jerk of his head. "You get that taken care of, boss?"

"Eh. For now. Goddamn fool's never gonna learn, though."

It was a voice I knew instantly. A voice that had haunted my dreams for days. The voice of the devil himself.

"Same old shit, at least once a week. I'm starting to think the son of a bitch likes it, Mike."

His walkie-talkie squawked loudly upon his belt as if to emphasize his point.

I couldn't turn around even if I tried. My feet seemed cemented to the floor, my ass Crazy-Glued to my seat. My every muscle tensed up. My cheeks, ears, and neck burned with terror. I felt naked, so vulnerable sitting there as *he* walked up behind me. I could hear the blood rushing through my head, felt my bowels lurch. I wondered if he heard them too.

"You decided not to haul him in this time?" Deputy Linder asked his superior.

"What good's it gonna do? Guy's gonna learn his lesson faster if I take him home and let Bella knock him over the head with her rolling pin a few times than if he's sleepin' it off in the tank."

"True," Mike laughed. "Good point."

"Friggin' Sal. Betcha a million dollars his liver looks like that roadkill you scraped up last week over on Bartleby."

"But he'll never change."

"Nope. His kind never do."

Sheriff Burt Baker walked past my chair then, and I could have reached out and touched him. Loose change jingled in his pockets. His gun belt squeaked with his movements. The weapon looked so impossibly huge, there at his waist. I couldn't stop staring at it.

He glanced back at me. I gasped as our eyes met.

Burt Baker reached to pour himself a cup of coffee from the brewer atop the file cabinets.

"This stuff any good?"

"I wouldn't," Mike replied. "It's probably toxic by now."

"What else is new."

Baker poured himself a cup of coffee before turning back to Mike and me.

"So what's going on here?" he said.

"I, um . . . you—" I started, but I could say nothing else. I wanted to run from that place, wanted to flee down Main Street, wanted to leave this town and never look back. But I couldn't. My feet felt as if they had melded with the cold, hard floor. My knees were like Jell-O.

"Pretty slow day here at home base," Mike said. "Mr. Kyle was just—"

"You're Dan Mackey's brother," Baker interrupted. "Darlene's kid."

The murderer's eyes seem to burn into my soul. I felt like a mouse about to be devoured by a big, ugly snake. The old acne scars around Sheriff Burt Baker's dark features seemed deeper than ever before, his flesh mottled and craterous.

I wanted to spit in his face. Even where I sat, across the room from him, I was quite sure I'd hit my mark.

"I . . . um . . . y-y-yeah," I said at last, through clenched teeth. "Th-that's me. R-right."

"That brother of yours, he's one hell of a basketball player."

I nodded, stared at that picture of Mike's twins again and wished I could be in there with them.

"I watched him win the state championship for Stokely High last year," Baker said. "Swear to God, I've never seen a white boy play like that."

I said nothing. Just kept staring at that picture of Disney World.

"You play?"

"Wh-what?" I squirmed beneath Sheriff Baker's penetrating gaze.

"Your brother the only athlete in the family? Or do you play too?"

How I wished he would stop looking at me. His eyes narrowed, as if he were interrogating me. I wanted to hide under Mike Linder's desk and never come out.

"Just him," I wheezed.

"Yeah. You look like more of a bookworm. Probably like to read, draw, crap like that?"

I said nothing. Just squirmed in my seat, felt a salty trickle of sweat drip down my forehead and into my right eye. It burned there, like acid.

"Hm," the sheriff said finally, no longer interested in whether I planned to follow in my brother's footsteps or pursue more artistic interests like reading and drawing and crap like that. *Thank God.* He walked to the desk next to Mike's, sat his cup of coffee there (COPS DO IT "BY THE BOOK," read the logo on the side), and eased into his chair. He opened a manila folder atop his desk and his brow creased as he studied some paperwork inside there.

I began to breathe again. Tentatively.

"So, anyway," Deputy Linder said. "You had something on your mind, Kyle. What was it you wanted to tell me, buddy?"

The sound of a single raindrop outside the building might have been louder than my whisper at that moment. I could barely hear my own voice. Not that it would have mattered anyway, as my thoughts came out so jumbled and incoherent: "I . . . I need to . . . need t-to t-t-talk to you . . . we . . . D-Dan said . . . you . . . b-but . . . I . . ."

Sheriff Burt Baker looked up from his desk, smirked at me, and then turned toward Mike.

He said, "That must have been *his* bike that night."

I felt a sudden wet warmth in the crotch of my

Fruit-of-the-Looms. A chill ran through my body like shards of ice cutting straight to the bone.

Sheriff Baker offered me a haughty smile before returning to the paperwork on his desk.

I exhaled loudly, realizing that Baker hadn't said anything about my bike at all. I had misunderstood him. Instead of "that must have been his bike that night," he'd simply said to his deputy, "Cat must have his tongue, right, Mike?"

It should have been funny. I should have stifled a chuckle of relief. But I didn't.

My terror got the best of me.

And so I did it.

I chickened out.

"Nevermind, Mike," I said. I shot to my feet, almost knocking over my chair. My voice was thick with tears as I backed away from the desks, moving for the door. "It's n-nothing. F-forget it. I . . . I have to go. I . . . I h-have to . . . M-Mom . . ."

"Kyle?" Mike started. "What—"

"I forgot I, um . . . I have to b-be somewhere," I said. "I have to g-go. I'm s-sorry."

Deputy Linder's brow furrowed as he watched me retreat. "Okay. If you're sure . . ."

Sheriff Baker winked at me.

The hairs on the nape of my neck stood up. I fumbled for the door, never turning my back on the men until I was out of the building.

I collided with an old man in a soggy gray jogging suit as I staggered out of the Sheriff's Department and turned to flee toward home. His wide yellow eyes glared into mine and he smelled of Old Spice overkill.

"Watch where you're going, junior!" he snapped at me.

But I barely even heard him.

Chapter Sixteen

Mom came into my room that night while I lay in bed half-heartedly thumbing through a Superman comic book. I didn't mind her visit, though her true motives remained a mystery to me long after she was gone. I hadn't really been reading my comic book anyway. The whole time I tried to follow Superman's adventures around Metropolis I could only think about what Sheriff Burt Baker had said to me earlier that day.

You look like a bookworm. Probably like to read, draw, crap like that?

Never in my life had I known true hate before then.

I loathed everything he represented. Everything he was about.

Lies. Hypocrisy. Murder and deceit.

Finally I tossed my comic book aside, deciding I abhorred Clark Kent and his alter ego nearly as bad as I hated Sheriff Burt Baker. Mr. Goody-goody in his red-and-blue tights always did the right thing. Super-man wasn't afraid of anyone or anything.

And then I saw Mom standing in the doorway.

At first she just stuck her head in the door tenta-tively, as if she were some vampire disguised as my mother and thus could not cross the threshold into my domain without an invitation. She coughed softly, twice, to get my attention.

"Kyle, are you awake?" she asked, even after she saw me lying there with the light on.

"I'm awake."

She had just gotten out of the shower. Her hair lay across her shoulders in wet black curls. She wore her favorite teal bathrobe, and she smelled like strawber-ries. Despite her hard cheekbones and the crow's feet around her eyes, I could see the gorgeous woman my mother had once been. Beneath her tired exterior I could envision the stunning Southern belle who had stolen my father's heart in high school, and I was quite sure that if Mom would only allow her beauty to shine more often through the ugly veil of her addiction, she would have been the most beautiful lady on Earth. To me, at least. If.

"I see you've cleaned up your room," Mom said.

"Yep."

"Looks good. Except for the funny book lying in the middle of the floor."

I shrugged, didn't even wince like I used to when she called them "funny books."

She leaned over, picked up my Superman comic and set it next to my lamp. She took a second to ad-just it so it was perfectly square with the edge of the nightstand, as if admiring fine art.

"You should take care of these, Kyle," she said. "You never know, they could be worth a lot of money someday."

Mom made herself comfortable beside me on the bed. I felt a pang of embarrassment when her robe fell open slightly and I glimpsed a pale inner thigh stippled with light freckles and maybe even a hint of dark pubic hair. I cleared my throat, looked off toward my closet, and though Mom pulled her robe tighter around herself she didn't seem to notice my embarrassment. I felt a sick feeling in the pit of my stomach. Not a pleasant thing for a child to notice, that. Such unwanted sights force a growing boy to recognize his mother as Woman, with parts no different from those ogled during clandestine peeks at his cousin Toby's *Playboy* collection, smooth pink places identical to those he will one day kiss and touch in the way adults kiss and touch one another behind closed doors.

I shuddered, mortified by such unwanted revelations. I suddenly found myself wondering if Mom had done *it* with anyone since Dad died.

That would be like spitting on my father's grave, I decided. I could never handle such a thing.

"My darling Kyle," Mom said. "It seems like only yesterday when I brought you home for the first time. You were so tiny . . . just two big blue, curious eyes staring up at me from that blanket."

I said nothing. Didn't know how to respond. I just lay back, listened to Mom's voice, and felt an odd sort of comfort in the way it fell into a mellow rhythm with the sound of the rain outside. It reminded me vaguely of those old jazz records Dad used to love when he was home on leave, the ones he would listen to in the den every Saturday night with a glass of Scotch in one hand and a thick novel open on his knee.

"I remember how proud your big brother was." Mom offered me a sad little smile, but she seemed so far away. "He wanted to take you to school for show-and-tell."

One hand caressed my cheek. My mother's skin was soft, still warm from her shower, but something about her fingernails made me uneasy. They were the nails of a person who no longer feels it is worth the effort to maintain every minute detail of her appearance. The nail on Mom's right middle finger was broken off at its tip—as if she had used that digit too many times in the past, and those years of wear and tear were finally beginning to show—and the polish she had last applied on all of her fingernails was cracked and chipped like the paint of a building condemned many years ago.

Mom's eyes were wet. She looked like she might start crying any moment, or perhaps she already had wept for a spell but had taken the time to compose herself before she came into my room.

"Mom?" I said. "Is everything okay?"

"Everything's just peachy," she said, though her cheerless tone belied her words. She adjusted my covers, pulled them up to my chest. "I just wanted to talk for a moment. Can't a mother check in on her baby boy before bedtime?"

I resisted the urge to scoff at her "baby" comment. I couldn't help it. It was a boyhood reflex, that immediate desire to insist *I haven't been a baby for a long time, thank you*.

"You were probably eight or nine years old the last time I tucked you in. Do you remember?"

I nodded, tried to recall the last time she had done so. It had been even longer than the three or four years she estimated, I thought, though I did not argue with her.

"Kyle—"

"I miss it," I said, before she could go on.

"What's that?"

"I miss it. The way you used to tuck me in."

She looked shocked. "Gosh. Really, sweetie? I guess . . . I guess I just assumed you were getting too old for me to do that anymore."

I shook my head. "Not yet."

I meant it. Despite my distaste for her "baby boy" comment just a few seconds previous, I did not ever want to grow up. Not if growing up meant being alone when the darkness came. No, during those last few days I had decided I could wait as long as necessary.

Mom sniffled, leaned down, and kissed me on the cheek. Her wet hair hung in my face. I breathed in the aroma of the Head & Shoulders she had used a few minutes ago, and unlike the strawberry soap I had smelled when she first came into my room, this new scent nearly made me sneeze. She hadn't quite rinsed all of the shampoo out of her scalp, and there was something a bit too cloying about that smell, like a powerful chemical in which my mother had bathed, hoping to wash away her deepest darkest secrets.

"That girl's funeral is tomorrow, you know," she said from out of nowhere. As if she had just remembered it, and hadn't been dwelling on that sad event all day like everyone else in town.

"I know," I said.

"It's supposed to be a pretty day, too. Supposed to clear up quite a bit."

"Really?"

"Ironic, isn't it?" Mom laughed, but there wasn't the slightest bit of humor in it. "A beautiful day for a funeral."

I could see it in her eyes. My mother and I were thinking the same thing. I was only five years old the day we buried my father, yet I recalled the whole terrible affair no less vividly than if I had been ten times that age. It had been such a bright, sunny morning. Almost everyone who came to Dad's funeral had worn sunglasses. I'll never forget that one trivial detail for as long as I live. The sun had created a beatific halo effect behind each of the mourners as they stood above my father's grave, an effect that seemed to denote flawless sincerity, yet how could I trust all those giant, sweaty-browed grownups with their expressions of sympathy and promises of prayer if I could not see their eyes?

Mom looked off toward my bedroom window, at the raindrops slithering down the glass like so many wet, silver worms leeching away at our modest home. The storm hummed a low, mournful song above our heads. Tears gathered in the corners of my mother's eyes, but they never spilled down her cheeks.

"Are you going?" I asked her, when I thought she might sit there like that forever, just staring out at the rain.

"To the funeral?" Mom sighed. "Oh, to be honest, Kyle, I haven't even thought much about it. I suppose I should. Everyone else will be there."

"Probably," I said.

"I'd have to take a couple hours off work, though, and Mr. Norton would never allow me to do that."

I stared up at my mother, heard her teeth grinding together as she sat there on the edge of my bed in her own little world. I could tell she wanted a drink. Couldn't wait for it. She would undoubtedly imbibe the second she left my room. I felt strangely hollow inside about that, though, and wondered if I really cared at all anymore. Perhaps that was the most frightening thing about the whole situation—the utter apathy with which I had grown to view Mom's af-

fliction in those days when I had so many other trying matters on my mind.

"I thought I might go," I said.

Mom blinked at me.

"To Cassie Rourke's funeral. If it's okay, I mean."

She gave a little shrug, but did not offer her bless-
ing just yet.

"I didn't know her," I said. "So maybe it's dumb. But
I'd like to pay my respects, ya know? It seems like the
right thing to do."

Mom reached over, caressed my cheek again. She
nodded slowly, and there was something almost sar-
castic in her tone when she assured me, "If you want
to go to the funeral, Kyle, I'm not going to stop you.
In fact, I think that would be quite commendable."

I frowned.

Finally she stood, messed with my covers again
until they covered every inch of my body up to my
nose.

"Comfy?"

"Mm-hmm."

"Good." She yawned, turned to leave. "Get some
sleep, sweetie. I'm sorry I bothered you."

"It's okay."

"I love you, Kyle. You know that, don't you?"

"Yeah," I said. "I know."

I wasn't lying. I did believe her. I never doubted for a
second that my mother loved me, despite all the fights
and the hard times her addiction had inflicted upon
us. Mom just had a hard time *showing* us her love back
then. I'm sure it wasn't easy without my father around,
trying to raise two boys to be good honest men in a
world that was anything but good, a world that grew
more dishonest with every passing day. But Mom did
love me. I was sure of it.

"Everything I do, Kyle, I do it for you," she said, so

low I could barely make out her words beneath the never-ending drone of the rain outside. She swept her wet hair out of her eyes, tucked several locks of it behind her small, red ears. "For you and Danny. I may not always make the right decisions, or know all the answers, but I try. I try damn hard."

"I know," I said.

"I'd do anything for my sons."

"I know."

She crossed her arms in front of herself, as if the temperature within my bedroom had dropped to several degrees below zero. "That's my job, you understand? To take care of my boys. And a mother's job is never done."

I wished she would leave. I had no idea what she was talking about, and where minutes before I had enjoyed my mother's company I now felt uncomfortable beneath her glassy wet gaze and all this talk of taxing motherly duty lasting into eternity.

"Anyway," Mom said, "I love you. Sweet dreams, hon."

I watched her turn out my bedroom light and walk out of my room then, her shoulders slumped.

She moved down the hallway like a ghost in the night. Silently. As if she never had been there at all.

I lay awake in the darkness for a long time after that, wanting to cry but not sure if I should. I did not know if those few awkward minutes my mother and I had shared together were entirely good or bad, and perhaps that was the most frightening thing of all.

Chapter Seventeen

That night I dreamed of Cassie Belle Rourke's funeral, and when I awoke at 3 A.M. gasping for air, my pajamas soggy with cold sweat and piss, I could only lie in the darkness until dawn. So afraid.

In my nightmare, Cassandra Rourke's funeral was held out at what I once called my Secret Place. Old Father McKinney from the First Lutheran Church of Midnight officiated. Everywhere I looked, the Snake River Woods were filled with citizens who had come to see Cassie Rourke laid to rest. When there was no more room to stand around the Well and throughout that grove in the middle of the forest, folks sat atop the Old Shack's rusty tin roof. Several of them were even perched in the trees around me, unmoving black shapes watching the proceedings at hand.

They seemed to be watching me, throughout it all. But I couldn't be sure.

Because their eyes were missing.

Mom was there. Danny, too. Mom's hair was wet,

as if she had just stepped out of the shower, but there were dark bags under her eyes and the fancy red dress she wore appeared more appropriate for a wild night on the town than the morbid show at hand. In her right hand she gripped a bottle of Jack Daniels, but it was broken in half. She brought it to her mouth every few seconds, sipped thirstily at nothing but the cold night air.

Beside Mom, Dan looked resplendent in his black suit and Florida Seminoles letter jacket. His hair was wet too, slicked back. His tie clip was shaped like an airplane. He held a basketball under one arm.

The word GONE was written on my brother's forehead in something that resembled dried mud or shit.

Dan smiled at me, winked at me, but I did not smile back.

Cassie Rourke's family was present too, of course, their bodies hitching with sobs and their faces glistening masks of wet sorrow in the night. They leaned over the open black chasm of the Well in the middle of the Snake River Woods as if expecting their daughter to rise from its depths at any moment, laughing and proclaiming the whole thing had been one big, malicious joke. Standing just outside of the gathering, inspecting his fingernails and occasionally trimming one with his bright white teeth as he waited for his cue, was chubby Malcolm Vaughn, owner of the Vaughn Funeral Home on Monge Street. Bernadine Fallon-Hyuck was there, too, editor-in-chief of the *Midnight Sun*. Also present were Hiram Bentley, Midnight's esteemed mayor . . . Dr. Sarah Ling, my hometown's resident optometrist . . . not to mention old Miss Shit-Bird and her daughter Prudence Schifford, who taught English and creative writing classes up at the community college. Somewhere in the crowd I even spotted Steven Doyle, a young man who had left Midnight to join the Air Force the previous winter but had been killed during his first visit back home when a drunk driver plowed into him on I-85.

Sheriff Burt Baker showed up as well, which was no big surprise. And Henry. Their heads were bowed, but I couldn't help but notice the way their mouths were upturned in hateful, knowing grins. Every so often, as the services progressed, they would nudge one another, snickering obscenely as if sharing some hilarious private joke.

Father McKinney's eulogy was barely audible. His skin looked eerily bluish in the night. His hands shook as he stood before the Well, his Bible open before him.

Then I noticed it wasn't a Bible he read from, as he laid Cassie Rourke to rest. It was a fat white tome titled *The Joy of Sex*.

Finally Father McKinney took a step back, closing his sacrilegious substitute for the Good Book with a *thwap* of cold finality, and gestured for the mortician to do his thing.

There was no coffin. Instead, Cassie Rourke's nude corpse was propped up on Burner in the doorway of the Old Shack. An off-white sheet speckled with dark blotches of rust-colored blood enshrouded them both. One of the dead girl's arms flopped out when Malcolm Vaughn and two shadowy volunteers from the trees hefted her body, Burner and all, and carried her to the middle of the grove beside Father McKinney. A rust-colored maple leaf was stuck to her wrist.

Burt and Henry Baker started clapping when the men threw her down inside the Well. Up and over she went, Cassandra Belle Rourke and my bicycle as one.

The whole town followed Baker's lead, began to applaud when they heard the splash at the bottom.

Everyone but me.

"Ashes to ashes, dust to dust," said Father McKinney. "Welcome to the Hotel California."

My pajamas were so drenched with sweat once I woke from my nightmare, several minutes passed before I realized I had pissed in my bed.

I listened for the forlorn tapping of the midnight rain against my window, but the storm had slacked off at least for the time being. The only sounds in the house were the soft *tick-tick* of the heating ducts beneath my bedroom window and Mom's deep, masculine snore across the hall.

Then I smelled it. That pungent ammonia stench. My nose scrunched up. I realized I lay on a cushion of warm dampness.

I rolled over, saw the yellow discoloration of my bedspread beneath me.

"Great," I whispered. I jumped out of bed, instantly ashamed. "Shit!"

I felt so low. Mom was going to be pissed. I could hear her already, despite how well we had gotten along earlier that night:"Jesus Christ, Kyle, didn't you outgrow that bedwetting crap years ago?"

I rolled my eyes, sighed.

I pulled all the sheets off my bed, stripped off my pajamas, and took everything to the utility room on the other side of the house, where I threw that big ball of stinking wet cloth into our washing machine. I dumped a big scoop of detergent on top of my mess, then turned on the washer, realizing by the time it started to rumble and shake as if it were about to explode that I did not care at all if the noisy thing woke my mother this early in the morning.

Let her bitch, I figured.

It certainly wouldn't be the first time. Nor the last.

August 10

Chapter Eighteen

The weatherman had been right. It was a beautiful day for a funeral.

On the day the people of Midnight, North Carolina, laid Cassandra Belle Rourke to rest, the rain went away for a while. Of course, it came back like a bad rash later that night, after the funeral was over, but how uncanny it seemed, the way Mother Nature appeared to have planned it all out so perfectly. The clouds above Midnight had drifted away by ten or eleven that morning like curious bystanders at the scene of a violent crime, onlookers who disperse when they are convinced there really is nothing to see, and on an afternoon that should have been gloomy and gray, the sun came forth to shine upon my hometown like a heartless tormentor whose happiness mocked those gathered to mourn.

It just didn't seem right. I almost wished the rain would return. Funerals should be held in foggy, overcast weather, days suited for black umbrellas and somber moods drenched with a constant drizzle smelling of mildew, mud, and sorrow. Yet the day we buried Cassie Rourke would have been perfect for family picnics in Washington Park. I should have been riding Burner through the streets of Midnight that afternoon, should have made my way to Bobby Wisdah's house, where we would spend all day laughing and splashing one another in his parents' Olympic-size pool.

Instead, the citizens of Midnight had congregated beneath the clear blue skies to cover a sixteen-year-old girl with dirt . . . as the killer himself looked on. . . .

Once again I cursed myself for leaving Burner in the woods that night as I walked across town to the Trinity Baptist Church on Tenth Street. I wondered where he was at that very moment, how long before his captor came looking for me.

It wasn't a long walk to the church—Trinity First Baptist was less than a mile and a half from my front door, in fact—and considering the day had turned out so warm, I didn't even wear a jacket. Every color in the town seemed twice as vivid, more alive than ever before, as the sun came out for a while and the dampness went away. I felt as if I could see into forever as I walked through town to that grand building where the majority of Midnight's population was already gathered.

I arrived about ten minutes after the funeral began. The church doors were open, and I could hear the low drone of the preacher's voice as I approached the building's white brick steps. Occasional sniffles, sobs, and whimpers drifted out of there as well on the day's warm breeze, like sorrow itself escaping from the church to spread its spores of melancholia elsewhere.

The place was packed. The pews were full, and everywhere I looked people were lined up elbow-to-elbow along the walls and against the church's massive stained glass windows like an overdressed crowd at a Standing Room Only rock show. I blushed, my cheeks burning as I searched for a place to stand. I felt as if everyone were watching me. Finally I found an empty spot along the back wall of the church, and I squeezed in between two old ladies who smelled like talcum powder and butterscotch candy.

Up front, Cassandra Belle Rourke's casket was already closed. It looked so *small*, I couldn't help but think, so much shorter and oddly compact than I had imagined it would be. It was the color of marble, with the slightest hint of a girlish pink hue.

I felt claustrophobic just looking at it.

Above and behind the coffin stood Pastor James Brady, a middle-aged man with salt-and-pepper hair cut so short he resembled a square-headed Marine as opposed to a man of God. He wore large wire-rimmed glasses and a dark gray suit, a tie the color of dried blood. In a voice more soft and soothing than any I had ever heard he explained how death should not be a time for sadness, but a time for rejoicing. We should all be *happy* for Ms. Cassandra Belle Rourke, he insisted, for she now lives in a place where pain and suffering and death do not exist and never will.

Maybe I had arrived too late, and missed too much of his sermon to appreciate the context, but I could not agree with the reverend. I wanted to believe that today should be a happy day, a day in which Cassie Rourke did not cease to be but instead passed on to the most perfect place imaginable, but then Pastor Brady had not seen the things I'd seen. *He* had only witnessed how peaceful she looked before they closed her up forever and her soul went to be with Jesus . . . *he* had not watched, mortified, as my town's own Judas Iscariot snapped her skinny neck like a stick . . . he had not seen the terrible yellow-black bruises left upon her by a frustrated young man whose mutilated member restricted him from doing the things he *really* wanted to do to her. . . .

It took me only a minute or so, despite the hundreds of people gathered in that single room, to spot him. The person I hated more than anything on this Earth. He sat in the fifth pew to the right of Pastor Brady's pulpit, beside an obese red-headed lady in a dark green dress.

Sheriff Burt Baker was not in uniform on this day. He wore a bulky navy blue suit. His hair was slicked back, for once not greasy-looking but recently washed. His head was bowed as he listened to Pastor Brady's message of hope, and every so often he nodded solemnly as if agreeing with the holy man's words.

I glared at him, wondering how he could ever show his face at this funeral. I clenched my fists, and they turned the mottled pinkish marble color of Cassandra Belle Rourke's casket.

It should have been *him* up there, I thought, lying in that cold metal box. Baker and his good-for-nothing son, locked up together in the darkness for eternity.

It wasn't fair.

It shouldn't have been that innocent sixteen-year-old, whose mother rocked back and forth in the front pew like a woman in the throes of a violent seizure. It shouldn't have been the sister of that little boy in his tiny black suit and miniature blue tie, a child who did not cry but buried his face in his father's chest and tried like hell to understand everything transpiring around him (*I know where you're coming from, kid*, I wanted to say to him). It should have been Sheriff Burt Baker we committed to the earth that day . . . not the daughter of that sour-faced man who sat listening to pastor James Brady's sermon with a look of unbridled rage upon his face, an expression of vengeance so out of place in a house of worship that Clinton Rourke frightened me more during that moment than a million Burt Bakers combined.

None of it was right.

We shouldn't have been there. *She* shouldn't have been in that coffin.

Calvin Mooney should not have been sitting in jail, awaiting indictment for a crime he did not commit.

We all should have been at home. Happy. Enjoying the weather.

Everything was wrong.

After Pastor Brady's sermon, we all filed outside to the two acres of cemetery behind Trinity First Baptist. I remember how massive the whole scene appeared to my twelve-year-old eyes, how that multitude of tombstones scattered over the rolling hillside brought to mind some clever trick with mirrors God had performed for us in hopes of lifting our spirits on that sad, sad day. If I hadn't known any better, I might have suspected the resting places of my hometown's dead stretched on and on into infinity, beyond the borders of my hometown. Only when I shielded my eyes from the sun did I see the rickety wooden fence beyond the rear row of graves, the immense pasture in the distance where a number of fat brown cows grazed like tiny alien figures cruelly apathetic to the rituals of humans mourning lost loved ones.

Birds chirped gaily in the treetops to our right, where the Snake River Woods flanked the eastern side of the church property about two hundred yards away. The cemetery's grass had been mown recently, and that strong summery smell reminded me of backyard barbecues and carefree sprints through the icy spray of neighborhood sprinklers.

Cassie Rourke's grave waited like a hungry black maw in the middle of the cemetery, in the slender shadow of a large white tombstone. Twelve folding chairs were arranged to the left of it in two neat rows, for the decedent's immediate family, and a thick blanket of faux grass discreetly covered the pile of dirt that would soon cover Cassie Belle Rourke.

PRECIOUS DAUGHTER, TAKEN TOO SOON, AWAITS US IN GOD'S ARMS, read the fancy cursive text upon the dead girl's shiny new headstone. CASSANDRA BELLE ROURKE: SEPT. 9, 1961—AUG. 5, 1977.

Four young men in matching black suits carried her casket out to the cemetery. They moved so slowly, it seemed as if hours passed between the time they came through the church's doors and they eased Cassie Rourke's pinkish coffin onto that rusty-looking contraption that would eventually lower it into the earth.

Around the time Pastor Brady began to say a few more words I did not really hear, his voice sounding tired and his forehead looking sweatier than ever as he stood over Cassie Rourke's small casket, I began to think of my father's funeral. I turned, and I could see the square gray shape of Dad's tombstone toward the top of the hill. It was located in the last row of graves closest to that cow pasture, silhouetted by the too-bright sun. I envisioned the bronze and silver stars engraved upon that fat gray marker beneath my father's name and rank, could see in my mind's eye the single cheap bouquet of plastic flowers Mom left there when she visited Dad's grave the previous Father's Day.

I felt a hard pang of guilt when I realized this was the closest I had come to my father's grave in over a year.

That hit me hard.

I was ashamed.

Crazy as it sounds, I remembered more about the terrible day we buried my father than about the way Dad had looked and smelled and talked. I could recall every minute detail of the day I said good-bye to him forever, though I had only been five years old when he died. As I watched Cassie Rourke's body being interred into the ground behind Trinity First Baptist Church I could almost hear the phantom melody of "Taps" drifting over the cemetery on the day's cool breeze. I remembered that short, stocky man in the Military Policeman's uniform who had played the tune in memory of my father, recalled the way his cheeks puffed out as if in morbid imitation of some blond-haired, blue-eyed Louis Armstrong.

I remembered how Dan and Mom had handled the whole thing.

Dan was thirteen years old the day we buried my father. I remember how tall he seemed to me even then, and how he did not look like himself as he stood above Dad's grave with tears running down his face. Yet at the same time my big brother had displayed an odd sort of dignity through it all. He just kept dabbing at his eyes with his crooked black tie, his moist stare never leaving that big brown star-spangled-banner-draped box in which our father lay. Meanwhile, our friends and family had been forced to restrain Mom several times when she tried to throw herself upon Dad's coffin, refusing to let him go. Throughout the funeral she fell to her knees and clutched at the bright green grass as if she might fall off the world should she lose her grip upon it, and once Dan placed his small, pale hand over her mouth when she started cursing my father for leaving us behind when we needed him so badly.

"Mom, don't do this," he'd said. His face was red as he pulled her away from Dad's grave and spoke to her as if their roles had been reversed. "Please . . . it's gonna be okay."

That was the moment, I believe, when I realized *Dan* would get us through this. Not Mom. Not that chubby preacher who could only maintain eye contact with any of us for a second or two before he quickly looked away as if our sorrow were somehow contagious. Not the condescending sympathy offered by so many well-meaning but oblivious neighbors. But Dan. Even at thirteen years old, he had been my rock. My role model. My portrait of strength when I had nowhere else to turn.

My big brother was the closest thing to Dad I had left.

April 17, 1970, is a day I will never forget, yet more often than not it is the minutiae of our forever-altered lives before and after Dad's funeral that I remember most vividly. The little things that made up that dark day, the trivialities of life we would never again perform in the same way. From that morning when we all got up to get dressed, putting on our best for Dad one last time, though neither Mom nor Dan nor I mentioned exactly what we were dressing for . . . to that evening, when Mom did not know we saw her sneak outside and shove the folded-up flag she'd been given at Dad's funeral deep into the bottom of our overflowing garbage can at the end of the drive . . . to later that night, when it was all over and we laid down knowing our father would never again reprimand us for staying up too late, knowing we would never again hear him laughing at Johnny Carson in the living room, would never hear his deep snore across the hallway or his deep voice on the phone, calling to check in on us when he was away on a tour of duty.

Nor would I ever forget the way Mom stared down at me as I lay in bed that night, her eyes all red and swollen and ugly as she tried her best to explain to me about death and heaven and all the things a mother does not completely understand herself, though she tries her best to help her children comprehend it all so *they* might sleep at night. She had tried. I had to give her that. She had tried.

I thought the Rourke funeral would never end. More than once as Pastor Brady droned on and on I thought we might stay out there amidst the multitude of leaning tombstones and the cloying scent of mown grass and cowshit from that distant pasture until the end of time. Or at least until—as Brady spoke of more than once—the glorious day when the "Prince of Peace" returned "to take us home with Miss Cassie."

I wanted to go home. I wished I had never come. All I could think about was my father, and I wished I had just stayed away. . . .

When Cassie Rourke's funeral was over I don't think there was a dry eye out there on that hill behind Trinity First Baptist, beneath the blinding sun. Everywhere I looked trembling hands dabbed at leaking tear ducts, shoulders hitched with sobs, and an occasional anguished wail broke out from the dead girl's immediate family to echo about the meadow like utmost grief made tangible.

Once I thought I even glimpsed a tear trickling down Sheriff Burt Baker's pitted cheek, as he stood there on the edge of the crowd with his hands in his pockets and his fat brown head tilted toward the heavens. His tie clip, I noticed, was a pin in the shape of a miniature gold badge. At some point he had donned sunglasses to shield his eyes from the sun. They were orange tinted, aviator style, and the fact that his murderous eyes were hidden made him seem ten times more devious than before.

"Let us pray," said Pastor Brady.

By the time the reverend had whispered his solemn "Amen," I felt mentally drained. My knees were weak, and I was no longer sure I would have the energy to walk all the way home. The distance to my house on Old Fort Road seemed ten times farther than from there to Tallahassee, Florida.

My head swam. I felt dizzy.

I especially thought I might pass out atop the grave of some poor soul who had left this Earth long before I was born. As I made my way down the hillside with the rest of the departing mourners, I suddenly realized that Sheriff Burt Baker was walking right behind me.

I didn't dare turn around.

"You do what you gotta do, Sheriff, that's all I'm sayin'," I heard a gruff voice demand. It took me a few seconds, but I realized it could only belong to Clinton Rourke. The dead girl's father. He sounded as if he had something caught in his throat.

I swallowed, bit my lip. Felt so conspicuous. I wished I could hide behind that large angel monument I passed on my left, but it was too late.

I kept walking.

"You make that nigger pay for what he did to my little girl. You hear me? Don't you dare let them say he's unfit to stand trail. 'Cause you know that's bullshit."

"I know what you're going through." Sheriff Baker's tone was soft, consoling, and I imagined his hand on

Clinton Rourke's back as they walked. "This has gotta be real hard for you. But you know Calvin Mooney's fate is not up to me, Mr. Rourke. I've done my part. I've arrested the man who hurt your daughter. Now the Polk County Justice System's gotta do the rest."

"He's gonna walk," said Clinton Rourke. "He killed my little girl, and he's gonna *walk.*"

"You don't know that," Baker said.

"Some Slick Willy goddamn lawyer has his say, they'll let that black bastard off just 'cause he's retarded. You wait and see. That's the way the courts work."

"Look, Mr. Rourke—"

"Meanwhile, my little girl will still be six feet underground."

A loud sob. One of the men cleared his throat. I kept walking, not wanting them to know I was intentionally hanging back just to overhear their conversation. As I made my way down the hill I quickly stepped to one side, around an infant's tiny, lamb-topped tombstone, and fell into line behind a very old, stooped black man in a wrinkled brown suit whose trek down to the parking lot appeared as if it might take forever. I strained to hear every word behind me, and as I did so I stared at the horizon, toward the Blue Ridge Mountains west of town. I could see the bruise-colored threat of another storm looming in the distance.

"Mr. Rourke—" the sheriff started again.

A sound like a pained growl. The men were right beside me now, inches from my left shoulder. "Where's the justice for my little girl, huh? He *killed* her. He raped her. He's gotta pay for that. *We've* gotta make him pay for that."

I kept walking, putting some distance between us. But not too much.

"You know Bonnie hasn't slept since that morning you came to the house and told us what happened?" said Clinton Rourke. "She sees that nigger in her dreams, she says. Sees him raping our little girl over and over and over. She sees him hitting her. I don't know if she's gonna make it, Sheriff. She says she doesn't wanna live anymore. I tell her she has to make it through this, 'cause we've still got our little boy, but she doesn't hear me. She doesn't even seem to know I'm there. She just stares off into nothing, and then she'll start shaking all over and makin' this terrible sound like . . . like something dyin'. Doc Rehm started her on Valium yesterday, but they might as well be aspirin. So far they haven't done a damn bit of good."

Neither man said anything for a long awkward minute or two. I almost thought they had taken another path through the cemetery and were no longer behind me, but I could see Sheriff Baker's patrol car ahead, in the far right corner of the church parking lot. I knew they must still be headed my way, if they hadn't stopped walking altogether.

"That son-of-a-bitch ought to *die* for what he did to my daughter," Clinton Rourke said. "God knows I'd do it myself, slow, if I could get him alone for just five min—"

"With all due respect, Mr. Rourke," Baker interjected. "I don't think we should talk about this anymore. I'm not sure you want me to hear where this conversation is leading."

"I don't care!" Rourke wept. "You just do what you gotta do, sheriff, you hear me? You make him pay. 'Cause by God, if you let him get away with what he did to my little girl, her blood's on *your* hands!"

"Now listen, sir—" Sheriff Baker replied, but then I could hear no more of their conversation. Both men's voices were drowned out by an awful chorus of female sobbing as I rounded the church and left the cemetery behind me.

I dared not stop or even slow down.

Urgently, I headed back toward town, passing Sheriff Baker's beige patrol car in the far corner of the church's parking lot as I went. It reminded me of some predatory beast sitting in wait for a two-legged snack to venture too close to its grille. Its undercarriage and tires were spattered with chunky red mud, and something about that made the vehicle appear all the more ominous . . . tarnished, like its owner, where both should have been shiny and pristine.

I gave it a wide berth.

I wondered if Burner was in the trunk even now, waiting for me to come rescue him. If he lay where Cassie Rourke's cold, stiff body had lain days before, all beaten and bloody and bruised.

Several times as I made my way back home I wiped tears from the corners of my eyes with my best Sunday shirt, but I did not turn around even once. I kept walking at a steady pace, not quite running but certainly wasting no time at all, as I imagined *him* following close behind me in his patrol car, a big black shape behind the wheel of a silent rolling death machine.

Finally I sprinted up the steps of our patio, found the key Mom always kept for me under our welcome mat. I unlocked the door with trembling hands, slammed it behind me the second I was through. Locked it and threw the chain. Stood there with my back against the door until my breathing gradually returned to normal.

I had never been so happy to be home.

Chapter Nineteen

That evening, Mom called to me from the den as I sat in the middle of my bedroom floor. My door had been shut all day, and I hadn't even come out for dinner ("Just remember how I slaved over a hot stove so you wouldn't go hungry, Kyle, and that's *after* I worked my ass off all day at the plant," she said, but I paid her no mind). I felt safe in my own little world, and I had decided at some point that I would be perfectly happy staying there forever. Perhaps Mom could just slide me sandwiches and saucers full of water under the door when I got hungry. I could expel my wastes out the window, into her once-precious rosebushes.

I was bored out of my skull, hated the sight of rain more than ever. It had started pouring again just a few short hours after the funeral, as if the morning's sunny weather had been a figment of every Midnight citizen's wild imagination. The storm seemed like a curious whisper at my window. I had chosen to pass the time by putting together a model of a '67 Firebird that Dan bought for me on my last birthday, but I just couldn't find the enthusiasm to continue. My hands kept shaking, and I ended up with less glue on my miniature Pontiac than on the newspaper I had spread out on my bedroom carpet so I wouldn't make a mess.

I abandoned that project after about an hour. I returned the unfinished model to its box, then slid the box into the back of my closet, on the top shelf behind my baseball mitt and a broken pellet gun that had belonged to Dan when he was my age. I sighed, wadded up the sticky newspapers in the middle of my bedroom floor before shoving them into the Spider-Man wastebasket beside my night table.

I'm not sure what ever happened to that model, though I do suspect that if it had not been a present from Dan I might have found obscene pleasure in throwing the Firebird against the wall and watching it shatter into a thousand pieces, judging from my mood that day.

I collapsed upon my bed and wondered what the hell to do next to pass the miserable time away.

I had been lying there like that for a couple minutes—staring at my *Star Wars* poster on the wall as if it held all the answers, watching the way the shadows of the raindrops at the window made Darth Vader's shiny black helmet appear all blotched and dirty—when Mom called out to me from across the other side of our house.

"Kyle? Could you come here for a minute, please?"

At first I pretended I didn't hear her. I rolled over on my back, stared at the ceiling.

"Kyle!"

God, how I wanted to be light years away from Midnight, North Carolina. If I crossed my eyes, the white of my ceiling almost resembled some infinite, snowy wasteland. It seemed to stretch out into forever, past the roof and the dark, cloud-choked sky above, and I envisioned myself floating upward, drowning within the soft white up there before coming out the other side safe and sound with all of my worries gone forever. Perhaps a better place lay beyond that vast, swirling expanse of nothingness, I imagined . . . a place where big brothers never went away and mothers loved their sons more than the bottle and fathers never died in far-away lands with funny-scary names like Dông Hà and Da Nang and law-enforcement officers served and protected and honored their badges and would never *think* of taking another human life. . . .

And then I uncrossed my eyes. Blinked several times fast.

It was just my ceiling again. My problems remained.

The rain droned on and on.

"Kyle!" Mom called again a few seconds later, from the living room. "Come here, son!"

"What is it now?" I said under my breath, rubbing at my eyes. I really did not want to be bothered, and I wished Mom would just pass the evening at hand by drinking herself into oblivion.

I groaned when she called me again.

"What do you want?" I shouted back at her in my most annoyed tone.

"Come here for a minute, son!" she said. "In the living room! Now!"

I groaned again, stood.

"Kyle!"

That was followed by a giggle.

I froze, thought I had imagined it at first. But then it came again.

Mom was laughing in there. A high-pitched, girlish

giggle. I didn't know what to think. I hadn't heard my mother's laughter in years. Not like that. Not so real.

It sounded almost . . . musical.

But then I heard another voice in the living room, saying something to my mother I couldn't quite make out.

I frowned. *Who . . . ?*

A deep, masculine chuckle came next. Basso and unclear, more a buzzing vibration through my bedroom walls than the distinct sound of laughter, but there was no denying I heard it.

I felt weird all over. Almost the same way I had felt that night Mom came into my room and her robe fell open, though I did not understand why.

Who was Mom talking to? I wondered. We never got visitors anymore. My mother's ugly temperament had long ago alienated any family friends we'd had when Dad was alive. Traveling salesmen knocked on our front door every now and then, but Mom always ran those folks off within a second or two.

For a fleeting moment I perked up at the possibility that Dan may have come home early.

My heart fluttered.

But then I forced myself to abandon such wishful thinking.

I didn't want to go to the living room. At all. I hated meeting new people, particularly adults. I hated the way they stared down at you and made you feel so insignificant while you shifted your weight uncomfortably from one foot to the other, kept your hands in your pockets and prayed that their conversation would veer toward things other than *you* so you could sneak away below their line of sight.

God, how I wanted to crawl under my bed and never come out. For a second or two I pondered my only possible route of escape, through the window into the storm outside, but I knew that was silly. I had to do this.

"Kyle!" Mom called again.

Alas, I had no choice. She wouldn't give up easily, I knew. As I left my bedroom and headed down the hallway, I dragged my feet, walked with my shoulders slumped. I stared at the floor and gave several exaggerated sighs like I used to do when I was much younger and would put on a good show of pouting because I didn't get my way.

I heard the music before I was out of the hallway. It was turned so low at first I couldn't place its origin. But then I saw Mom had carried her little GE transistor radio—the one she always listened to when she washed dishes or cleaned the house—into the living room from the kitchen. It sat atop our television behind her, and from its single dusty speaker Crystal Gayle asked, "Don't it make my brown eyes blue?"

"I'm busy," I lied once I entered the living room, and though she could hear me just fine above the music, I raised my voice more than was necessary to advertise my sour mood. "What is it?"

Mom stood in the center of the room. She smiled at me, beckoned for me to come closer. "Oh, quit being so grumpy, hon. It's not like you're doing anything important in there."

I blinked several times fast, unable to believe my eyes, when she stepped toward me.

My mother was *beautiful*. I hadn't seen her in such formal clothing since . . . hell, I couldn't remember the last time I had seen Mom dressed like that. She looked like she was getting ready to go to church. Or maybe to a fancy ball. She wore a long green dress, more makeup than I had seen on her face in a long time. But not too much. She still looked very classy. Golden hoop earrings dangled from her ears. Her hair was pulled back into a tight ponytail save for two long, curly locks framing either side of her face. The lilac smell of her perfume filled the room, and though she had splashed on the stuff a tad too liberally, it was not at all an unpleasant scent.

Before me, I was sure, stood the woman my mother could have been had she never started drinking. It was almost surreal. Like stepping backward in time. Or into an alternate universe.

"Mom?" I said. My voice came out hoarse, hardly more than a whine. I cleared my throat, started over. "Mom? W-wow. Wow. You're . . . you look *really* nice."

She reached out to me. "Oh, Kyle. You're so sweet. Come here."

"Why are you dressed like that?" I asked. "Are you going somewhere?"

She didn't seem to hear me. Her eyes darted toward a spot in the room behind me.

For the first time, I realized someone sat at the back of the room, just outside of my peripheral vision.

"Oh—" I said with a start, turning. "Hey—"

"There's someone I'd like you to meet, Kyle. You know Sheriff Baker, right?"

My mouth hung open. The air in my lungs seemed to turn to concrete. My surroundings seemed to shrink in on me, and all I could see was . . . *him*, in my tunnel vision.

Larger than life.

Right there in front of me.

Smiling at me.

In my home.

He sat hunched forward, as if awaiting his cue to stand. His khaki uniform was slightly wrinkled, but his badge seemed to glow. His shoes had been recently polished. A hint of curly chest hair was visible where he had unbuttoned the top two buttons of his shirt, and I wondered with a pang of nausea somewhere in my gut if my mother liked that.

The murderer's eyes were a bright, bright blue. The same color as Burner. They were almost mesmerizing.

In one huge brown hand he held a glass of scotch on the rocks. The ice jingled musically against the sides of the glass as he rose from his chair. From *Dad's* armchair, the one he used to sit in when he watched reruns of *Hogan's Heroes* or read the *Midnight Sun*.

This was sacrilege. A slap in my father's face.

His gun belt squeaked as he moved toward me, like something alive and in terrible pain.

I tried to breathe. I couldn't.

"Huh," I said. "Huh . . ."

He glanced at Mom, and she licked her lips, returning his troubled frown.

I said, "You—"

Sheriff Burt Baker grinned as he took my hand in his. I didn't offer it. He just grabbed it. His grip was gentle, yet I could not stop thinking about how those same hands had committed murder. How they had snapped Cassandra Belle Rourke's neck like a pencil.

He smelled like sweat and motor oil masked with cheap cologne.

"Hello again, Kyle," Sheriff Burt Baker said. "How are you, son?"

I couldn't move. I knew I would pass out any second. I prepared myself for the taste of old shag carpet.

"Wha . . . Mom?" I stammered, jerking my hands away from the killer in khaki before me. "I don't . . . h-how . . . ?"

"Say hello," Mom said. "Don't be shy."

My eyes grew wider than ever. I watched him watch me.

Time seemed to stand still.

"I . . . I . . . M-Mom? Wh-what is this?"

Mom mouthed for me to say hello. She looked desperate. As if, should I ruin this moment, I would shatter any happiness she had ever known.

Sheriff Baker looked back at her and she quickly smiled.

"I don't understand . . . what is this?" I said again, glaring at them both. It was all I could do not to hiss my words through my teeth, not to spit my hatred all over his uniform. I envisioned globules of my saliva catching in the black curly hairs beneath his throat. *How's* that *for sexy, Ma? You people make me* sick.

"What are you . . . why . . . wh-what are you doing here?" I said instead.

"Kyle! That's not very nice!"

Mom gave me a stern look, but then smiled again as if life had never been finer when the sheriff looked back to her.

"Oh, it's all right, Darlene," the sheriff said. He held up the most gigantic hand I had ever seen in a placating gesture. "Kids are always intimidated by the uniform, I think. I'm used to it."

That seemed to appease Mom. At least for the time being.

"You can relax, Kyle," Baker said. "I'm not here to arrest anybody."

"You're . . . no?" I didn't know what I was saying. I felt light-headed, so confused.

He winked at me, made a clicking sound with his tongue. "Unless, of course, you've done something wrong."

I said nothing. Just kept staring at him, dizzy with disbelief. My teeth chattered together. I felt so, so cold.

"What is this, Mom?" I asked her yet again. "Why . . ."

"Kyle, there's something I've been meaning to tell you," she began to explain at last. "I guess I've waited long enough. You do have a right to know."

I waited. Not breathing. Not moving. Not wanting to believe the filth that would soon fall from between my mother's lips, as I somehow knew what was coming.

I needed to pee.

"The sheriff and I," Mom started. "That is, Burt and me . . . we . . . well, Kyle, we—"

Baker cleared his throat, stared at his shiny black shoes.

"We're sort of . . . um—" She looked to him, as if for help. "We've been . . . seeing each other, for the past couple months, and . . . oh, gosh . . ."

One hand went to her chest. Mom's cheeks turned a bright rose color.

"Hey, shh," said the sheriff. He moved toward her, gestured for her to stop. He set his glass of scotch atop my television, put one big arm around her. "Let me, hon."

Hon? I was going to hit the floor any second. There was no doubt in my mind.

The sheriff reached behind Mom, turned off her radio.

As if he owned my house and everything in it.

I wanted to scream. Scream at him to leave and never come back. I wanted to scream until my voice was gone and my throat was raw and bloody.

"What your mother's trying to tell you, Kyle, is that she and I . . . well, we've been spending a lot of time together for the past couple of months. We've been . . . dating. It's nothing serious. It's not like I have that much free time these days anyway, if you know what I mean. But your mother, when we get the chance, we . . . well, we just . . . we have a lot of fun together, Kyle. We really enjoy one another's company. That's all. Like I said, it's nothing serious, but we thought you should know. It's only fair."

"What?" I barked at him.

Burt Baker stared at me.

Mom stared at me.

"H-How . . . whaa . . . Mom? What . . ."

"It's okay, honey," Mom said. She stepped toward me, out of Baker's embrace, but I took two quick steps back.

Don't you fucking touch me, the look on my face must have said.

"We understand what you must be feeling."

"You . . . I . . . n-no . . . no, you don't, Mom. . . ."

"Darlene," said Sheriff Baker, with a little sniffle. He adjusted his gun belt, nodded sadly. "I think I know what's going on here."

"You do?" Mom and I said at the same time.

"Yeah," Baker said. He looked at me. "I do. But it's okay, son. Really. You have nothing to worry about."

"It's . . . I don't understand. . . ."

"I'm not trying to replace your father. You have my word. I'd never try to do that."

Burt Baker's right hand covered his heart, offering a picture of utmost sincerity.

Then his arm snaked back around my mother's shoulders. As if he would never let her go, no matter my feelings on the matter.

"That's not what he's trying to do, Kyle," Mom added. "Not at all."

"I know I could never replace your father," said the sheriff. He took a second to kiss my mother's forehead. I shuddered. "No one can. But I want you to know . . . I am here for you, if you ever need anything."

He winked at me, and I wobbled where I stood. The rain on the roof above seemed deafening, like the hoof-beats of a thousand demonic horses approaching to signal the dawn of Armageddon.

"Are you okay, honey?" Mom asked me.

At least one long, awkward minute passed before I answered.

"No, Mom," I said, my voice cracking. "I'm not okay at all."

"He's not trying to replace your father," she said again, quickly, as if she had lost the ability to think for herself and could only repeat the sheriff's filthy lies. "Really."

"You see, Kyle," the sheriff explained, "your mom and I have a lot in common. My wife, Connie, passed away ten years ago. Ovarian cancer. It was rough, the worst thing I've ever been through in my life, and I thought I'd never date again. I thought it'd be like . . . like *betraying* her, you know?"

"Right," said Mom.

"But it's not. It took me a long time to realize this, but I know Connie would want me to move on with my life. She would want me to be happy. In fact, I'm quite sure my wife . . . and your father too, for that matter, are probably looking down from heaven right now, and they're pleased to see we're not wallowing in misery. We haven't forgotten them—Lord, no—but we're happy. We're making it. Day by day. The best we know how."

Mom smiled at me, nodded. Her eyes were moist.

I could not look at them. I looked everywhere around the room, my gaze constantly shifting and darting about from the floor to the wall to the ceiling and then back to the floor, but I could not meet the murderer's eyes.

I wanted to leap upon him, tear out his throat with my bare hands. How *dare* he mention my father. How dare those words fall from his ugly lips.

"We thought you should know, Kyle," Mom said. "I do apologize for not telling you sooner. I guess I was just waiting for the right time to tell you."

"Wh-why?" I said.

"It's not like we were trying to hide anything from you, you understand?" Mom went on. "There's nothing *to* hide, really. We've just tried to be very discreet about it. No one but our families need to know."

"Why?" I asked her again. "How . . ."

"It's okay, son," Baker said. "We understand what you must be going through. But there's nothing for you to worry about. Just be happy for your mother. Know that *she's* happy."

"I can't believe this."

"I'll take good care of her, I promise."

"I can't believe this."

"Kyle—" Mom started.

"I can't believe this!" I screamed at them, at the top of my lungs.

I ran to my room. Slammed the door as hard as I could, locked it.

Thunder boomed overhead, rattling the windows. Setting me even more on edge.

"Kyle Mackey!" my mother shouted, from the living room. "You get back here right this instant!"

I ignored her.

"You come back here and apologize, young man! That was very rude!"

I didn't. And I wasn't going to. No matter the consequences.

I heard him trying to console her in there, felt the buzzing vibrations of his basso tone in the wall against which I cowered. I thought I heard my mother weeping. But I didn't care.

I shook my head back and forth, back and forth, refusing to believe any of this.

It couldn't be happening. It *couldn't!*

I waited until I heard the front door shut, about ten minutes later, before I got up. Waited until they left on their precious little date, and I heard the sound of a vehicle moving away from our house and up the street.

That cinched it. I was alone. So terribly alone.

She had left with *him*—with that *bastard*—without attempting to reconcile her shattered relationship with her son. Didn't she realize that's what I wanted? Didn't Mom know I secretly wished she would come knocking at my door, demanding I open up or by God I was grounded for so long Dan would be out of college the next time I was allowed to come out of my room? Didn't she understand that I *wanted* her to chase after me, to hold me, and tell me everything was gonna be okay?

No. She had left in the arms of a murderer. She had deserted me.

I decided during that moment that I hated not only Sheriff Burt Baker, I hated my mother as well.

Never in my life had I felt so betrayed.

Things could not possibly get any worse.

August 11

Chapter Twenty

Six days after the Apple Gala, and only two days after he was arrested for the murder of Cassandra Belle Rourke, Calvin "Rooster" Mooney escaped from the liar's custody.

At least, that's what the citizens of Midnight all believed. What Burt Baker led them to think.

I knew better.

Mom had already left for work that morning when I wandered into the living room, lazily scratching my butt through my pajamas. I was glad she was gone. I didn't wish to speak to her so soon after discovering her betrayal of our family, of my father's memory, and for that matter I wondered if I would *ever* want to see her again.

Putting such thoughts out of my mind as best I could, I planned to pass the time by watching a few cartoons, maybe imbibing in a blueberry Pop-Tart or two.

Once upon a time I thought Saturday morning cartoons were the greatest invention since primitive man discovered he could create fire. Those early hours of every Saturday seemed so magical. How I dreaded seeing noontime roll around when the likes of Bugs Bunny and the Super-Friends were replaced by adult programming such as NWA Wrestling and the Champion Bass-Fishin' Hour With Bobby J. Flukhas. Now, however, watching cartoons had become nothing more than a beloved distraction, something to take my mind off everything that had happened in my hometown. I tried to avoid watching television at all, for that matter, lest it reminded me of my failure to do the right thing with some sudden "News Flash" or "Late-Breaking Top Story."

Case in point . . . less than ten minutes after I plopped down on our ratty old couch, and the thing squeaked like some living creature protesting my intrusion upon its private territory, a smiling, middle-aged man with perfect white teeth and immaculately coifed sandy blond hair suddenly replaced Wile E. Coyote and his ill-fated efforts to destroy the Road Runner on the TV. . . .

"We interrupt this program to bring you a Special Channel 5 News Report," said the anchorman. He spoke very softly, slowly, as if his audience were a bunch of drooling idiots who could otherwise barely comprehend the implications of what he told us. The slender black stripes on his bright yellow tie looked like prison bars. "This morning the Polk County Sheriff's Department issued an All-Points Bulletin for Calvin Tremaine Mooney, the thirty-year-old man who was arrested earlier this week for the murder of Cassandra Belle Rourke. Sources say Mooney escaped from the Polk County Jail shortly after seven A.M., after allegedly attacking Sheriff Burt Baker during a routine inspection of his cell."

The man looked down at his papers, licked his lips before continuing.

"At this time, authorities are warning citizens that Mooney may be armed, and he should be considered dangerous. Sheriff Baker urges anyone with information leading to Mooney's whereabouts to please call 704-555-1819 immediately. Again, that's 704-555-1819."

For the next few seconds Calvin Mooney's mug shot was displayed, giving everyone a good, long look at this harmless man they were being told to fear. To hate.

I shook my head, stared at the floor, but flinched when Burt Baker appeared on my television.

He stood outside the offices of the Sheriff's Department, hands upon his hips. His bumpy brown forehead was shiny with sweat. The shoulders of his rumpled uniform were stippled with drops of the day's cool drizzle. Baker rubbed at his Adam's apple every few seconds as he spoke into a microphone some off-camera reporter had shoved into his face. Once he pulled out a dirty-looking blue handkerchief, dabbed at his cheeks and forehead with hands that trembled slightly.

I guess he was supposed to look rattled. I wanted to throw something at the TV screen.

"He got me good, I'll admit it," the murderer said, wincing. "Poked me right here, in the throat, with two fingers. Hurt like a son of a . . . anyway, I can promise you that'll be the last time this guy lays a hand on anyone in my jurisdiction."

Burt Baker should have won that year's Oscar for Best Actor. Forget Peter Finch and Faye Dunaway. They had nothing on him.

"Sheriff, what provisions are currently being taken

to apprehend Calvin Mooney and bring him back into your custody?" the reporter asked.

"I've got my best men working on it," Baker replied. He looked directly into the camera, as if personally consoling every worried man, woman, and child in Midnight. "I assure you this won't take long at all. I made the mistake of letting my guard down this once, but it will *not* happen again. That's what I get for trying to be compassionate, trusting the best in people, I suppose. In any event . . . what happened, happened. Now we've got to focus—*I've* got to focus—on apprehending this felon and bringing him back to justice A.S.A.P. One thing Polk County knows is that I've never been the kind of sheriff to sit around on my duff and let business take care of itself. This little . . . problem . . . will be handled quickly and efficiently, and I can promise you it's just a matter of time before Calvin Tremaine Mooney is back in jail, awaiting trial for the murder of Cassandra Belle Rourke."

"Thank you very much for your time, Sheriff," said the reporter.

The camera started to pan back to him.

But then Sheriff Baker held up one hand. He pulled the microphone back toward his face, gestured for the cameraman to give him one more second.

"Hold on there, chief," he said. "I'm not done."

The reporter gave him one last chance to spread his propaganda. "Please, Sheriff, be my guest."

Sheriff Baker looked so sincere as he stared into the camera. If I hadn't known he was a lying bastard, had not witnessed his murderous acts with my own eyes, I might have bought into his unholy deception just like everyone else. . . .

"I want everyone to be careful out there," Baker said. "Calvin Mooney might not look like much, but this is one *very* dangerous man we are talkin' about. He's sick. Some kinda pervert, gets his kicks off hurtin' women. He's already had his way with one poor girl, and I'd die before I'll let another innocent person fall prey to his twisted desires. Just be careful, folks, is all I'm saying. Be careful. We'll get him. I promise. Soon."

Damned if I didn't see tears in the sheriff's eyes. For the second time in the last twenty-four hours. I thought I might throw up.

Worst of all, though, was the realization of what was to come.

Calvin Mooney—the man we all called Rooster— was a dead man. He just didn't know it yet.

Sheriff Baker hadn't "accidentally" let Calvin Mooney escape. He hadn't been overtaken, "poked in the throat with two fingers" by that lanky, buck-toothed black man whose mind knew only childlike wonder and not a hint of violence. The sheriff could have broken Rooster in two, if the urge overtook him.

I hated Burt Baker more than ever, as his little "plan" became so clear to me. . . .

It should go without saying that in small Southern towns such as Midnight circa 1977, things worked much differently than they do now. Though people did not talk about it, racism was still alive and well. Despite the victories earned by civil rights activists a decade before, Dr. Martin Luther King's dream of equality had only begun to take awkward baby steps at best. While bigotry was not as blatant as it once had been below the Mason-Dixon Line, and its prac-titioners refrained—more or less—from advertising their disdain forthright, such outdated ideals were far from nonexistent. I saw it every day, though I could not fully comprehend the cruel implications of it all at the ripe old age of twelve. The days of WHITE

FOLK ONLY and NO COLOREDS signs in dusty storefront windows were long past, yet hate still festered beneath the surface in my hometown like an ugly sore that no longer oozes but leaves a nasty scar nonetheless. When I was a child, the truth about tolerance displayed itself not through public lynchings or even flaming crosses illuminating the night out toward Jefferson Circle (the area of Polk County populated predominantly by black folk), but in subtle Sunday morning smirks given the region's small but boisterous African Zionist Church by passing Caucasian families. How far Midnight had progressed in matters of race and equality was evident in Mayor Hiram Bentley's routine dismissal of motions brought forth in town meetings requesting the reparation of the roads on Jefferson Circle, despite frequent allotments of thousands of taxpayer dollars for the continued upkeep of streets leading into wealthy white developments like Fleming Heights and Foxwood Terrace.

It wasn't something that was out in the open, Midnight's racism. Most of the time, my hometown hid it well. I soon deduced, however, that things might have been simpler, *better*, had the bigotry that lurked in Midnight been more obvious. The way things were back then, it was like a volcano waiting to blow at just the right time.

Sheriff Burt Baker knew all this. He was well aware of the fact that most folks in his county considered a man with skin the color of Calvin "Rooster" Mooney's guilty from the moment he was born. He knew someone with Mooney's intellect could not defend himself against vigilantism, especially when said street justice was doled out by bloodthirsty fellows who considered a "nigger" less than human to begin with.

As far as Polk County's redneck contingent was

concerned, that man as dark as my hometown's namesake had killed a girl. A white girl. Now, it was just a matter of time before Sheriff Baker's satanic plan came to fruition.

Midnight was about to change, I feared. I could feel it coming, and I had never been so afraid. I no longer wanted to live there. I wanted to leave. I was ashamed of my hometown, and of what I knew it would soon become.

The place was about to implode.

I did not hear the rest of what the anchorman said. I just sat there, numb, as he droned on and on: "In other news, New York Police arrested twenty-four-year-old David Berkowitz yesterday for the infamous 'Son of Sam' shootings that have plagued the city for the last thirteen months. Oddly enough, it was a series of unpaid parking tickets that led to the alleged killer's arrest, say authorities. . . ."

August 13

Chapter Twenty-one

In the days following Calvin Mooney's so-called escape, Midnight became an unfamiliar place to me. Just as I had suspected. Yet I never could have imagined the chaos that would ultimately transpire in the space of just two or three days.

How could this be the town I had grown up in, I asked myself several times throughout it all. Before long, I hardly recognized Midnight, North Carolina, and that fact alone terrified me even more than the things I had seen in the Snake River Woods on the night of August 5.

I felt like a stranger in a strange land. A small, skinny alien in a mad world filled with hateful, red-faced creatures hungry for revenge. So hard to believe that these monsters had once been my neighbors. That these roads had once been my stomping grounds. Now, they were as unfamiliar to me as the dark side of the moon. Or Mars. Or Tallahassee, Florida.

Everywhere I looked, burly rednecks in flannel

jackets carried giant black shotguns and hate in their eyes, searching for the man they believed to be Cassandra Belle Rourke's foul killer. Ugly curses and cruel epithets echoed through the wet gray streets of my hometown from sunrise to sunset, punctuated by the staccato farting of mud-spattered pick-up trucks decorated with Confederate flags and NRA stickers. Floppy-eared coonhounds the color of rust and dried shit sat in the beds of those white-trash death machines, baying at the chaos or, perhaps, the distant scent of the hunted. Every so often, a shotgun blast would split through the chaos from somewhere across town, louder even than the thunder that never stopped booming above Midnight, and every time I heard such an ominous sound I wondered if it was finally over. If Calvin Mooney lay dead, and somewhere in the center of my hometown a new "hero" had been born amidst the smell of blood and sweat, chewing tobacco and gunpowder.

I imagined Rooster's head on a wall, eternally gawking from some proud hick's living room wall like a prize blackbird. I envisioned him smiling that goofy, buck-toothed grin of his even in death, and I wept for him. More than once, as I stared out my bedroom window at the loud, drunken posses cutting through my backyard to get to the Snake River Woods with no respect for the boundaries of private property, I could not distinguish between the summer rain trickling down the glass and my own salty tears flowing down the pale doppelganger face of my reflection.

The few times I dared to leave my home and venture into town, I could feel the rage coming off my neighbors like the stench of body odor. I could no longer look any of them in the eyes. I felt so ashamed that I knew them, even more ashamed that I had liked a few of them. Particularly unsettling, however, was the fact that I was distantly related to one or two of them.

I hated them. I thought I had known them, but I had not. They were all like hairless werewolves to me, the way they had changed. . . .

Case in point: Mr. Willy Putnam, owner of the hardware store on King Street. Gone was the round little man in the GOD BLESS AMERICA cap who had called me "Hotshot" for as long as I could remember, always gave me a piece of peppermint candy anytime he would see me around town. In place of that kind middle-aged gent lurked a bloodthirsty thug, a short but no less imposing figure whose high-pitched war-cry of "Die, Nigger, Die!"—which I heard him bellow one afternoon when I sneaked across town for a peek at the burgeoning chaos, as Mr. Putnam led a group of heavily armed men over the railroad tracks behind old man Gash's junkyard toward the broken-down homes on Jefferson Circle—seemed to become the motto of those who had taken it upon themselves to become Calvin Mooney's judge, jury, and executioner.

Once or twice I even heard a rumor that the local chapter of the KKK planned to get in on the action. They were based over in Asheville, called themselves the White Knights of the Lord's Army. Supposedly they were scheduled to roll into town early the following week, and they planned to help Polk County wrap up this nasty business once and for all.

Go figure.

Calvin "Rooster" Mooney was the most loathed man in Midnight, I knew—in the *history* of my hometown—and though I did not want to admit it, I knew he would not be alive by the end of the week.

To this day, I do not know how I lived with such

knowledge, yet still kept what I saw that night in the woods to myself.

I was angry. Pissed off. My hatred for Sheriff Baker knew no bounds. Yet I was also still so very *afraid*. My rage did not dilute my terror, or that instinct of self-preservation.

I waited. Praying that the answer would come to me. Somewhere, somehow. Some way.

August 14

Chapter Twenty-two

That evening I sat in the living room devouring my nails while Mom watched a new show called *Three's Company* and laughed like it was the funniest damn thing she had ever seen.

Her laughter made me sick. It hurt my ears and sounded more like the braying of a lascivious donkey the louder and louder it got.

All day Mom had pretended as if there were nothing wrong between us at all. She sipped a cup of brandy-laced coffee and watched TV, only getting up to refill her mug and—once—put a load of dirty clothes in the washer. I played her game, chose not to bring up her recent indiscretions no matter how badly I wanted to give her a piece of my mind. I sure did not wish to talk about Sheriff Baker, even as I knew we *should* discuss what Dan would undoubtedly have called the "elephant in the living room" before our relationship became irreparable and I really did start hating her.

Somewhere around the time Jack and Janet were

trying to talk Chrissy out of moving to a commune with a fast-talking guru named Swami Rama Mageesh on *Three's Company*, the phone rang.

Mom hardly batted an eye at first. She shook her head, laughed at something on the television, and sipped from her mug.

The phone rang again.

"Ah, crap," she said, as if hearing it for the first time. "What is it now?"

Why don't you ask your stupid boyfriend? I wanted to say, in the snottiest voice I could muster. But I didn't.

The phone rang again.

"Get that, Kyle, would you?" Mom said.

I grunted. Stood. Went to the kitchen and picked up the phone.

"Hello." My tone was flat. Disinterested.

"Hey-hey!" came my big brother's voice, from three hundred forty-eight miles away as the crow flies. "How's it hangin', tiger?"

An instant rush of bliss nearly took my breath away. He sounded so close, as if he were talking to me from just a house or two down the block. Tears gathered in the corners of my eyes, but they were tears of joy.

Nevertheless, I did not miss a beat: "Twelve inches long, four around, and slightly to the left."

"Ha!" Dan laughed loudly in my ear. God, it felt good to hear that. "You've learned well, grasshopper."

I giggled.

In the background, on Dan's end of the line, I could hear several people talking. I imagined a dorm room full of college students laughing and partying and carrying on when they should have been studying. One girl had a very annoying high-pitched laugh that reminded me of the cawing of a crow gone insane.

"So how's things, little bro?" Dan said.

"Okay, I guess. Man, it's great to hear from you!"

"Same back atcha."

"I miss you so bad, Dan."

"I miss you too. Boy, do I ever."

"So why haven't you called before now?"

"I did!" Dan said. "Night before last. Mom said you had already gone to bed."

"Whaaat?" I scowled in my mother's direction, but lowered my voice so she could not hear me from the other room. "Dammit. I sure would have liked to talk to you, Dan."

I wondered if she had kept Dan's call all to herself on purpose. While I could not understand her motives for doing such a thing, I figured I wouldn't put it past her.

"It's okay," Dan said. "You know Mom."

I rolled my eyes, sighed. "Yeah, I do."

"Anyway, we're talking now, right?"

I said nothing. Just basked in the moment. Loving it. Never wanting it to end.

"God, it's good to hear your voice, Kyle."

"Yours too," I said. I sniffled, cleared my throat. "So what's it like down there? How's Florida?"

"Hot. It's very hot. Dude, I've been here a week, and I've already got a sunburn like you wouldn't believe."

"At least it's not raining all the time."

"Jeez, man. You gotta be kidding me. It's *still* raining up there?"

"It never stops," I said.

Neither of us spoke for the next few seconds. There was so much I wanted to tell my brother, so many things we had to cover. I didn't know where to begin!

"So," Dan said. "I'm on a payphone, bro. I can only talk for a few minutes. Tell me whatcha been up to the last few days."

"Not a whole lot," I said. "Just hanging out. Trying to avoid Mom. You know."

"Cool. And . . . anything else?"

I could hear it in his voice, the way it went low and serious all of a sudden. I gnashed my teeth, dreaded the next words out of his mouth. But there was little doubt in my mind where he was going with this.

"So did you do it?" he whispered. "Please tell me you did."

"What?"

"You know."

"No, I don't."

"Come on, Kyle. It's me. Don't play dumb, okay?"

"I . . . um . . ."

"You didn't, did you?" Dan said. "Jesus. You didn't do it."

"Umm . . ."

"It's been over a week, Kyle! I can't believe it's been this long, and you haven't told anyone!"

God, it hurt, my brother talking to me like that. I would have preferred he shouted at me, berated me . . . either would have been far more endurable than the sound of utter disappointment in his voice.

"Why didn't you go talk to Deputy Linder, like I told you to?"

"I tried, Dan. I did."

"What do you mean you *tried?*"

"I went to see him."

"And?"

I glanced over my shoulder to make sure Mom couldn't hear our conversation. She was still engrossed in *Three's Company*, though, hadn't even bothered to ask who was on the phone.

I quickly turned back toward the phone on the wall when she started scratching at her crotch like a man.

"I was going to tell Mike what I saw. I swear to God I was. But then . . . then *he* walked in, just when I was about to tell Mike everything."

"Baker? Shit."

"I was so scared. I froze up. I didn't know what to do."

Dan didn't say anything. I wished he would. But the silence on the other end of the line further cemented the fact that I had let my big brother down. The quiet itself was like a stake made of ice slicing through my heart.

"He was *right there*, Dan. In front of me. He looked at me. He *talked* to me."

"Hmm," said Dan.

"I'm sorry," I said.

"Don't tell me you're sorry. Tell that to Cassie Rourke. Tell Calvin Mooney."

"What was I supposed to *do?*" I whined.

"You know what you have to do."

"Mom's dating him, you know," I said, barely above a whisper, before he had a chance to say anything else. I think I expected that to get me off the hook. Perhaps with these new developments Dan might suddenly jump off my back and realize exactly what I was going through.

But that didn't happen.

"She told me several weeks ago," he said instead. His tone was sad, devoid of hope. "Ain't that a load of crap?"

"Why didn't you tell me?"

"I didn't want to upset you. It was bad, Kyle. Real bad."

"You fought about it?"

"That'd be one word for it. Dude, it was like World

War Three. I'm surprised we didn't wake you that night."

Neither of us said anything for a minute or so. In the living room, I could hear the theme song to *Three's Company* blaring as the show ended for another day.

"What are we gonna do?" I asked my brother.

"I'll handle Mom," Dan replied. "You just focus on what *you* have to do."

"God, Dan. I've never been so scared."

"Can't blame you. But you don't have a choice about this, bro. You can't pretend you didn't see it."

I said, "Yeah, but . . . *how?* This is the sheriff we're talking about, Dan. He's not some homeless person. He lives up on Foxwood Terrace. People know him. People *like* him."

"I told you already. Go see Deputy Linder. He'll help you."

"I tried that," I said. "It didn't work. I can't go back there."

"You can't just give up, though, Kyle!"

"I know. But I can't go back there."

"You could call him."

I let out an exasperated sigh, but Dan ignored it.

"Hell, call him at home, if you have to. Tell him what you saw in the woods. Then hang up."

"Maybe," I said, but my heart wasn't in it.

"It's gone too far, Kyle. Baker needs to be stopped."

"I know."

"You are the only one who can set this right. If you don't do what you need to do . . . what you *have* to do . . . Cassie Rourke will rot in the grave without vindication. Calvin Mooney will be punished for a crime he didn't commit."

"I'm not denying something's got to be done, Dan," I said. "I just don't know that I'm the one to do it."

"Damn it, Kyle. You are the one. You're the *only* one. Were there any other eyewitnesses out there that night?"

I let out an exasperated sigh. "No."

"Call Deputy Linder," Dan said. "As soon as you get off the phone with me. I mean it."

"I just . . . I *can't*, Dan."

"Yes, you can. *Please*, Kyle."

"I'm sorry."

"Fine. Okay. Tell me why, then. Why can't you do it? Why can't you pick up the phone, make a ten-second call to Deputy Linder, then hang up."

"Because he's got my bicycle, Danny!" I nearly shouted into the phone. I glanced back at Mom, but she had nodded off. She licked her lips in her sleep as if lapping up delicious pools of alcohol even in her dreams. "He's got Burner, and I'm sure he knows who I am!"

"What the hell are you talking about?" Dan said.

"He's got my bike. Baker's got Burner. Or some-body does. Henry, maybe. I don't know. But he's gone. Someone has him. And they're gonna come af-ter me, Dan. They're gonna get me. . . ."

"No. Wait, Kyle . . . let me get this straight—"

"That night after the Apple Gala," I said, my tone so tired and defeated, "I forgot my bicycle in the woods. I ran away, without thinking, and I left Burner there. I know it was stupid. I went back for him the next night, but he was gone. Now all Baker has to do is find out who owned that bicycle, Dan. Once he does that, I'm history."

At first I thought I was hearing things, on the other end of the line. I frowned.

Dan started laughing. My big brother was *laugh-ing* at me.

Had he gone crazy?

"I don't believe this!" Dan said, between chuckles. "Holy shit . . ."

"I don't think it's funny," I said, dabbing at my tears with my T-shirt. "Not at all."

"You thought—" Dan could barely get out what he was trying to say, he was laughing so hard. Yet there was something in that laugh, I realized, that was not borne of anything truly comical. It was the throaty chuckle of a man who has been sentenced to die, but has been granted a last-minute reprieve by the governor. A laugh of relief.

"*What*, Danny?" I said, irritated. But I let a nervous chuckle slip out in spite of myself. I couldn't help it. Dan's laughter had always been so infectious. Perhaps his insanity was too. "What is it?"

"You can rest easy, little buddy," Dan said. "Trust me."

I wiped my eyes again, hard. Sniffled.

"I can't believe I forgot to tell you, man! I feel so stupid."

"Tell me . . . what?"

"I guess with all the chaos last Sunday, running late for the airport and all, it totally slipped my mind. I am so sorry. No wonder you're a nervous wreck, dude!"

"*What*, Dan?" I said, impatient as hell. "What's going on? Please. Tell me."

"I got your bike, Kyle. It's okay."

"You . . . *what?*"

"I got Burner. I went back for him that night."

"Oh, my . . . you . . . what . . . ?"

"I didn't say anything to you about it because I didn't want you to be mad at me. It wasn't that I didn't believe you—what you saw out there and all—but I had to see the place for myself. I had to see if they left anything behind, you know? Like, evidence or something. Plus, I wanted to make sure *you* didn't leave anything behind."

"I did," I said.

"Yeah. You sure did! Do you realize how lucky you are?"

"Not lucky." I wept softly into the receiver. "I have you."

"It's okay, Kyle," Dan said. "Burner's safe. The sheriff doesn't know a thing."

"God, Dan . . . I can't believe it. . . ."

"Who loves you, bro?"

"You do," I said. "You do."

"And don't you ever forget it."

". . . all this time . . . I thought he *knew*. . . ."

"Shh. It's okay. What are big brothers for, right?"

"Where is he? Where's Burner?"

"In the storage shed," Dan said. So nonchalantly. I could almost see him throwing a thumb over his shoulder, giving me a little wink. "I could barely fit him in there, with that piece of shit lawnmower Mom bought last summer. But he's waitin' for ya."

"Wow," I said. "Oh, Dan . . ."

"You know what this means, Kyle," he said softly. "You have no excuses now. You've got to . . ."

"Yeah," I said. "I've got to."

"You'll do it, then?"

"Yes. I'll do it, Dan. I promise."

I still could not believe it. It all seemed like a dream. So surreal . . .

"Well, sport," Dan said after another minute or so, shattering my reverie of indescribable relief, "I guess I'd better get off here. Lemme shout at Mom for a sec, would ya? And I'll talk to you again soon."

"You'd better," I said.

I turned toward the living room.

"Mom?"

Her chest rose and fell, rose and fell. Her hoarse snore filled the living room.

"Mom!" I said, louder.

Still, she did not budge.

"I think she's out," I said into the phone. "Probably for the night."

"Has she been drinking?" Dan asked.

"What do you think?"

"Don't worry about it, then. I'll catch her later, I guess."

"Okay. I love you, Dan. Thanks again."

"Love you too. Bye now."

I waited until I heard the *click* of a severed connection on his end before I hung up the phone.

I walked back into our living room then, and despite the fact that Mom was once again passed out—probably dreaming of her new lover, a man who had betrayed us all and shit on my father's memory—I found myself smiling from ear to ear for the first time in several days. I couldn't believe it. Burner was safe after all! If what my brother said was true, Sheriff Baker had no clue whatsoever that I had witnessed the dark deeds he and his son committed out there in the Snake River Woods.

That cinched it. Dan was right.

I had the upper hand in Baker's evil game.

And it was time to take care of business.

Chapter Twenty-three

The game had changed. My whole *world* had changed, now that I knew my bicycle had been returned safely back home where it belonged.

I checked, just to be sure, as soon as I got off the phone. Not because I didn't trust my big brother, of course, but because I couldn't wait to see Burner.

It seemed to take me forever to walk out to the storage shed. The wet, knee-high grass lapped at the backs of my legs, and I wondered how long it would be until Mom made me mow it since Dan had shirked his duty.

And then I could think of nothing else but Burner as I opened the shed's heavy wooden door. Its rusty hinges squeaked like the gateway to an ancient tomb.

There Burner sat, just as Dan had promised. His shiny blue body stood out against the dusty darkness of the storage shed, amidst Dad's old tools, the toys my brother and I had outgrown years ago, and the battered old lawnmower Dan always hated trying to crank worse than he hated using it.

He was safe. My bicycle had been waiting out there for me all along. Locked up. Hidden.

He had never been in the hands of a murderer.

I was safe.

Burner seemed to wink at me when the beam of my flashlight struck him. As if to say, *Where have you been, old friend? I was starting to feel a bit lonely in here. . . .*

I fell to my knees beside him, almost numb with relief.

"Burner," I said. "You're home. . . ."

I sat like that, on my knees next to him in a pitch-black room that smelled so much like grass and gasoline, for so long I lost track of time. It felt like hours.

Finally, I wheeled Burner out of there, back onto the front porch where he belonged. It was in that spot, in the far left corner behind the weathered old porch swing no one used since Dad died, where my bicycle had always waited for me in happier times.

I had never been so happy. I couldn't wait to ride him again. I thought about taking off right then, speeding down Midnight's dark streets atop my best friend in the world like we used to do when I was supposed to be in bed.

But I didn't.

Because I had things to do.

Now that I no longer had to worry about Sheriff Burt Baker scouring Midnight for the owner of that sleek blue Schwinn Scrambler with the razor fender and the BMX-style handlebars—if he did not already know, if he had not been using his foul relationship with my mother to toy with me like a cat toys with a mouse before it tears the smaller creature limb from limb—I knew Dan was right. My big brother always was right, and he had proved it once again.

While doing the right thing would not be easy, I had no more excuses. No longer could I sit and allow an innocent man to take the blame for what I knew that son of a bitch had done.

Shortly after Mom rose from her coma on the couch and retired to her bed (without saying a word to me, but of course I couldn't have cared less), I sneaked into the kitchen.

Using only the dim moonlight coming in through the window over the kitchen sink, I slid open the drawer beside the refrigerator where we kept our phone book. I dusted the book off with one hand, and several small black rat turds fell onto the floor from atop its cover.

I quickly rifled through the book, found what I was looking for right away.

There was only one Mike Linder in Midnight. A Mike W. Linder, Jr., at 2777 Whitman Way.

I took a deep breath.

And picked up the phone.

Chapter Twenty-four

"Hello?"

The voice was young. Female. One of Deputy Linder's daughters, I assumed. She sounded very sleepy, as if the telephone had awakened her.

I swallowed, suddenly feeling very self-conscious.

"Er . . . um . . . c-could I speak to Mike, please?"

"It's almost eleven-thirty. May I ask who's calling?"

I froze. I hadn't expected that.

I deepened my voice, changed it as best I could.

"Umm," I said. "Could you tell him . . . umm . . . *Bob* is calling, please?"

I rolled my eyes, felt stupid. But maybe it would work. Just maybe.

"Okay," said Mike's daughter. She sounded disinterested, but not rude. "Hold on a second."

Clunk. She set down the phone, went to get her father.

I waited, felt my heart slamming in my chest like a big bass drum. I feared I might start hyperventilating by the time Mike came to the telephone.

About a minute later, someone picked up the phone. Mike's daughter again. She sighed, as if she had better things to do than play answering service for her father.

"Bob who?" she said.

Crap!

"Uhhh . . ." I didn't know how to answer that. "B-Bob . . . Bob S-Smith."

I said the first thing I could think of, and as soon as it fell from my lips I cringed, aware of how horribly contrived it sounded. How made-up-on-the-spot.

This wasn't going to work.

"Hold on," she said.

I held on.

After what felt like forever, Mike Linder came to the phone. I heard him mumble to her as he approached the receiver, "Only Bob Smith I know died two years ago, honey," but then he was as polite as always when his deep, friendly voice said to me, "Mike Linder speaking. What can I do you for?"

"H-hey," I said.

"Hello. Who is this?"

"Hey," I said again. I cleared my throat. "L-listen."

"Pardon?"

More firmly: *"Listen."*

"Who is this—"

"Don't believe what the liar says," I told him. I spoke just above a whisper, in the deepest voice I could muster at twelve years old. "Calvin Mooney never laid a finger on that girl."

"Huh? What—"

"Sheriff Baker is a murderer. He snapped Cassie Rourke's neck, after Henry beat her. I saw it."

Silence. I couldn't even hear Linder breathing. The phone line cracked and popped between us, a sound like distant flames lapping hungrily at the respect and admiration Sheriff Baker had won the past few years from the citizens of Polk County.

I waited. Let it sink in for a few seconds. I clenched my free hand into a tight white fist as I listened to the midnight rain begin to fall harder, batting against the kitchen window like hail.

"Do you understand?" I said finally, when nothing was forthcoming from Mike Linder.

For a second or two, I thought he might have hung up on me.

When he did speak again, his voice was tense. As if he did not want to believe what I told him, yet something in what I said rang of horrible truth.

"That's one hefty accusation, you know. Burt Baker's a good man."

"It's true," I said. "And no, he's not."

"Who is this anyway?" he asked.

"A friend."

Thunder rumbled above my house. I wondered if lightning could travel through phones, electrocuting anyone foolish enough to talk on one in the middle of a storm.

I heard him swallow. "Assuming this isn't some kinda sick joke . . . how the hell would *you* know this? You have proof?"

"I saw it myself," I replied. "Saturday night, after the Apple Gala."

"Christ."

"It happened in the Snake River Woods. Out at the old shack. Do you know the place, Mike?"

"I'm familiar with it," he said.

"Good," I said. "Look into this. Please. Cassie Rourke wasn't raped. Henry Baker couldn't rape her if he tried, I don't think. But he did beat her. And Sheriff Baker killed her."

"This is all too much too fast," Mike said. "Who *are* you?"

I ignored his question. "Check into it, Mike," I said. "Please. Don't let Burt Baker get away with this. He's a murderer. Not Calvin Mooney."

"But how—"

"Calvin Mooney never hurt a fly," I said.

And I hung up.

My breath gushed out of me like something solid. I leaned over the kitchen sink, felt weak but at the same time oh-so-proud of what I'd done.

I couldn't believe it.

I had done it.

I stood there over the sink, staring out at the storm, for at least half an hour. I couldn't remember the last time I found solace in such sounds, the way the rain and the thunder seemed to envelop me in a warm pocket of comfort that I wanted to huddle inside forever.

What happens now? I wondered.

I waited. Smiling. Knowing it could only be good.

August 16

Chapter Twenty-five

Doing the right thing had changed my outlook on life entirely. I felt like a new man!

Gone was the melancholy stupor that had been crushing me since the night of August 5. I could rest easy, knowing that justice would soon be served. Morning couldn't arrive fast enough. I assumed it was only a matter of hours before Mom called me into the living room and we both listened as a WHLP anchorman explained how Calvin Mooney was a free man and Sheriff Burt Baker had been arrested for murder.

I wondered if I would be called upon to testify. Strangely enough, I felt nothing more than a twinge of anxiety at the thought of having to do that. Perhaps I would be a hero, when all was said and done! Just like my brother had been when he won his scholarship to FSU, when he took the Stokely High Yellowjackets to the state championship and his picture was on the front page of the *Midnight Sun* not once but *twice* in one week. I nearly felt invincible as

I basked in the warm afterglow of knowing I had finally done the right thing with a simple phone call to Mike Linder. While my fear did not dissipate entirely, of course, it seemed to linger in the back of my mind more like a distant memory of something slightly unpleasant than any wicked black dilemma that had ruled my life for the past eleven days.

Deputy Linder would protect me. I was sure of that. He was going to make everything right again.

My soul seemed renewed with an almost intoxicating vigor. I wondered if Mom experienced a similar heady rush every time she twisted the lid off a brand new bottle of liquor.

I couldn't wait to tell Dan.

Chapter Twenty-six

"Elvis is dead," Mom informed me that afternoon.

I hadn't intended to speak with her. I was on my way to the kitchen for a snack of cheese and crackers when her voice came to me from the living room.

I peeked in there to see her sitting on the couch. Her hair was unkempt, tangled. She looked very pale. A new bottle of Wild Turkey whiskey sat between her legs. It sloshed like the belly of a sated pet as she brought it to her lips.

I thought I was seeing things at first, that it was merely the reflection of the rain streaking down the big bay window across the room, but when Mom returned the bottle to the space between her legs I realized she was crying. Tears streamed down her face, and as she spoke to me a huge snot bubble swelled and popped in her left nostril.

"Mom?" I said.

"Elvis is dead," she said again. "I can't believe it."

I stared at her, confused. A book lay open on her knee, facedown. A worn-out old copy of *To Kill a*

Mockingbird. She must have been reading it before she saw the news.

I followed her moist, red-eyed gaze to the television, where a grainy still photograph of the hefty King of Rock n' Roll, clad in glittering gold sunglasses and a white suit sparkling with a hundred rhinestones, faded away to a small yellow caption on a stark black background: ELVIS AARON PRESLEY, JAN. 8, 1935–AUG. 16, 1977.

"Oh," I said. "Okay."

I did not mean to sound as if I didn't care, of course. But then, I *didn't.*

I cringed when Mom blew her nose on the baggy pink T-shirt she was wearing (MOTHERS MAKE THE WORLD GO 'ROUND, read the logo over her breasts) and then I moved off down the hallway, frowning.

"What a sad, sad day," I heard Mom say behind me.

I don't know why I entered Dan's bedroom instead of my own that evening. Perhaps I was merely trapped in a daze, wondering what the hell was happening to my mother.

Sometimes I wondered if she wasn't losing her mind, bit by bit.

Mom had *never* liked Elvis. In fact, on more than one occasion, I had heard her claim he was a "pig," and that his music "turned her frigging stomach." Yet she wept for him that evening worse than I had seen her mourn anyone since the day we buried my father.

I shook my head, decided I would never figure her out, so why even try.

Once again, Dan's room felt like a warm sanctuary for me. It always seemed to set my mind at ease, going in there, and in some strange way I imagined my big brother was right there with me any time I ventured into his private domain.

214

I rifled through his albums for a few minutes, but couldn't find anything I was in the mood to listen to. I shrugged, sighed, fell onto Dan's bed and just lay staring at the ceiling with a wistful smile upon my face. I allowed the roar of the rain outside to fill the room, my head, my entire world.

Things were going to get better, I knew. And fast. I wondered if Deputy Linder had already confronted his superior. If he had called off the search for Calvin Mooney seconds before he slapped cold steel handcuffs on the real killers. On Burt and Henry Baker. I imagined him reading Sheriff Baker his rights, and that made me smile.

Knowing that everything was going to be okay plus the constant hum of the rain against the house soon worked like a powerful sedative upon me. I could not remember the last time I felt so relaxed, so calm. . . .

I rolled over, breathed deeply of my brother's scent on his bedspread.

Before long, the sound of the midnight rain faded, and I fell fast asleep.

SHERIFF BURT BAKER ARRESTED FOR MURDER! read the headline of the *Midnight Sun* in my dream. Its font denoted a celebratory tone, the text spelled out in pink and yellow and orange and red cartoon letters surrounded by firework-like blasts of the same colors. Swirls and sparkles and bright gay stars, like a party invitation.

Also in my dream: Burt Baker. On his knees in the town common. Surrounded by every last citizen of Midnight.

They were stoning him.

The sheriff thrashed about, begging for mercy, but even the town's youngest toddlers—children barely old enough to walk—were getting in on the action as the clouds above my hometown rolled away and the sun beat down upon us like the proud smile of a great, fiery god.

Baker screamed as he was pummeled about the groin by a series of sharp rocks thrown by Deputy Mike Linder's twin daughters. They giggled sweetly as they worked.

At some point he turned to look at me where I stood within the crowd.

"Does this make it all better?" he asked me, through an ugly mask of blood and dirt and snot and tears. "Do you think this brings her back?"

"No," I said to the killer. "It doesn't."

I hefted a rock of my own.

"But, man, it feels so good."

I awoke on the floor a few hours later, though it felt like only seconds had passed since I drifted off. Apparently I had rolled out of Dan's bed in my sleep. My head throbbed, and a tingling pins-and-needles sensation ran through my elbow. I must have hit my funny bone on the frame of the bed on the way down.

I laughed at myself. Besides feeling stupid for falling out of the bed, the pins-and-needles tingling in my arms was one of those pains that for some reason you can't help but chuckle over, even as you grit your teeth and wish it would go away. A pain that almost tickled in some weird way.

"If my big brother could see me now," I groaned.

I prepared to stand, and that's when I saw the cigar box under Dan's bed. About two feet back. It had been shoved up against the rosewood body of an acoustic guitar Dan hadn't touched in years, and was surrounded by a wrinkled red tank-top that had been kicked under there and forgotten, a hardcover copy of a book called *The Deep* ("A New Novel By the Author of *Jaws!*"), an old eight-track tape of The Who's *Tommy*, and a fuzzy herd of dust bunnies.

The cigar box was old, its once-bright colors faded and its corners scuffed. There was something about it that seemed to beckon to me, though I did not know why.

I couldn't help myself. My curiosity got the best of me once again. . . .

I slid the cigar box out from beneath my brother's bed. PRIMO DEL REY, read the logo on its lid.

Lightning flickered at the window. Thunder vibrated through the foundations of my home. I could feel it in my butt as I sat there Indian-style beside Dan's bed.

I stood, set the box up on Dan's mattress. Sure, I felt a tad guilty at this invasion of my big brother's privacy, knew what I was doing wasn't really right, but I rationalized my actions by telling myself that Dan wouldn't mind. We were more than just brothers. We were best friends. We had nothing to hide from each other. Ever.

I expected to find a few dollar bills inside the box, some loose change. Maybe a couple old arrowheads Dan had collected during his own boyhood adventures around Midnight. I had a few of those myself in a shoebox under my bed, and I wouldn't have sold them for all the money in the world. Perhaps, I thought, I might find a key or two inside there as well—the kind that turns up and you can't remember for the life of you what that key opens so you hold on to it forever just in case you do ever need it.

I certainly did not expect to find anything too terribly exciting.

But then, I was young and naïve.

I rose, plopped down on the edge of Dan's bed.

Opened the box. As soon as the lid fell back, the undeniable aroma of women's perfume wafted up into my nostrils. It wasn't overwhelming, that smell, but it was there nonetheless. And it was strong. Inside the box.

I felt the tickly threat of a sneeze coming on, like a wave threatening to break in my skull, but it never came. I licked my lips, shifted my weight uncomfortably upon the bed. The smell of a female, especially a flowery aroma so potent and alive as the one which escaped from that old cigar box despite having been sealed up inside there for God knows how long . . . it made me feel funny down below in a way I could not explain at the age of twelve.

That is not to say that I did not like it, of course. I did. That perfume smell immediately brought to mind every tiny crush I ever had, every girl who ever smiled at me in gym class or sat beside me in Vacation Bible School. For the record, I never went through that female-hating stage most grammar school boys wear on their sleeves like some prepubescent badge of honor, and I think even if I had I would have dropped it like an ugly jacket I was glad to outgrow the second that glorious woman-smell met my nostrils. . . .

I was hooked. I had to know what was in that box now, even if it killed me. . . .

The first thing I saw when I opened it was a worn paperback copy of *The Hobbit*, by J.R.R. Tolkien. Beneath that lay a dog-eared ticket from the Kiss concert Dan had gone to see with a bunch of his high school friends shortly after graduation. Also hidden in there were two slips of yellow notebook paper scribbled with what I assumed were girls' phone numbers (KIM, said one, BECCA the other). I frowned when I saw those, wondered what his steady girlfriend Julie would have thought about such souvenirs. Underneath the girls' phone numbers lay an unused postcard from Myrtle Beach, South Carolina, and an imitation-leather key-chain with the Ford logo on it. But that wasn't all. As I thumbed through these items, placing each upon the bed before me as if taking a detailed inventory of Dan's private property, a cigarette rolled into one corner of the box. That made me frown. Far as I knew, my brother had never been a smoker. I picked the cigarette up, sniffed it. Scrunched up my nose. It sure didn't smell like any cigarette I'd ever seen. It had no markings, and almost looked homemade.

Then, at the bottom of the box, beneath everything else my brother had chosen to hang on to for whatever reason, I saw the neat square pile of pink notebook paper.

The pages were all undersized, as if torn from a colorful legal pad. There were three or four of them, all stacked together beneath *The Hobbit* and the Kiss tickets and the key-chain and the funny-smelling cigarette.

I realized instantly that those pages were the source of that strong perfume aroma. I could almost taste it.

The first thing I noticed about them was the purple ink used to write those notes to my brother. Upon each hot pink page were several short paragraphs written in what looked like a girl's neat handwriting. She wrote in a style that could not seem to decide whether it wanted to be cursive or print, but alternated between both, and she liked to dot her every "i" with a cute little heart.

The second thing I noticed, as I gave those pages a precursory glance, skimming over them without really reading any of the letters' contents yet . . . was the signature at the bottom of each.

They had all been signed C.B.R.

CASSIE.

Or a variation on that name and those initials.

The room grew cold.

"D-Dan?" I stammered. "I d-don't . . . what is this?"

I stared off into nothing for a minute, trying to make sense of what I had just found. I was confused. In a daze. The storm lapped at the window a few feet away from me like the slimy wet tongue of a pervert.

My hands trembled slightly as I started with the page at the top of the stack, reading it aloud to myself in a low, uneven whisper:

Dear Danny,

> *i enjoyed talking to you Saturday night. Although i'll bet it would have been better for both of us if your girlfriend hadn't been there (haha).*
>
> *Just kidding. She seems pretty cool, I guess. what was her name again?*
>
> *i would like to give you my phone number, if you wouldn't think bad of me. Just remember— if my daddy answers don't worry. his bark is a whole lot worse than his bite.*
>
> *i can't wait to hear from you, Danny. Please call me. i'll be waiting.*

> *Hugs and Kisses,*
> *CASSIE*
> *555-4845*

I swallowed a lump in my throat that felt approximately the size of one of my brother's basketballs. My heart slammed in my chest.

I shook my head back and forth, unable to comprehend this new development before me.

It couldn't be. No *way.*

What the hell did this mean?

I didn't want to read on. But I did. I held my breath as I picked up the second pink letter, no longer wanting to smell that heady perfume aroma which permeated each page like the scent of one very flirtatious ghost:

Danny,

i can't stop thinking about our night together. i miss you so bad. Every minute i am without you hurts so bad i want to DIE.

God . . . what did you DO to me?

You made me feel so special, Danny. i want to see you again soon.

You are so sexy. My hunky basketball star.

Love,
C.B.R.

I couldn't stop shaking my head.

This wasn't right.

"How . . . what. . . . ?"

Dan *knew* her?

I felt dirty, didn't understand any of it, yet at the same time I did. So much more than I wanted to.

Everything I thought I knew, everything I believed, suddenly seemed like only one possibility. If not a dirty lie altogether.

I grew light-headed as I perused the third love letter to my brother, and with every passing second a terrible taste—like the taste of a dead girl's rotting flesh—filled my mouth and caused my bowels to lurch:

Danny . . . my love:

i know you're worried about my age, but that shouldn't matter to you now. What's done is done, right?

Heck, Mom and Dad don't even know you exist.

Sometimes you have to look at the big picture. Think about it this way . . . our ages wouldn't mean a thing if you were 30 and I was 27, now would it?

think about that.

AGE IS JUST A NUMBER!

It hurts when you ignore me, Danny. i gave you something special, and now you want to act like i'm nobody.

i thought you were different than all the other boys. I thought it meant something more with us. Something REAL.

You're not a boy, Danny. You are a MAN.

MY man.

Is it HER? If it's Julie, maybe you should get rid of her. If you do it now, i'm sure she'll understand . . . but if she finds out about us from someone else, it's going to be a lot harder for everyone involved, don't you think?

i don't know what I'm trying to say. i probably sound like an idiot. All I know is . . . I think I love you, Danny.

Can you feel it too? Don't lie.

What can SHE give you that i can't?

C.B.R.

I read that one again, and as I did so my vision grew blurry. I felt a headache coming on.

None of it made any sense.

The last letter I had pulled from the cigar box, however, was the one that I am quite sure made my heart stop for several long seconds. My body had grown numb from the neck down and the room started spinning around me by the time I got to the end of it:

> *SCREW YOU, DAN, if you can't be a MAN and do the RIGHT THING!!!*
> *IT TAKES TWO TO TANGO, YOU KNOW.*
> *Wait till people see you're not the MR. PERFECT they all thought you were!*
> *you're just like all the rest. you make me SICK.*
>
> C.

What the hell was going on here? My head swam. I felt ill. The room seemed to spin around me. I gripped the edge of the bed to keep from rolling off it again.

I couldn't believe the implications of those letters. . . .

Why had Dan neglected to tell me that he knew Cassie Rourke when I had confided in him about what I had witnessed in the Snake River Woods?

Was it possible that my big brother—the one person whom I loved and trusted unconditionally, whom I thought I would love and trust unconditionally till the very end of time—might have had something to hide?

No. It couldn't be. I would not allow myself to consider such a thing. I felt ashamed that such terrible thoughts could even enter my mind.

The possibility of something like that being true . . . my God, it would have killed me.

I could not deny, however, what I saw with my own eyes.

Dan *had* known Cassie Belle Rourke. And her letters to him hinted that they had been much more than just friends, once upon a time.

The thing that bothered me most of all, however—the thing that made me want to run screaming into the midnight rain, never to return lest I should learn the horrible truth about what had happened between my brother and that girl who was brutally murdered the night of the Apple Gala—was the fact that those last two letters suggested a relationship turned sour.

I could almost feel the animosity burning off the last page, radiating from Cassie Rourke's words like lavender fire.

What had happened between them? What had my brother done?

I didn't know.

I could no longer be sure about anything at all in my world.

And that is why—as the storm beat madly against the sides of my house and my brain swirled with a million conflicting emotions and the cloying smell of Cassie Belle Rourke's perfume seemed to grow stronger and stronger the longer her letters lay on the bed before me until it might have filled the whole room—I leaned over the side of Danny's bed like a man on a rapidly sinking ship . . .

And I threw up all over his bedroom floor.

August 17

Chapter Twenty-seven

School was scheduled to begin in just four days, but as the storm throughout Midnight loomed with no visible end in sight—not only the barrage of constant thunder and lightning, I mean, but also the chaos surrounding the search for Calvin Mooney—rumors ran rampant throughout my hometown that the first day of school might be delayed for a week or two. Normally, as with the cancellation of school due to snow several times each winter, this would have been the greatest news ever to a kid who would rather stay at home and do nothing all day then sit behind a desk and listen to some crotchety old teacher drone on about chlorophyll, long division, and dangling participles. For once, however, the news of the school year's possible postponement was no cause for celebration. To me it simply meant, during those dark days following the Apple Gala, there would be no homework or good friends or even bullies like my grammar-school archenemy

Craig Stoody to take my mind off the far more sinister matters that had tortured me so mercilessly of late.

I was stuck at home with my doubts and fears and mistrust of everyone and everything I had once held so dear.

The rain continued, on and on, as if intentionally mirroring my foul mood. It pummeled my home like a giant hammer, and everywhere I looked dirty gray water ran down the streets of Midnight like precious lifeblood leaking from a thousand different cuts the storm had opened in the places I once loved. A growing number of Midnight's side roads were blocked by bright orange sawhorses and detour signs, hastily constructed barriers warning of flooded routes that had become, in effect, lesser tributaries of the Snake River. A number of electrical wires and phone lines had been severed by the storm, and they lay atop the asphalt here and there throughout town like so many black snakes ready to strike at unsuspecting citizens. At any given time we could all expect our power to flash off and on, sometimes remaining interrupted for up to a day or more.

Midnight itself seemed stuck in a constant state of gray back then, the town's very atmosphere one of gloom and despondency.

It was like a disease.

A disease that had infected us all.

Chapter Twenty-eight

Even now, so many years later, I don't know what got into me that morning. Perhaps I was simply in such a foul, antagonistic mood toward everyone and everything around me, I grew blinded by my burning desire for quick, easy vindication.

I wanted to lash out at somebody—*needed* to lash out at something.

I had called Deputy Linder already, and I told him what I saw. Dan assured me Burner was safe, and I had seen the evidence for myself out back. Yet those were very small victories when all was said and done. There were still other matters that ate constantly at my brain like a nasty black worm devouring all reason and common sense. . . .

Someone had to pay for the fact that my brother had known Cassie Rourke. Someone had to suffer in the same way I had suffered since discovering that my mother was involved with a beast who committed murder, then blamed it on a poor handicapped man.

I was young. I was foolish. I was pissed off. Thinking clearly had become a foreign concept to me, and even my fear took a backseat to the hatred I felt for Cassandra Rourke's killer after those most recent developments.

That is why, just a few minutes after Mom left for work, I called Sheriff Burt Baker myself.

And I told him what I saw, out there in the Snake River Woods.

Mom headed off to work that day around six A.M. I heard her getting ready, singing softly to herself in her bedroom as I lay in my own bed listening to the radio.

I waited until I heard her station wagon pull out of the driveway and rumble on down the street before I got up and went into the kitchen.

On the table beside an empty bowl and a box of Corn Flakes I found a note she had left for me. It explained how she'd gone in to work early so she could "milk a little Over-Time"; otherwise she was afraid "the next time the power goes out it might just stay out, 'cause it sure ain't free."

I shrugged, yawned, but then frowned when I saw the post-script at the bottom: "P.S. Burt says hello. You really should get to know him, honey, 'cause I think you guys would get along GREAT."

I shook my head. Made a sound that was half-exasperated groan, half-animal growl. I clenched my fists, hated the note even more for that exaggerated "GREAT" with which she had ended it, in all capital letters.

I felt more than GREAT as I crumpled up her piece-of-shit note and tossed it toward the wastebasket in the far corner of the kitchen. I missed, but I didn't pick it up. I left it lying in the middle of the floor like a small white turd expelled on Mom's linoleum by a constipated gremlin.

Then I saw his number, on the wall beside the phone, an amendment to Mom's little "emergency list" slightly above and to the right of the contact information for our family physician, Dr. Laymon:

BURT
555-8405

My stomach lurched when I saw it. She had drawn a fat, swirling heart around the killer's name with a red Magic Marker. Like a naïve, lovesick schoolgirl defiling her personal belongings with odes to short-lived puppy love.

I stood there for a minute, staring at his name. Waiting for my nausea to subside. I asked God to forgive me for the thoughts filling my head. I did not want to hate my mother, but I found it harder and harder to fight such feelings the more I learned about her.

Then, I quickly wiped away the tears gathered in the corners of my eyes. I swallowed. Took a deep breath.

I picked up the phone.

And dialed the sheriff's number.

"Hello," Burt Baker said, halfway through the fourth ring.

I recognized the murderer's voice instantly. It was slurred just slightly with sleep, the voice of a man who has only been out of bed for a few minutes and has not yet had time to don the face and tone he uses to go out into the world. But it was him. No doubt about it.

My breath caught in my throat.

"Hello?" Burt Baker said again, louder. "Baker residence."

"I know what you did," I said, deepening my voice

as much as possible. The last thing I wanted was to sound like a twelve-year-old kid. Especially the very twelve-year-old Baker might recognize as the son of the woman he'd been dating.

"Come again?" he said, without the slightest bit of worry in his tone.

"I saw what you did to Cassie Rourke, in the woods."

"You . . . what? Who the fuck is this?"

"It doesn't matter," I said. "All that matters is, I know who *you* are . . . Sheriff."

"Who are you? What the fuck do you want?"

Bingo. I couldn't help but notice how his voice cracked a bit that time. He hid it well. But it was there.

"This better not be some kinda jo—"

"It's not a joke," I interrupted. "I saw what you did to Cassie Belle Rourke after the Apple Gala. Henry hurt her, and you killed her. You blamed an innocent man. But you're not going to get away with it."

"Who . . . wha . . . look here, man—"

"I made sure you won't get away with it."

He sounded like a lost little boy when he asked me again, "What do you want? Tell me."

"Nothing," I said. "Except justice."

I hung up.

My heart beat faster than ever before. I held one hand against my chest, breathed deeply.

But I felt good.

Damn good.

"Checkmate, you son of a bitch," I said, recalling the one time Dan tried to teach me how to play chess, but I hadn't grasped it at all.

It seemed to be my brother's favorite saying that night:"Checkmate."

It felt good. It felt right.

So I smiled, and I said it again:"*Checkmate*, Sheriff Baker. Your move."

Chapter Twenty-nine

Less than twelve hours later, the sheriff did make his move.

And I wished I could take it all back.

I wished I could forfeit our game entirely, if it would change anything.

But it was far too late for that.

"He's dead, Kyle. Oh, my God, I can't believe he's dead."

"Mom?" I sat up abruptly, my mind still foggy with sleep. My heart raced from being jolted awake. My head throbbed. "What's wrong?"

I realized I must have fallen asleep on the couch at some point earlier that afternoon. I'd slept for quite a while, too, because Mom had already arrived home from work. She had *just* gotten home, I assumed, as her purse still hung around one skinny arm. She still wore her work clothes, and several strands of her curly brown hair were pasted to her sweaty forehead.

I blinked several times fast, sat up. For the next few

seconds I wondered if her words had only been part of a very bad dream, perhaps a nightmare about the day we learned my father had been killed in Vietnam.

But no, this was now. And this was no dream.

"He's dead," Mom said again, through a shiny mask of tears. "I can't believe this has happened."

"Who's dead?" I moaned, stretching. "Elvis?"

She either did not hear my smart-ass comment or paid it no mind.

"He was such a good person. God. Him and Terri both, all the things they used to do for us after your father died . . . how could I have been so . . ."

"Who are you talking about, Mom?" I asked her. "What's going on?"

"It's like it's not real, you know? Like it's this . . . nightmare. He can't be dead. It's impossible. I just saw him at the grocery store a couple nights ago. He can't be gone. Can you believe it, Kyle?"

I suspected I would not believe it. No way. *If only she would tell me what the hell had happened!*

"Oh, God," she cried. "It's so awful. . . ."

I waited for an explanation. I began to chew at my nails as a dark blanket of worry descended upon me. Somehow I knew . . . this was for real. This wasn't another one of Mom's drunken rants or bouts of depression. Something had happened.

Something very bad had happened.

"It was a car accident," she said. "I'm not sure about all the details yet. I just heard it from Sarah Mohler."

"Okay," I said, following her so far. Sarah Mohler was our next-door neighbor, a lady who had gone to school with my mother and remained one of Mom's on-again, off-again friends. She was also the biggest gossipmonger I ever met, back then or ever since.

"She says it happened over on Highway 76. Supposedly he died instantly . . . thank the Lord he didn't suffer . . . but . . . oh, God, Kyle . . . how do they really *know* that, if they weren't there? I can't imagine what Terri and the twins must be going through . . . the poor things. . . ."

I barely listened to my mother's rambling now. I could only focus on what she had told me, what I knew it all must mean as the pieces fell into place.

Even if I did not want to believe it.

"No," I said. "Mom . . . please tell me that's not true. . . ."

It was too much too fast.

Terri . . . the twins . . .

Mom leaned over to embrace me, but I practically leapt out of her grip, from the sofa to the television.

I had to know for sure.

I turned on the TV.

And there it was, the Hour's Top Story on Channel 5. My heart leapt into my throat.

"No," I said. *"No. . . ."*

"Earlier this afternoon," explained a tan young anchorman over grainy footage of something crumpled and warped that used to be a patrol car being pulled from a muddy roadside ditch, "Deputy Sheriff Mike Willem Linder was killed when his patrol car careened off of Highway 76 and hit a telephone pole. He was pronounced dead on arrival at Polk County Memorial Hospital at approximately 3 P.M."

The anchorman put on his most somber face then, paused, and looked straight into the camera. Straight at me.

"Again, folks, we regret to report that Deputy Mike Willem Linder, of the Polk County Sheriff's Department, died today in a tragic accident off of Highway 76."

I shook my head back and forth, and clenched my fists as if the man on the television might take it all back if I only *dis*believed what he had told me strongly enough.

"Deputy Linder was thirty-nine years old. He is survived by his wife, Terri, and twin fourteen-year-old daughters, Staci and Traci. Funeral services are expected to be held early next week."

This couldn't be happening. A great weight lay upon my chest. I couldn't breathe. I fell to my knees, and the television grew blurry before me.

The young anchorman's voice was barely above a whisper as he concluded with, "We'll be right back with more Channel 5 News after these messages."

I continued to shake my head back and forth slowly, not hearing anything else on the television, just the sound of my own sniffling and Mom's incoherent babbling somewhere behind me. The din of the storm outside filled my head like the truth of the whole matter personified, batting at the window and trying to get inside to wreak havoc.

I wanted to scream. I wanted to raise my head to the heavens and shout at God.

It wasn't fair. It wasn't supposed to turn out like this.

Deputy Linder's death had been no accident, I knew.

He had gotten too close to the truth.

After I called him and left my anonymous message, I knew Mike had wasted no time in investigating my allegations. Perhaps he had questioned Calvin Mooney's guilt, or maybe he had come right out and foolishly accused his friend of murder. . . .

And Sheriff Burt Baker had once again cleaned up any loose ends that threatened to expose him as the monster he really was.

Tears streamed down my face like the torrents of rain at the window. Shame filled my soul.

"I'm sorry," I said to Mike's wife, Terri. To his fourteen-year-old daughters, Staci and Traci.

I wanted to die. I wished it had been *me*, in that patrol car.

I might as well have killed our old family friend myself. . . .

August 18

Chapter Thirty

"Kyle!" came my big brother's voice the following night, all the way from Tallahassee, Florida.

"Dan."

Mom had gone out earlier that evening. Where I did not know, though I suspected she was with *him*.

I tried not to think about that.

Dan must have been eating an apple, judging from the loud, wet smacking sounds in my ear (*crunch-scrape, crunch-scrape* went his big front teeth as they worked away at the fruit), and his words were nearly unintelligible amidst all the noise. "What's crack-alackin', little brother?"

"Mm," I said. "Not much."

I should have been ecstatic to hear from my brother again. Instead, I just wished he would leave me alone.

At least until I could figure everything out, find out what had happened between him and Cassandra Belle Rourke.

Dan's voice was a stranger's on the other end of

the line. No, his voice had not changed. He was still my brother. But something darker lurked beneath his soft Southern accent and deep post-puberty tone. Something sinister. Something I could no longer trust.

The person I loved, whom I had idolized as long as I could remember, had become an enigma to me overnight.

What obscene secrets did he have to hide? How had he known her, and what had he done to her?

Did I even want to know the answers to those questions?

I wasn't sure. I couldn't think straight. I was so, so confused.

"Hello?" Dan said. "You there, little bro?"

"Yeah," I said. "I'm here."

"*O-kay.*" I could hear the puzzlement in his tone. It hadn't taken him long to pick up on my mood.

Good. I wanted him to hear it. I *wanted* him to know I was none too happy with him. At least for now.

"You sure sound happy to hear from me, Kyle. Like I just told you your dog died or something."

"I don't have a dog," I said. Cold.

The sounds of his apple-mastication ceased. I could almost hear my brother's frown. "I know that. God. Excuse the hell outta me. Did I interrupt something? What's up with you?"

"Nothing."

"Kyle, what is it? What's the matter?"

"Nothing, Dan. I'm fine."

"Is there something you want to tell me?"

"Nope."

Thunder boomed overhead, rattling the window above the kitchen sink, so loud that I barely heard what Dan said next:"So did you do it? Just tell me you did it, and I'll let you go."

Ah. So *that's* why he was calling. Not to see how I was doing. Not to check in on his little brother.

But to keep up the fucking charade.

I bit my lip. One hand went to my roiling stomach. I began to feel things about my brother I had never felt before. Things I did not want to feel, but could not help even if I tried.

They made me want to die, those feelings.

"Yeah," I said, but my voice was barely more than a sick croak. "I did it."

"Good man! I'm so proud of you."

I shrugged, although he could not see my gesture. I made a bored, noncommittal grunt.

"So why so gloomy, little bro? You should be very happy. That's a mighty fine thing you did. You'll see."

I said nothing.

Again: "I'm so proud of you, Kyle."

Still, I said nothing.

"You there? Earth to Kyle. . . ."

"I should be proud of myself, Dan," I said finally, fighting back tears. "But I'm not."

"What do you mean? Why not?"

"Mike's *dead,* Dan. Deputy Linder is dead."

"What . . . what are you talking about?"

"He's dead. The news said he was killed in a car accident, but I know better. *I know better.*"

My brother said nothing. He sounded as if he might start hyperventilating on the other end of the line.

"Baker killed him," I said. "Don't you see?"

"Oh, God," Dan wheezed.

" 'Cause he knew too much."

Dan made a hissing sound through his teeth.

"It's all my fault. He's dead now because *I* got him involved."

Dan said, "No. No. Look. You can't blame yourse—"

I didn't want to take it out on my big brother. I really didn't. But all I kept seeing as his voice came to me over the phone line were those love notes. Those letters from a dead girl, in the box under his bed.

"Did you know her?" I said quickly. My voice cracked as I said it, and it came out in a very low, nearly inaudible whisper, yet I knew he heard it because even the sounds of his strained breathing immediately went silent. He could not mistake what I had said. It was there. Between us, like a sharp electrical shock over the phone line. And I could not take it back even if I'd wanted to.

"What?"

"Did you know her, Dan? Tell me the truth."

"Who . . . Kyle, what are you talking about?"

"You know."

"No," he said. "I don't."

I could hear it in his voice, though. I did not have to tell him. He sounded guilty. He knew damn well what I was talking about.

"Look, Dan, I gotta go," I said. "I'll talk to you later, okay?"

"Kyle, what's the matter with you? What are you—"

"Bye, Dan," I said.

I hung up. On my big brother. It was something I had never done before, and would never have even thought about doing as recently as several days before.

But then, so much had changed since the night of the Apple Gala.

By the time the phone was back in its cradle, my face was drenched with tears. I ran to my room, praying he would not call back.

He did, of course. A few minutes later. The phone rang and rang and rang—at least forty times, I'm sure, though I didn't bother counting—but I ignored it.

I had never been so confused in my life.

Everything I had ever believed had turned out to be a lie. Everyone I ever loved turned out to be a liar.

The lies in my home stank of rot. Their stench filled up every room, permeating the air with the smell of treachery. Blood. Betrayal. And death.

It was an odor far more powerful, even, than that of Mom's addiction.

Chapter Thirty-one

My heart might have stopped when I heard the short, sharp *whoop* of a police siren outside, followed by the reptilian hiss of tires on wet pavement.

I ran to my bedroom window, pulled aside the curtain. I could see nothing at first. I made a fist, quickly rubbed a small circle in the condensation so I could see outside.

The night surrounded my house like an enormous wet blanket. Beneath it, a soft drizzle fell upon our lawn, giving the property a surreal silvery-blue look like something out of a dream.

The room grew cold as an icebox when I saw Sheriff Burt Baker's beige patrol car parked in front of my house, down by the curb.

It didn't move. Its engine idled softly, like the purr of one very large, contented feline.

I could see Baker's thick round shape behind the steering wheel, like some satanic force twice as black as the night around him.

And another shape, in the seat beside him. Some-one smaller.

Henry? I wondered.

Had they finally come to silence me? Was this the end?

How would they do it? I wondered. Would the sheriff snap my neck the same way he had snapped Cassie Rourke's, so effortlessly?

I swallowed, and my throat was as dry as the hottest, barest desert wasteland.

I wondered if he was watching the house. Watch-ing *me*.

What was he waiting for?

I nearly pissed my pants when his back-up lights came on, like two bright white eyes in the night.

"What do you want?" I whispered. "Leave me alone. . . ."

The patrol car backed slowly into my driveway then, as if I had summoned it. I gasped. From where I sat I could hear gravel crunching beneath the car's tires like the brittle bones of infants snapping and popping beneath an ogre's feet.

I glared at his shape inside the vehicle, wondering what he planned to do.

A second or two later the car stopped, about halfway up the length of my driveway. For a second I thought Baker might keep reversing until he backed right into Mom's station wagon. But then his brake lights glowed an eerie bloodred, giving my whole front yard the look of some low-budget horror movie.

I moved back from the window, sure I would be spotted if I stood in that crimson glow for too long.

My heart thudded in my chest. I was so sure of it now—I was going to pee in my pants. I could not stop it.

I knelt on the floor, and dared to peek through the window again.

For the next few minutes the only movement outside was the thick cloud of exhaust farting out from the sheriff's patrol car in a steady blue-gray stream. It billowed into the air like the hot, rank breath of a demon, partially obscuring my view of Burt Baker and his passenger and whatever the hell they were up to.

I glanced down at my hands, realized I had balled them into fists so tight they had gone numb.

How could I have been so stupid? I asked myself. I had signed my own death warrant for sure when I had called and told him what I saw.

I wished I could take it back. God, how I wished I could take it back.

He had come for me. He had arrived to clear up the final loose end in his evil scheme.

"Go away," I said, trying to will him off of my property. *"Please . . ."*

It didn't work. The car sat there like a sleek tan shark in the vast sea of night outside my house. Going nowhere.

I bit my lip, and this time I growled through bared teeth, "Leave me alone, you bastard."

The passenger door of the patrol car yawned open then.

Baker laughed. It was a deep, basso chuckle that cut the night like a sword slicing through silk, and it did not seem to come from twenty or thirty feet away from me but from right there in my bedroom with me. I shuddered. I could hear the radio inside his patrol car as well. He had it turned up so loud I wondered if he might be *trying* to disturb everyone on my block in the wee hours of the morning.

I watched, listened, waited. Squinted through the darkness, trying to make out *who . . .*

When I recognized her, I shook my head. I could barely stop myself from slamming one of my fists through my window.

My mother. Of course. I scowled at her through the window as she got out of the car, staggering slightly. Her dress looked as if she had taken it out of the washer earlier that night and thrown it on without a second thought toward ironing it or trying to make it look halfway presentable.

There was a run in one of her stockings, I saw when she came closer. I could see her slip winking out at me from one side of her skirt.

My mother grew blurry as she approached the front door. Tears filled my eyes as I watched her pass through the crimson glow of the sheriff's brake lights like something crossing out of one dimension and into another.

She had only begun to scrounge through the depths of her bulky brown purse when Baker honked his horn twice fast.

Mom giggled. Turned. Blew the killer a kiss.

I heard her let out a little belch.

At last, the sheriff drove away. The sound of his patrol car's engine rose and fell like that of an oddly shaped starship as he took off down the street faster than was really necessary.

A few seconds later I could hear Mom trying to get the key in the lock.

"Frigging thing," I heard her say. "Don't give me a hard time. . . ."

From where I sat, so still by the window, it sounded as if she were just scratching at the wood around the lock in hopes that it magically allow her to enter if she kept doing that long enough.

Finally, the door opened.

By the time I heard my mother stumbling down

the hallway, toward her bedroom, I had already sneaked back into bed. I closed my eyes, pretending to be fast asleep.

Please don't come in here, I prayed.

I heard her belch again.

A few minutes later she started singing Cher in the other room, though she sounded like a retarded Elvis impersonator more than anything else.

I rolled over, groaned, covered my head with my pillow, and tried to drown out the awful sound of it.

But that only helped a little.

August 19

Chapter Thirty-two

The next evening Mom sent me to the grocery store across town for a gallon of milk and a carton of eggs. Seems she planned on playing the perfect mother, for some reason—perhaps to make up for her wild night out on the town with Midnight's own Jack the Ripper. A batch of homemade chocolate chip cookies would await me after dinner as long as I didn't mind helping out with that one chore.

Much to my chagrin, however, she also informed me just before I headed out the door that we "might have a guest for dinner."

Him.

It was as if she had intentionally waited to tell me that *after* I agreed to go for her.

Truth be told, I didn't really mind running to the grocery store for Mom. The fact that *he* might pay us a visit before the night was over notwithstanding, Burner and I had a lot of catching up to do. I was delighted to have my old friend back—to say the least—and at least my trip to the grocery store would allow us time to enjoy one another's company, to do all the things boyhood companions are supposed to do when they are released from domestic captivity and allowed to roam free like wild animals.

I couldn't get out the door and onto Burner's soft silver seat fast enough.

"Be careful, Kyle!" Mom called after me from the kitchen, but Burner and I had already taken off like a bullet by the time she said it. The door slammed shut behind me, and the sound of it was like a harsh punctuation mark upon her attempt at concern.

"I will!" I shouted back at her, my voice bursting out of me in a staccato machine-gun effect as I bounced down the steps of our front porch atop my bicycle. "Don't worry! I'll be back in a few!"

Gravel sprayed into the air behind us like hard gray flames from the ass-end of a rocket as Burner and I zipped out of our driveway and into the street. A cold drizzle struck my face and hands like tiny shards of ice as we headed toward town, but I did not mind. I stuck out my tongue, tasting the rain, loving it, and despite the evening's damp chill I felt warm all over, shrouded in that euphoric feeling of ultimate freedom I always experienced each time Burner and I attempted to shatter the sound barrier.

Once we reached the town common, I purposefully took the long route around Midnight's business district to the Big Pig Grocery on Brady Boulevard. The alternative would have been to venture down Main Street, and despite my mood as Burner and I flew down Midnight's damp back alleys and muddy side roads, I shuddered at the thought of passing by the Sheriff's Department.

The sun had begun to dip beyond the Blue Ridge Mountains by the time I reached the grocery store, and the drizzle had died away—at least for a little while. Only a cold, misty fog coated Midnight's slick wet streets, brushing against my ankles like something sinister lying in wait as I pulled into the Big Pig parking lot.

I screeched to a halt in front of the store and hopped off of Burner, propping him up on the sidewalk beside a squat black newspaper machine selling copies of the *Midnight Sun* for fifteen cents.

I hurried inside then, and wasted no time in picking up that gallon of milk and carton of eggs Mom needed.

I fell into line behind two old men who waited to pay for their own groceries, and after a couple minutes I sighed impatiently, started tapping my foot. Apparently the pretty blond teenager running the cash register (DIANE, read her name tag, above a cartoon image of a smiling, bow-tied sow: "THANKS FOR SHOPPING AT BIG PIG!") could not be bothered to speed things up a bit. She smacked her gum loudly as she worked at her own leisurely pace, and I was quite sure the End of the World would dawn before she finished ringing up the single loaf of bread and six-pack of toilet paper being purchased by the large red-headed woman at the front of the line. Meanwhile, I watched more than a few lines around me—lines *not* designated "Express Lane," as it were—clear out in what seemed like record time, the shoppers handing over their cash one after the other like twitchy, smiling actors in a chaotic loop of film footage sped up for comic effect.

I sighed again, rolled my eyes.

"Oh, come on," I whispered. "This is ridiculous. . . ."

But then my mood suddenly changed. My childish impatience turned to hot, burning fear as I caught gruff-voiced snippets of the conversation taking place between the two old men in front of me. Rarely did anyone over the age of fourteen or fifteen have anything to say that interested a kid like me in the least, so at first their geezerly gossip had been little more than faint white noise to me as we waited there in line.

Then I heard one of them mention a single name, a word that made my breath catch in my throat, and I *had* to know what they were talking about. . . .

"Calvin Mooney," said the first guy in line.

And I suddenly went tense.

"That's what Dirk Stuber told me, anyway." The speaker had a long face covered in wrinkles, wore an ugly green button-up shirt and a cap that said KISS MY ASS, I'M RETIRED. In his little red shopping basket he carried a jar of olive oil, a can of beets, and two packs of hamburger buns. "Stopped me on the way into the store. Said his son, Davey, was the one drove the ambulance. Guy was dead before they got there, though."

"Well, it's about damn time," said another senior citizen standing directly in front of me. He was the tallest person I had ever seen. He wore a pinkish golf hat with a bright yellow ball on top, baggy slacks the color of babyshit. In the crook of one liver-spotted arm he carried a fat brown bottle of cooking sherry. "Henrietta and I were starting to wonder just what the county's been payin' Burt Baker for all this time."

"My sentiments exactly. Gonna have to be some changes 'fore he gets my vote again."

Finally, the line moved forward. The old man in the KISS MY ASS cap laid his groceries upon the counter and lowered his voice a bit but not too much as he turned back to his friend and posited, "I know it ain't the popular opinion these days, Carl, but I've said it all along . . . they let these black bastards run wild, like a buncha fuckin' monkeys, sooner or later it all comes to a head. That's what got us into this mess in the first place. This Mooney character shoulda been in some sorta institution a long time ago, you ask me, 'stead of out walkin' the streets."

The tall guy shook his golf hat. "Damn shame is what it is."

I flinched when a third guy broke into the conversation from behind me.

"Come on now, Sam, that's not fair," said the new man. His was the first voice I'd heard since stepping into the Big Pig that did not seep with a thick Southern accent. It was a kind voice. A younger voice. "Personally, I gotta wonder whatever happened to a fellow being innocent till he's proven guilty. . . ."

I nodded as I glanced back at him. He was a chubby middle-aged man with a belly that barely allowed him to squeeze into the checkout line with us. In one arm he held a bag of potato chips and a can of Spam. In the other he carried a case of Budweiser.

The two older gentlemen stared at him as if he were a giant turd that had grown legs and the ability to talk.

"Didn't Calvin Mooney deserve a fair trial just like anybody else? That's all I'm sayin'."

I had to know what was going on. I swallowed, took a second to find my voice, and quietly asked, "What happened?"

The senior citizens at the front of the line turned around, looked down at me as if I were an insect they had nearly stepped upon.

"T-tell me," I said. "Please. What h-happened?"

"They got Calvin Mooney," said the tall man in the golf attire. "Finally."

"What?"

"Shot him dead, kid," said Mr. KISS MY ASS. He pulled a five-dollar bill from a wallet bulging with green and handed it to the cashier. "Out on Forty-fourth Street. Caught him lookin' in some white girl's window."

"No," I said. I covered my mouth with one hand. I felt light-headed. The cool air in the grocery store tasted bitter, and seemed to grow thick as dog fur clogging up my lungs. "*No* . . . th-that can't be right. . . ."

The first man in line grabbed his bag of groceries, then thanked the cashier by pinching the bill of his KISS MY ASS hat as if in some crude display of redneck chivalry, and said to his fellow senior citizen before heading off, "Now let's just pray he burns in hell."

I felt weak. Dizzy. I could hardly breathe. The store seemed to swirl around me as if reality itself had become a sloshing liquid thing. . . .

I couldn't stop shaking my head. Back and forth. Back and forth.

"No," I moaned. "What have they *done?*"

Milk and eggs for Mom's cookies were the furthest things from my mind now. Feeling numb, I let my groceries tumble out of my arms and onto the counter behind the tall man in the golf hat.

I squeezed past him then, and I fled for the exit at the front of the store, my heart pounding at what felt like a hundred thousand beats per minute. . . .

"Hey!" I heard someone say behind me, or maybe I imagined it. I don't know, because I did not turn around.

I burst from the grocery store, and left Burner propped up against the building for now. In a matter of seconds I had crossed the Big Pig's vast parking lot. I dashed madly across the street, forgetting to look both ways, not knowing where I was going nor caring at all about the mess I made all over my jeans as I splashed through a dozen puddles on my way.

I did not stop running until I burst through the

doors of the new Sears & Roebuck store at the end of the block.

"Help you?" said the man behind the counter. He was a balding middle-aged gent with wire-rimmed glasses that looked too small for his wide, round face. On the side of his neck perched a thick brown mole the size of a small nation. "I gotta close up shop in a few, son."

He gave me an expression that seemed to indicate he had better things to do than bother with stupid kids, but I paid him no mind.

I turned from the man with the mole to the six small televisions for sale against the wall to my right.

They were all turned to the same station. To Channel 5, and the WHLP Evening News.

All my questions were answered.

It was true.

Oh, God, it was *true*.

I fell to my knees, right there on the floor in the middle of the Sears & Roebuck, as I watched. And I listened. And I learned.

Out of the corner of my eye, I could see Mr. Friendly staring at me with his mouth hanging open. Vigorously he scratched at his stubbled chin, apparently wondering what the hell was wrong with this weird-ass kid in the middle of his store.

Must be retarded or something, I could almost hear him thinking. . . .

"Indeed, ladies and gentlemen," said the blond anchorman on the six identical Zenith television sets before me. He seemed to speak directly to me, his voice sounding oddly choral as he explained, "Earlier this evening, Calvin Mooney, the man arrested ten days ago for the murder of Cassandra Belle Rourke, was shot and killed by an unknown assailant. Mooney had escaped from the custody of the

Polk County Sheriff's Department this past Friday. Though details are scarce at this time, the WHLP News Team will bring you further information as soon as it becomes available. This has been a Channel 5 News Flash. We now we return you to your regularly scheduled program."

And that was that. It was over, as if Calvin Mooney and his life had never been worth more than one very brief mention to begin with.

Rooster did not matter. He never had.

He was black. He was mentally handicapped.

He was a murderer, as far as my town was concerned.

He had been dead long before Burt Baker ever opened that jail cell and allowed his little scapegoat to temporarily walk free.

The bastard's plan had worked. To say the least.

I could not stop staring at the television, dumbfounded by everything I had learned during those last few minutes, even after the anchorman's grim expression was abruptly replaced with an episode of *M*A*S*H*. I knelt there, shaking my head back and forth, not wanting to believe any of it though I knew I had no choice, while an ecstatic Radar informed Hawk-Eye and B.J. that he'd been accepted into the "Famous Las Vegas Writers School."

I made a gagging sound, covered my mouth with one hand.

"Hey," said the man at the counter. "You sick or somethin', kid?"

I just kept shaking my head, as if I might keep doing that for the rest of my life. The laugh track on the TV pierced through my skull, seemed to gnaw at my brain like a plague of hungry ants.

"Hey," the man barked at me again. "You okay?"

"N-no," I croaked. "No . . ."

Finally, I stood. I wobbled there for a minute before staggering out of the store and onto the sidewalk. The door slammed shut behind me, and I could already see Mr. Friendly turning the COME IN! WE'RE OPEN sign over to CLOSED, PLEASE CALL AGAIN in my peripheral vision. I doubled over, feeling as if I might vomit, but I hadn't eaten dinner yet so nothing came out but a single hoarse dry-heave.

Jesus . . .

It was all too much too fast.

They had killed him. Calvin Mooney had paid for Burt Baker's crime, and now the whole terrible ordeal was over as far as Polk County was concerned.

Cassie Belle Rourke's death had been avenged.

"You . . . *bastard*," I cried, gnashing my teeth and balling my fists. "I hope you fucking *die. . . .*"

My stomach kept roiling, my bowels lurching like something parasitic nesting inside me, as I crossed the street, ready to retrieve Burner and head back home at last. A passing brown sedan (BAKER FOR SHERIFF IN '75! read the bumper sticker on its dented rear end) splashed me with muddy water, but in my stunned daze I barely seemed to notice. Though my clothes and hair were dripping wet, my pants soaked with mud as if I'd just gone running through a pigpen, I could only focus on Burner, propped up against the front of the grocery store on the opposite side of the massive parking lot before me.

I couldn't get to my bicycle fast enough.

In those last few seconds before the game took a whole new turn, I seriously considered mounting my old friend right then and there, just riding away to some place far, far away. To a town where no one had ever heard of Midnight, North Carolina, or Cassie Belle Rourke or Calvin Mooney or a foul creature by the name of Burt Baker.

The thought of it sure was tempting. . . .

But then I chose to hang around. At least for a while.

Because that's when I saw the sheriff's son, young Henry Baker, come strolling out of Betty's Flower Shop, next to the Big Pig Grocery.

I froze where I stood. All thoughts of deserting my hometown suddenly vanished, as I watched him cross the parking lot.

He was headed right for me. . . .

His hair was wet, slicked back, and it appeared to have been trimmed a bit since the last time I saw him. He had shaved his Vinnie Barbarino sideburns. His mustache was still a thin, wispy thing that looked more like a stain on his upper lip from drinking chocolate milk than facial hair. As he came out of the store he held a small bouquet of pink carnations in the crook of his left arm. His other hand was busy stuffing his wallet into the back pocket of his tight black jeans.

My heart slammed in my chest. I swallowed a lump in my throat, but it just seemed to grow twice as large.

After a few seconds I realized that Henry had not seen me. He appeared to be in his own little world, and his strut across the parking lot had not faltered in the least the closer he got to me. I exhaled loudly, forced myself to start walking again when I realized he had not seen me, but just to be safe I veered off toward the left side of the lot to prevent crossing into Henry's line of sight. All around me, tires hissed on wet pavement and shopping carts creaked like ancient beasts made of steel as business continued booming at the Big Pig on into the twilight. I kept my eyes on Henry Baker the whole time, however. I watched as the sheriff's son approached a Ford pick-up parked crookedly in a space designated HANDI-CAPPED PARKING ONLY. He whistled as he walked, and I recognized the tune as Deep Purple's "Smoke on the Water." His truck was the same make and model as the one my brother owned, but Henry's was the color of diarrhea, and something about that made me chuckle beneath my breath as he opened the door and climbed inside.

By the time Henry started up his vehicle, and it rumbled like something with a bad case of indigestion, I had reached Burner. I grabbed his handle-bars, swung one leg over his seat, but I didn't take off just yet.

As thunder rumbled in the distance, somewhere beyond the foggy gray peaks of the Blue Ridge Mountains, I stood there staring at Henry's silhouette behind the wheel of his truck. His head jerked up-ward several times fast. Even after his tics had passed, and his head was still, Henry just kept sitting there. His truck idled noisily, but he did not back out of his handicapped parking space.

What was he doing in there? I wondered.

Primping. He was primping in the rear-view mirror. Licking his fingers, fixing his hair. A quick sniff at his armpits.

Finally the truck's headlights came on. Henry took a second to roll down his window before pulling out of his parking space. I could hear Ted Nugent singing "Wang Dang Sweet Poontang" on the radio.

Tentatively, Burner and I rolled forward, off of the sidewalk and into the Big Pig's fire lane.

I knew it was risky. Knew I would most likely regret it . . . yet I *had* to know what he was up to.

Henry glanced in his rear-view mirror one last time, baring his teeth as if to make sure there were no unsightly pieces of food stuck between them, and then his truck headed out of the Big Pig's parking lot. He squealed his tires as he pulled onto Brady Boulevard, and the sound was like a woman's high-pitched scream splitting through the dusk.

"Let's go, Burner," I said, and then we were off too, following the Ford down the highway.

I coughed as Burner and I cut through the thick blue cloud of smoke left by Henry's display of automotive machismo. I pedaled as hard and as fast as I could, trying to catch up with his truck but at the same time making sure I kept a safe distance behind him.

After a few minutes my heart raced and my thighs began to burn with the flames of exertion, yet nothing could have stopped me from finding out where Henry Baker was going. What he was doing, and why he looked so eager to get there.

I *had* to know whom those flowers were for, if it was the last thing I ever did.

He didn't go far. Henry's truck turned left at the end of Brady Boulevard, took a sharp right onto Simms Lane, and about five minutes later took another right onto a road called Bartleby Drive.

Henry cruised slowly down the block, his brake lights flickering now and then like bright splashes of blood amidst the gathering darkness. The sound of the Ford's tires on the rain-slick road was not unlike a lecherous whisper in the night several hundred feet ahead of me. Finally, the pick-up pulled to a smooth stop at the mouth of a cul-de-sac, before a two-story house with beige siding and brown trim. KELLOGG, said the name on the mailbox out front. A giant Winnebago the same color as the house glistened wetly in the blacktopped driveway (a vanity tag on the back of it read HWYQUEEN), and on the front porch wind chimes tinkled in the evening's chilly wet breeze like long metal fingers playing an invisible xylophone.

Henry checked his hair again in the truck's rear-view mirror before he got out and slammed his door.

He jogged up to the beige house, the bouquet of carnations he had purchased at Betty's Flower Shop in hand, and ascended the steps of the porch in two quick, long-legged bounds.

He took a deep breath before knocking on the front door.

I noticed his head jerked upward three times fast while he waited, as if in premature greeting of whoever might come to the door.

A minute or so later he knocked again, glanced back over his shoulder toward the road as he did so.

I gasped.

Fortunately, he had not seen me. Burner and I had darted behind a large pine tree on the opposite side of the street as soon as Henry's truck had stopped, and I savored those next few minutes during which I was able to catch my breath. From the thick black shadows beneath that tree I stood over my bicycle, wondering what Henry Baker was up to while I gripped Burner's handlebars so tight their hard rubber grips felt like handfuls of needles against my palms. I barely even noticed the fat drops of rain dripping from the leaves onto my head, even after my hair was plastered to my skull and the dirty water trickled down my cheeks like frigid sweat without the salty smell.

Henry raised one pale fist to knock again when the patio light came on.

The door opened.

I rolled forward several feet atop Burner and squinted, trying to see whom it was Henry had come to visit. A feminine voice. Their muffled salutations drifted toward me in the night from across the road, yet I couldn't quite make out everything they said. Something from Henry about "sorry I'm late," maybe, an exclamation of "they're lovely" from her when he handed over the carnations, but I couldn't be sure.

A few seconds later, though, I did get a good look at Henry's friend . . . when she crossed the threshold and leaned into him for a deep kiss.

She was at least a head shorter than the sheriff's son, and probably two or three years his junior. She was very skinny, her feminine curves seemingly non-existent beneath a baggy gray Duke University sweater and blue jeans. Her long blond hair was pulled back into a tight ponytail that dangled all the way down to her tiny butt. While I could not deny her beauty, the girl had applied her dark eye shadow, rouge, and hot pink lipstick a tad too liberally; from the way the patio light struck her face I suspected her too-thick makeup might have been a mask for an imperfect complexion.

She reminded me, somewhat, of a slightly older, scrawnier Cassie Belle Rourke. With a few more pimples.

I did not even blink as I watched them. As she closed the door behind her, locked it, and followed Henry Baker to his truck. From my hiding place across the road, however, I did whisper one question that foolish schoolgirl's way. It came out like a guttural growl, from somewhere deep within my chest. . . .

"What are you doing?" I asked her, scowling at Henry Baker as he strutted around to her side of the Ford to open her door for her. "Don't you know what he *is* . . . ?"

But of course, she didn't. Judging from the expression on her face, she was impressed to no end with his chivalry. She didn't see the way he stared at her ass as she climbed inside the pick-up. She never noticed the way Henry's left hand balled into a fist several times fast just before he closed her door, as if he were groping for an invisible rope to keep his raging libido from pushing him right off the world.

Seconds later, they pulled off—but not before Henry had leaned over from the driver's seat to steal another quick kiss from his date—and they headed back toward town.

I followed them. Keeping at a safe distance once again.

But not *too* safe.

"He sure moves fast, doesn't he?" I asked Burner as we zoomed along behind Henry's truck down Bartleby Drive.

I was not referring to the speed at which his pickup cruised through the neighborhood, however.

"He used her up . . . and he threw her away. Now he's moved on to another one . . . that asshole. . . ."

Burner's only reply was the steady *click-whirr* of his recently oiled chain, the soft hum of his tires atop the asphalt, as I pushed my bicycle to its limit and beyond. My heart raced and fatigue threatened to overtake me as the Ford soon passed out of Midnight's business district and kept on going toward the county line.

But I refused to quit. I *had* to know. . . .

"Where's he going, boy?" I asked Burner. "What's he gonna do this time?"

Before long we crossed beneath the graffiti-laden bridge that was the old Junction 85 overpass, and Henry took an immediate right onto a lonely back road aptly called Shortcut Drive. A few minutes later he took another right onto Highway 76, and we soon passed the sprawling rust jungle of Old Man Gash's junkyard in our wake. Beyond its crooked chicken-wire fence, the jumbled silhouettes of at least a hundred long-dead vehicles seemed to leer at me with their shattered headlight eyes. My eyes grew moist as I thought about how Deputy Linder had died just two days ago upon this very road. I didn't know the exact spot where it had happened, of course, but I did not *want* to know. As I cruised along several hundred feet behind Henry's truck, beneath that infinite cloak of starless night, I stared straight ahead, refusing to gaze upon anything but the Ford before me.

Poor Mike. His family. *What a waste it all had been*. . . .

I gripped Burner's handlebars tighter than ever, banished such thoughts from my mind, and forced myself to focus on the task at hand as Henry's pickup took a hard curve to the left up ahead. His tires squealed like dying babies, and the thick, pungent smell of burning rubber filled the air.

For the next few seconds the truck vanished from my sight. . . .

I pumped at Burner's pedals more furiously than ever, never letting up for a second despite the agony burning within my thighs.

"Come on, Burner," I said, as if it were entirely up to my bicycle whether we caught up or Henry left us in his dust.

The wind buzzed in my ears, and the sound was almost deafeningly loud. Like a swarm of invisible bees attempting to impede my progress.

"Come on . . . we can't lose him now. . . ."

Burner shot forward obediently.

"Thattaboy," I said. "Thattaboy!"

We took the curve nearly as fast as Henry had taken it. Burner and I seemed as one, my hands melding into his handlebars and my butt merging with his seat, as we united to prevent inevitable disaster like some bizarre sci-fi hybrid of boy and Schwinn Scrambler. Burner's tires made high-pitched whining noises and my breath came out of me in a long, slow wheeze. Time seemed to stand still. Finally, though—*miraculously*—we came out of the curve unscathed.

As we straightened up, I quickly braked. A bit too hard, at first. Burner wobbled, threatened to spill over. My heart skipped a beat. I eased up on the backwards pressure I exerted upon the bike's pedals, allowed Burner to decelerate on his own. . . .

Before us, Henry's truck had slowed. It sat fifty or sixty feet away, in the middle of the road, its brake lights glowing ominously between the sheriff's son and me like crimson fire lighting the way to my doom.

At some point Henry had rolled down his window, and I could hear Lynyrd Skynyrd on his radio.

"Hey, little girl," Ronnie Van Zant queried in his imitable redneck way, "What's your name?"

Burner slowed to a smooth stop. Waiting. Not making a sound.

Had he spotted me behind him? I wondered. Did it end here, on this lonely road where Henry's father had already cleared up one loose end forty-eight hours before?

The night seemed to grow blacker around me. Henry's lights seemed to dim beneath it.

My ears played tricks on me. I imagined him opening his door, emerging from the pick-up to confront me at last.

I held my breath, wished I could stop the frenetic slamming of my heart. Surely he could hear it. Perhaps that was what had given me away.

269

I exhaled a long sigh of relief then as the song on Henry's radio suddenly grew faint in midchorus, and the pick-up turned left with a short, sharp yelp of its tires.

It seemed to disappear directly into the forest.

"What the—" I whispered.

Burner rolled forward. I squinted through the darkness to figure out what the hell had just happened.

Then I saw it.

A thin dirt road, partially obscured by the woods. KEEP OUT, read a bullet-riddled sign at the mouth of it.

I frowned, licked my lips nervously, and again resumed my chase.

Burner and I took off again, entering the woods behind Henry. After a minute or two I was forced to stand atop Burner's pedals to keep him moving forward, using all of my remaining energy to propel us up a steep incline. Ahead of me Henry's truck bounced along the winding, rutted path, its shocks squeaking and groaning every few seconds, its tires making low chuffing noises as they fought to gain traction in the sticky red mud. Trees leaned over the road like living shadows all around us, creating the illusion that we were traveling through a long, dark tunnel illuminated only by the bloodred glow of Henry's brake lights.

I didn't know how much farther I could go. Any minute I knew I would have no choice but to hop off of Burner, walk him the rest of the way up that hill. If I did that, though, I feared I would lag behind and Henry would lose me for good.

Several minutes later we reached Henry's destination at last. I somehow managed a sigh of relief amidst my exhaustion as the hill leveled off, and that muddy road widened into a flat dead-end grove surrounded on three sides by a wall of pitch black forest.

My eyes grew wide as I realized where Henry had brought his date.

It all made sense now. I should have *known*. . . .

Straight ahead, where the woods abruptly ended, I could see into forever.

Though I had never been there myself until the night in question, I had heard all about the place called Storch's Rim from older guys like my big brother and his best friend Chris Craven. The Rim was Polk County's own Lover's Lane, its make-out spot where Midnight's teenage contingent often went to park late at night, where they sneaked away to "get some" (as I'd heard Dan describe it more than once—although back then I always reacted with a puzzled "get some *what?*"). Every town has such a site, I believe, and the Rim was Midnight's own rendezvous point for adolescent lovers hungry for sweaty backseat romps and clandestine samples of beer or "wacky weed."

Unfortunately, my very first impression of Storch's Rim was not what I had expected at all. The stories I had heard from Dan and Chris, tales that hinted of a legendary place just outside of town that might have been heaven on earth. . . .

They had all been lies, as far as I could tell.

Frankly, I thought the Rim looked like a frigging dump.

I scrunched up my nose as I inspected my surroundings, unable to comprehend why people would drive up *there* to "fool around." While my knowledge of matters in the realm of love was admittedly quite underdeveloped—to say the least—I could not comprehend how a person attempting to impress his girlfriend could find anything the least bit "romantic" about the area before me. Here and there, strewn throughout the grove, was the detritus of folks who cared about little more than having a good time. To my left lay a crumpled Pabst Blue Ribbon can, to my right a shattered Coke bottle. Directly in my path lay something that looked like a deflated, flesh-colored balloon filled with crusty white spit. Burner and I gave that a wide berth. A few feet from the edge of the forest closest to me lay an empty cigarette pack and a blizzard of flattened butts. On the edge of the forest, sticking to the rocky ground like some off-white fungus growing there, was a pair of women's panties.

"Ugh," I whispered, hopping off Burner.

I watched as Henry's pick-up rolled on toward the edge of the steep drop-off that was the Rim itself, and for a second or two I wondered if the sheriff's son planned to keep rolling forward until he and his date flew right out into the nothingness over Midnight. Finally, though, the truck's brake lights flashed one last time, and the vehicle jerked to a stop within a mere inch or two of the thin yellow picket fence that feigned to protect those who came here from certain death.

Through Henry's open window, I heard the blond girl giggle.

"Silly. Stop trying to scare me," she said, and I shivered. Her voice sounded so, so close in the quiet night air, as if she stood right next to me.

On Henry's radio, Blue Oyster Cult sang about how Romeo and Juliet would be together for eternity.

Far below us, the lights of my hometown resembled a multitude of bright, unblinking eyes in the night. Only in the center of it all did darkness reign, as if God had obliterated the lights there with the single swipe of some gigantic celestial eraser where the Snake River Woods cut Midnight into two nearly symmetrical halves.

Henry killed the engine. Cut his lights. His radio grew silent.

I froze. The quiet seemed to descend upon Storch's Rim like a heavy blanket. The only sounds were the urgent chirping of a million crickets in the thick brown weeds upon the hillside, the lonely whisper of a soft breeze wafting through the nearby treetops. In the clouds above town a hint of bright white lightning flickered every few seconds, but no thunder rumbled behind it. As if the storm had considered beginning anew, but couldn't quite make up its mind.

Abruptly I changed direction, praying Henry would not see me, as I spotted a place to hide on the opposite side of the grove from which I stood. A large round boulder sat there on the edge of the forest, slightly behind and to the left of Henry's truck. While I could tell it was only as tall as my waistline or so, if I squatted down behind the boulder I knew I should be safely out of Henry's line of sight. I hoped. It would have to do for the time being, anyway.

The rock was as wide as a small car and decorated with a rainbow of sloppy graffiti (DAVEY Z'S A FAG, GREG-N-CHARMIN 4EVER, BLACK SABBATH 666) that looked as if someone had vomited all over it. I quickly ducked behind it, carefully laying Burner on his side next to me instead of propping him up by his kickstand. Just in case. I feared I would have a heart attack if a sudden strong wind came along to knock him over.

I sat there as still as that boulder, and I chewed at my bottom lip as I listened. . . .

Right away I knew what they were doing inside the cab of Henry's Ford. The sloppy wet sounds of building passion drifted out of its windows to echo throughout the grove. The sounds of deep kissing. I had heard Dan and Julie make those same sounds on more than one occasion, when they thought they were alone. But with my big brother and his girl-friend they were different noises. Slower. Gentler. Longing, yes, but nowhere near as desperate.

I didn't feel like taking a shower when I heard Dan and Julie make those noises. My stomach didn't flip-flop and I didn't feel sick.

"Yeahhh," I heard Henry say. It was a deep-voiced, lascivious sound that made my arms crawl with goose bumps.

"Mmm," moaned his date. "Henry . . ."

"You like that?"

"Mm-hmmm."

Their voices carried to me on the night's breeze . . . so dangerously close. . . .

"You taste like strawberries," Henry said, and she giggled.

More moist kissing noises. I glanced down at Burner beside me, made a face like I'd just tasted something awful.

"Has anyone ever told you what a great kisser you are?" I heard the girl ask Henry.

"Nope," Henry replied.

"Well, you are. You kiss like . . . like I've always imagined Clark Gable would kiss."

"Cool," Henry said. "Who's he?"

"Don't tell me you've never seen *Gone With the Wind.*"

"I've never seen *Gone With the Wind.*"

"You don't know what you're missing," she said. "It's very romantic, you know."

"If you say so."

They started kissing again. My stomach rumbled in time with the flickering lightning over Midnight, like thunder trapped somewhere deep inside my gut.

"Henry?" the girl said.

"Yeah?"

"Can I ask you something?"

"Sure."

"I don't want you to get mad at me. It's just something I've been wondering."

"So ask."

"Promise you won't get mad at me?"

"Now how can I promise that," Henry said, "when I don't even know what you're gonna ask me?"

"I just don't wanna hurt your feelings."

"Just ask me, already," Henry said. "I've got a thick skin."

She giggled. "Okay. I've just been wondering . . ."

Henry interrupted her by leaning into her again for another deep kiss.

"Mmm," she said, when they were done. Then she asked quickly, as if fearing she might lose her nerve if she hesitated further, "Why do you do that, Henry? Are you scared or something?"

Henry said, "Do what?"

"That. You just did it again. With your hand."

"Oh."

"I'm just curious. There. That's what I'm talking about. That thing you just did with your fist. And your head. Is there something wrong?"

Henry didn't respond right away. When he did explain, his voice was low. Uneven. As if she had hurt his feelings. "I can't help it, Sherrie. It's this thing I have."

"Thing?"

"Yeah. It's a condition. It's called Tourette's Syndrome."

"I've never heard of it."

Henry sighed. He sounded as if he had gone through all this countless times before, and it never got any easier, so he'd finally just memorized the def-

inition of his malady from some medical encyclope-
dia: "It's a neurological disease that manifests itself
through uncontrollable behavior, such as nervous
tics or vocal outbursts."

"Hmm," said Sherrie.

"I can't help myself. Every so often, I just . . . I just
jerk, like that. I take haloperidol for it, but it only
works about half the time."

"Happa . . . haplerduh—"

"Haloperidol."

"Can you get high off that stuff?"

"No."

"Darn. Do they hurt? Your nervous tics, I mean?"

"What?" Henry seemed perturbed by her question.
"No, they don't *hurt*."

"Is it contagious?"

"Are you serious? Of course it's not, Sherrie. Can
we just drop it?"

"Sure. Whatever."

Several long, awkward seconds passed. A car horn
honked in the valley below.

"So where were we before?" Sherrie said, just when
I'd started to think they had fallen asleep in there.

Henry said, "Hmmmm," as if in deep thought.

"Come here, lover boy."

They kissed again. Deeply. Wetly. This one seemed
to go on forever.

I cringed.

When that round of tonsil hockey was finished, I
heard the girl say, "I don't do this with just anyone, you
know."

"Do what?" said Henry.

"Park. With boys."

"Ah. Well . . . that's good to hear."

"I'm not easy."

"I believe you."

She fell into his arms then, and once again they began to swap spit.

"Mmm," moaned the blond girl. "Oh, Henry . . ."

"Can I?" I heard Henry ask a few minutes later.

"Yes . . . please . . ."

"You're so sexy," Henry said.

Another giggle.

"You drive me crazy, Sherrie."

"That feels good . . . like that . . ."

"Can I?"

"Yes," she said. "Please . . ."

I heard what sounded like a rustle of clothing. Like a shirt or a blouse slowly being removed. The pickup shook slightly with their movements.

"Oh, Henry . . ."

"Come here . . . mmmm . . ."

"You're stalling." She giggled. "Can't you get it off?"

"I'm trying. I swear to God . . ."

"Here," she said. "Let me."

"Oh, Jesus," Henry said a few seconds later. I imagined him staring at her naked boobs in the darkness, and I felt hot all over. I imagined him licking his lips, reaching out for her breasts as if they were some grand treasure that would make him king of the world.

"You like?" she asked him.

"Yeah. Oh, God, yeah . . . wow . . ."

"My turn now," she said.

"What?" Henry panted.

"I want to touch you."

"Oh. Okay. But, umm . . ."

"Can I? Please?"

"Umm . . . I . . ."

"Is something wrong, Henry?"

"N-no." Henry's voice cracked. "It's just that . . . I . . . ummm . . . er . . ."

"Don't be shy. What's the matter? Is it because you have a little dick?"

"What? N-no . . . it's not anything like that . . . not really . . ."

"Here," she said. "I promise, it'll be okay. . . ."

"N-no. D-don't," Henry stammered.

"Stop playing hard to get, Henry."

I heard the metallic rasp of a zipper being pulled down slowly.

"Oh, G-God, Sherrie . . . oh, God . . . n-no . . . wait . . ."

"You ready?" she asked him.

"I *can't* . . . look . . ."

"I *want* you, Henry."

"Sherrie, *no* . . . wait—"

And then, abruptly, the night grew silent again. The breeze had died in the treetops. For at least the next few seconds, even the crickets ceased their chirping.

It was as if the volume on the world suddenly had been turned down all the way.

I wondered if I had made a sound, if Henry and his date might have spotted me watching them from behind that boulder.

I waited. Not moving. Not making a sound.

Finally, I heard the girl's voice drift out of the open window again.

"Ugh!" she said, sounding sick. "What is this, Henry? *Jesus* . . . is this some kind of sick joke?"

When Henry spoke, his voice was so low I could barely hear it. It had deepened at least an octave, and now it reminded me of his father's voice.

"Don't make fun of me, Sherrie," he said. "Don't you dare make fun of me."

"I'm not making fun, Henry, I just—" She snorted through her nose, a laugh she tried—unsuccessfully—

278

to stifle. "What the hell is that? What happened to it?"

"It's not fucking funny!" Henry shouted.

Again she laughed. Her voice was high pitched and cruel as she taunted him: "What did you expect me to do with that . . . that's all I'm sayin' . . ."

"You shut up! You shut the fuck up! Don't you fucking laugh at me!"

But she did. Again. She snorted through her nose. "It looks . . . Jesus, Henry . . . it looks like a piece of roast beef. . . ."

And that's when Henry Baker snapped.

"Fuck you, you fuckin' whore!" he growled at her, and that was followed by the harsh, undeniable sound of flesh against flesh.

There was no doubt in my mind what had just happened. He had slapped her. Hard.

I gasped from my place behind the boulder.

The blond girl started crying. "I can't believe you hit me!"

"Laugh at me again!" he dared her. "I warned you!"

"Fuck you, Henry!" she screamed at him. "Take me home. I wanna go home right now!"

"Shut up." Henry sounded as if he had started crying. But his were oncoming tears borne obviously from shattered feelings as well as violent rage. "We're not going anywhere till you tell me you're fucking sorry!"

"Fuck you. I'm not going to apologize to you. Take me home."

"You heard what I said," Henry sobbed.

"God damn you, Henry, I wanna go home! Right now! Take me the fuck home!"

He slapped her again. Harder than before.

"You better fuckin' apologize, bitch!"

"Owww, Henry," she wailed. "Owww . . . you . . . *bastard!*"

No longer could I sit by and allow this to continue.

Henry had done the same thing to another girl that night after the Apple Gala, and now three people were dead because I had done nothing. I had to stop him. I knew it was risky, knew I might regret it, but I knew I would never forgive myself if another girl ended up bloody and bruised—*murdered*—at the hands of the sheriff's son.

I could *not* let it happen again. Even if it meant exposing myself to a killer.

When he hit her again, it was not the sound of a slap. This time the awful, resounding *wham* of a bony fist striking the girl's face echoed through the night like a gunshot.

"Do it *now*, Sherrie," he shouted at her. "I'm not playing. You tell me you're sorry!"

I burst from my hiding place in the woods, bounded for the driver's side window of Henry's Ford as if jerked to him on invisible strings.

Too many people had been hurt already. Too many people had died. I couldn't let this continue . . . not anymore. . . .

"Stop it!" I screamed at him, approaching his window before I had even conjured some coherent plan of action. My voice sounded so tiny, so high pitched, insignificant and infantile, but I did not let that stop me. "By God, Henry, stop it! Stop it now!"

Henry's eyes grew wide. His jaw dropped as he turned to me.

"Who the fuck—"

"Stop!" I said again, as he turned toward his open window. "Not again, damn you!"

"Why, you little . . . what are you—"

"He hit me," said the girl in the passenger seat. Her hands covered her breasts, and as she sat there trembling like a woman standing naked in a blizzard, she stared at me as if I were her personal messiah. I could see a small, blotchy tattoo over her right nipple. It looked like a rose, but I couldn't be sure in the darkness. Tears ran down her cheeks. Her left eye was swollen, purple. A trickle of blood ran from her lower lip down to her chin.

"Please," she cried. "Get help. . . ."

"You're not gonna hurt them anymore," I snarled at Henry.

An eternity seemed to pass as we stared into one another's eyes.

Then he blinked, several times fast, like a man coming out of a deep trance.

"You don't understand," he said. "She laughed at me—"

During that moment Henry Baker resembled little more than a very scared, very confused little boy. I could see it in his eyes. He had never meant for it to go this far. He really did not *want* to do the things he did.

He was just as afraid as me. Only he had dear old Daddy to drag him out of his predicaments.

But then he seemed to realize the levity of the situation, that he did not have to explain himself to me, and his expression morphed from one of humiliation to anger.

"Who the fuck are you anyway? Were you . . . were you fuckin' spying on us?"

"I won't let it happen again, Henry," I said. "I won't let you do to her what you did to Cassandra Rourke."

His eyes grew wider than I would have ever thought humanly possible.

"Whaaaa . . . how did you . . . you kn-know . . . ?"

It hit me then, what I had said. Terror gripped my soul, and my knees grew weak. A rash of frigid chills ran from the top of my head down to my feet.

The distance between myself and my bicycle

seemed like hundreds of miles. From the earth to the moon. Or worse.

"Waitaminute," Henry said, his face burning bright, bright red. "I know you. Yeah. You're Dan Mackey's little brother." He pointed a long, skinny finger at me. "Your mom . . . my dad . . ."

"No," I said, not wanting to hear about that at all.

He reached to open his door.

"Come 'ere . . ."

"No!" I braced myself to run. But to where, I was not sure. *For the forest? For Burner?*

"Let's just talk about this."

Henry opened his door. The sound it made as it yawned open reminded me of a dying man's final breath.

"No," I said, taking two steps back. "Henry . . ."

I squatted to the ground, not really realizing what I was doing until after the deed was done and it was too late to take it back.

"Come here."

Henry slid out from behind his steering wheel, his hands held out toward me in a placating gesture that was almost—but not quite—convincing.

He lunged for me.

I grabbed a handful of dirt and gravel and threw it into his eyes.

"Aggh, *fuck!*" Henry screamed, his hands covering his face.

"Run!" I said to the girl, but she was already out of Henry's truck and running for the woods.

Her sobs filled the night as she crashed through the forest like a very large, disoriented animal.

As she left me alone with Henry Baker.

Henry fell to his knees. He clawed at his eyes with one hand, reaching out for me with the other.

"Sh-she . . . she *laughed* at me," he cried. "I didn't mean t-to . . ."

I didn't wait around to hear his confession. His pale, quivering fingers were only an inch or so away from grabbing my shirt when I scrabbled across the grove to that graffiti-streaked boulder, ready to get the hell out of there. I tripped once, but wasted no time in getting back up.

I jerked Burner off the ground, nearly crushed my testicles when I jumped atop his hard blue seat.

We took off.

I didn't dare look back over my shoulder, to see if Henry had made it back to his truck. I didn't wait to hear the pick-up come rumbling alive. Burner and I just raced for home, bouncing violently back down the rutted path the way we had come, and I prayed we would not crash . . . prayed that Henry Baker's big brown truck would not suddenly appear behind us once we reached the highway, blinding us with its headlights, roaring after us like a demonic beast intent on swallowing us whole. . . .

Chapter Thirty-three

What had I done?

I asked myself that question a million times as Burner and I sped back toward my house at 2217 Old Fort Road. The rain began again, and its ice-cold drizzle seemed to chill me to the bone.

I had sealed my fate. It was only a matter of time now. . . .

How long, I wondered, until Henry talked to his father? A day? Several hours? Mere minutes, perhaps?

How long before Sheriff Baker knew *I* had witnessed their horrid deeds that night in the Snake River Woods?

It was inevitable, I knew. . . .

They would come for me. Soon.

How long did I have to live?

Of course, as I raced for home I never considered the possibility that they might be waiting for me when I got there. Though word traveled fast in places like Midnight circa 1977, such modern wonders as cell

phones, instant messaging, and the immediate ex-
change of information made possible by such tech-
nology might have seemed as distant as the
possibility of time travel or lunar colonization.

Alas, after I passed Glenn and Gerta Freeman's split-
level with its FOR SALE BY OWNER sign in the yard directly
across the road from my own, a second after I jumped
that final speed-bump just six feet or so from my mailbox so hard I bit my tongue and Burner nearly bucked
me . . . my heart sank. I skidded to a stop, made a star-
tled little "Uh-gaaa!" sound that echoed down Old Fort
Road like the hoarse caw of some injured alien bird.

For several long, long minutes I just sat there atop
my bicycle in the middle of the street, staring at it.

I couldn't move. I could barely even breathe.

Apparently they had decided to take care of business sooner than I'd thought.

"Oh, my God," I wept, as the frigid rain fell upon
me like all Midnight's lingering secrets suddenly
plunging to the earth once and for all. "Oh, no . . ."

KEEPING POLK COUNTY SAFE, read the motto on the
back of that slick beige vehicle sitting in my driveway.
SHERIFF'S DEPARTMENT.

The bubble light atop the patrol car's roof reminded
me of a dark cyclopean eye. An eye that slept for now,
yet one that could come to life at any moment, alert-
ing Burt Baker to my presence telepathically.

I waited for him to come barging out of my front
door like Leatherface in *The Texas Chainsaw Mas-
sacre*, a satanic brown hulk lumbering after me in
the uniform of a kindly civil servant.

I couldn't believe it. He was in there. The killer was
in my home, waiting for me.

I swallowed, and there was a taste in my mouth
that made me think of wet clothes neglected in a
hamper and left to mildew.

It was over. Here. Now.

I took a deep breath, rolled Burner slowly through the front yard toward my house.

The time had come to look the devil in the eyes, I decided. I could run; I could hide. That's what kids do, after all, ninety-nine percent of the time. They run away from trouble as fast as their legs will carry them. But my time had come at last.

I knew I could not run and hide forever.

After what I had done at Storch's Rim, Burt Baker and his son would get me. Eventually.

I licked my lips, swallowed nervously once again, and prayed they would do it fast.

"Please, God," I cried. "Just let them end it quickly. . . ."

Behind me, the rain plinked and plunked upon the sheriff's patrol car. From beneath the vehicle's hood came a dull, insectlike ticking. The sound of the engine cooling. He hadn't been here long.

My heart pounded frantically as I moved like a zombie toward my front porch. I winced, held one hand to my chest. Wondered if I was having a heart attack. The house no longer felt like my home at all as I drew closer to it. It seemed to loom over me so large and black and quiet. It had become a strange, dark site sheltering all the evils of the world.

I did not want to go in there.

But knew I had to. I had no choice.

It was time to end this.

When I reached the porch steps I let Burner clatter to the ground, not caring in the least whom my racket awakened.

My shoes made gentle chuffing noises as I ascended the steps. The sound echoed in the night, seemed to come from the Freemans' yard across the street. I flinched, glanced back in that direction, but saw nothing other than Sheriff Baker's patrol car from the corner of my eye.

Mom had been considerate enough to leave the patio light on for me (wonders never cease, I thought with a smirk as I approached the screen door). A swarm of loudly fluttering moths fought over its sickly yellow glow, their fat, feathery bodies bouncing off the bulb like tiny kamikaze pilots. A few of them tickled at my ears and neck, and I batted them away as I bent to retrieve the single gold key Mom kept hidden for me beneath our WELCOME ("To Everyone But Traveling Salesmen and Holy Rollers") mat.

My hands trembled as I unlocked our front door, wondering just where the sheriff would be waiting for me.

Behind the door? In my room? In my father's favorite armchair?

Or would I never know? Would a bullet pierce my brain before I took even a single step inside my home?

I pushed the door inward. Waiting for whatever was to come.

But nothing happened.

Several seconds passed before my eyes adjusted to the darkness of my living room, yet immediately a cacophony of strange noises arose from the other side of the house, seeming to leap out at me from the murky darkness to pummel me with their awful, awful truth.

I knew right away what I was hearing, though I certainly did not want to believe it.

I stumbled, grabbed on to the doorjamb to keep from falling to my knees.

My guts roiled. My face felt hot—and tingly, somehow—as if I had stepped too close to a raging bonfire.

"How *could* she?" I cried, as salty, stinging tears filled my vision and spilled down my cheeks.

And the sounds grew louder back there in my mother's bedroom. . . .

"Oh, Jesus!" her voice came to me from down the hallway. "Yes, Burt! *Yes! Yes!*"

Her sounds of passion were accompanied by a rude animal grunting. As if a wild dog had broken into our home, and it was back there mauling her now.

"Oh! Oh, God! Oh, *God!*"

I slammed my hands over my ears, not wanting to hear it. But those terrible sounds would not go away. They grew . . . rising to a fervent climax the longer I stood there. . . .

"That's . . . so . . . good!" I heard my mother moan in between harsh, rasping breaths of passion.

She had betrayed everything my father stood for. Everything our *home* had ever stood for.

I clenched my teeth, shook my head back and forth.

"No," I growled. "Shut *up* . . ."

"Yeah, baby," Burt Baker's voice came to me from out of the darkness, as he did vile things with my mother—*to* my mother—in the very room where my father had once slept. Where Dad had dreamed his dreams and dressed for work and loved Mom in ways that were so natural and so good and so *right*.

"That's good, Darlene . . . mmm-hmm, baby, that's so damn *good*. . . ."

I wanted to die. I tried to block out the mental images bombarding me like quick, choppy cuts on a movie screen. I didn't want to imagine him on top of her, didn't want to see them rolling about all shiny and slick beneath the sheets as I had once seen her doing with Dad when I'd walked in on them after a terrible nightmare. . . .

But I couldn't help it. My mind insisted upon torturing me. Showing me, again and again and again, what it must look like in there.

Him. On top of her. Grunting, grunting, grunting . . . groping my mother . . . touching her . . . putting his thing inside of her. . . .

The living room seemed to shift and then swirl three hundred and sixty degrees around me. I gripped the doorjamb tighter than ever, so sure I would pass out any second.

"You like that?" Burt Baker asked my mother. "Mmm-yeah, honey . . . oh, *Christ* . . ."

Mom's reply was a cross between a reptilian hiss and a long, sated whine. If I had not known better I might have suspected he was hurting her, from the sound of it.

Then: "Fuck me! Oh, God, Burt—harder! Harder! I'm gonna cum!"

It was the most unsettling thing I have ever heard. I felt so unclean, filled with a terrible knowledge I wished I could give back. During that cruelest of moments I did not feel twelve years old at all, but far, far beyond my years. Innocence died screaming. Somehow I knew that every last morsel of childhood naivety I had savored till then lay rotting in the grave. Like Cassie Belle Rourke. Like Mike Linder and Calvin Mooney. Like my father.

"Fuck me, Sheriff! Fuck me, fuck me, *fuck me!*" Mom's orgasmic shriek filled the house, and as it built to a crescendo, there was something almost musical about it.

As if she were singing it to him. A nocturnal song of filth from the mouth of a woman who had kissed me and fed me and . . . given birth to me. . . .

That did it. I could take no more.

I sincerely believe, as I look back now on those

next few minutes or so after I whirled around and headed back out onto my front porch, that I might have been certifiably insane. Everything that had transpired since the night of the Apple Gala—all my anger and fear and hatred and confusion and guilt and regret and sorrow—became a swirling maelstrom of emotions I could not have kept in check even if I tried.

My feet felt heavy, the air around me somehow thick and syrupy as if I moved through a fever dream, as I trudged through the wet grass of my front yard and around the side of my house.

I could still hear them by the time I reached the storage shed out back. Through the walls. A muffled duet of urgent grunts and groans resembling some dark tribal rhythm coming from inside my home.

"I hate you," I said. To both of them, and to everyone in the world all at once. "I *hate* you. . . ."

As I opened the shed's heavy wooden door, the squeaking of its ancient hinges echoed throughout the neighborhood, sounding so much louder than they did in the daytime, but I didn't care.

Somewhere down the block a dog barked five times, then twice more, before finally shutting up for good. As if it had decided no one was listening so why bother.

What are you doing? screamed a boyish voice from somewhere deep inside of me when I stepped into the shed. It was the rational side of myself, I know now, trying to stop me before it was too late.

Think about this, Kyle, it pleaded with me. *Surely you can't be serious. . . .*

But I ignored it. I told it to go to hell.

I did not know what I had come for until the second I saw it sitting there. Everything before me had converged into a disorienting, foggy blur—even the sounds of the drizzle around me faded away to little more than a dull background buzz like faint static on a radio station headquartered several counties away—beneath the distant sounds of Burt Baker having sex with my mother.

A mischievous grin spread across my face as I hefted in one pale, sweaty hand that single can of Banner Red Krylon spray-paint. The same paint Dan had used the previous summer to help his friend Chris turn an ugly puke-green dirt bike into a vehicle the color of freshly spilt blood.

I carried it with me back the way I had come . . . across the yard, to the driveway. Never thinking once about the consequences of my actions.

I shook that long white can violently once I'd reached my destination, shook it as if it were the source of every horrid thing that had happened to me since the night of the Apple Gala. Its metallic rattle seemed to fill the night like the mating call of some lonely robotic cicada.

I had always loved that sound. Not to mention the strong chemical smell of the paint itself.

I savored both more than ever as I walked around Sheriff Baker's patrol car, squatted down beside the driver-side front tire, and went to work.

The can hissed like an angry snake. My hands no longer trembled at all as I spelled out a single word in wide, vibrant crimson letters, a word that stretched across that side of the vehicle from below its side mirror all the way to its rear tire.

I stepped back to admire my handiwork when I was done.

The paint can dropped from my hand into the grass below.

The rain grew heavier as I stood there, pelting me with its icy spray and soaking my clothes, but I hardly noticed it at all.

I glanced toward the house. Then back to Sheriff Baker's desecrated patrol car.

And I smiled.

Lightning struck somewhere close by. The night lit up, and for those few seconds when my entire neighborhood was illuminated as bright as day, my impromptu message for Sheriff Burt Baker appeared to stand out in bright, bloody relief against his patrol car's slick tan body. The letters had already begun to run in the rain, dripping down the vehicle's undercarriage and onto the driveway in thin, wormy rivulets, but the word could not have been more clear if I had spent hours carving it into the hood with a rusty old key:

KILLER

It felt good. Damn good.

I licked my lips, tasting the dirty rain. Gave myself a thumbs-up gesture.

But then thunder boomed overhead, a resonating crash that seemed to originate right in my backyard.

The sound of it woke me from my trancelike state.

I sucked in a bitter breath of damp air, stumbled backwards and nearly tripped over the empty can of spray paint lying in the grass behind me.

When the night lit up again, brighter than ever, the hard reality of what I had just done to Sheriff Burt Baker's patrol car burned through me as if I had been struck by the lightning. An electric tremor of white-hot fear shot from the top of my head down to my toes, and the tiny hairs on my arms stood up.

I covered my mouth with one hand, and seemed

to view the vandalism from outside of myself, as if someone else had done the deed.

Not me. It couldn't have been *me*. . . .

What did I just do?

I glanced toward the house again. Back to the car. Toward the house.

Then down at my hands, which were smudged with sticky red paint like the bloody palms of a serial killer.

"No," I whined. "Oh, God, no . . ."

I ran to where I had left Burner sprawled by the porch steps. He even seemed to glare at me for a second or two as if he could not believe what I had just done. I pulled him upright, and the rain assaulted his shiny silver spokes with a sound like dimes being dropped through a slow-moving fan.

I glanced toward the patrol car, felt a sharp pain in my chest. From a distance the letters I had painted on the car's beige body appeared *black*, black as a word drawn in tar or some foul putrescence from beyond the grave. The message I had left for Burt Baker seemed to scream at me as I crawled atop my bicycle.

KILLER.

KILLER.

KILLER.

With one last nervous glance toward the house— had the noises inside there finally ceased? I couldn't be sure beneath the roar of the rain around me and my own frenetic heartbeat pounding like a bass drum in my skull—I pushed off down the driveway.

I had no idea where I was headed. I did not even bother to flee from the scene of my crime faster than the speed of light. Instead, I pedaled at a slow, almost leisurely pace back toward town.

It didn't matter anymore.

Wherever I went, *he* would find me.

I felt numb. Resigned to my fate. And so, so tired.

Chapter Thirty-four

We passed through my sleeping hometown like phantoms in the night, and at some point it almost seemed as if Burner took over completely, slipping into autopilot mode as I hunched over the handlebars in a stunned daze.

I barely noticed how the sharp sting of the rain upon my flesh had eased off to a soft, chilly drizzle once we reached the town common, or how the rain soon dissipated entirely by the time my feet left Burner's pedals and we took a hard left off Tenth Street into the parking lot of Trinity First Baptist Church.

Our momentum carried us up into the hillside cemetery behind the church. We came within an inch of crashing into a large white tombstone (D.H. BULLARD, read the name there, 1919–1974), but I jerked Burner's handlebars to one side just in time.

Though I had not known—consciously, at least—where Burner and I planned to go, it appeared we had reached our destination at last.

I jumped off of my bicycle, eased him to the ground beside a mossy gray stone that said only FLYNN.

And I headed toward my father's grave.

Behind me, the church was a monstrous black shape in the night. Its stained-glass windows resembled four giant, lifeless eyes watching me with a sort of drowsy, half-hearted interest. Off to my right, toward the westernmost edge of the cemetery, loomed the Snake River Woods, but I didn't dare look their way. They were so, so dark—darker than anything I had ever seen—and I feared if I got too close or even glanced in their direction they might suck me into another evil dimension.

A single light in the far corner of the church's parking lot bathed the cemetery in its bright white glow. It buzzed faintly, like a dying housefly. Beneath it, the hundreds of tombstones sprawled about the hillside cast long, slender shadows on the wet green lawn like open graves hungry for new corpses.

Despite all the monster movies I had watched over the years with my big brother at the Lansdale Royal Drive-In, no matter how many times we had stayed up for *Night of the Living Dead* on the Late Show even though I knew it would give me nightmares, I was not afraid. I might have been visiting the cemetery in the middle of the day, for all such thoughts of wandering ghosts or maggoty hands bursting from the earth frightened me.

I did not fear creatures otherworldly or supernatural at all. No, ever since the night of August 5, I feared only what was real. What I knew could truly harm me.

My fellow man.

I welcomed the darkness, knew there was nothing that could hurt me in that place of the dead.

At last I had found sanctuary. If only for a little while.

For the first time in more than a year, I knelt before my father's grave, and as I did so I felt a strange sense of peace. As if I belonged there all along, had been shirking my duty, yet all was forgiven now.

SGT. DANIEL EMMETT MACKEY, SR., read Dad's wide square tombstone. NOV. 1, 1936–APR. 17, 1970. Beneath that was an engraving of a purple heart flanked on each side by bronze and silver stars, and the words LOVING FATHER/DEDICATED PATRIOT.

A crooked bouquet of fake carnations sat at the head of Dad's grave. Mom had left it there last Father's Day, I was pretty sure. The flowers might once have been white, but now they were drooping and brown.

I took a deep breath, bowed my head, and clasped my hands in front of me.

"Dad," I said. "I'm here."

Lightning flickered in the starless black sky, beyond the pasture on the other side of the cemetery. A short, basso cough of thunder echoed beyond the Blue Ridge Mountains.

I sniffled softly, ran one hand through the bright green grass atop my father's grave, and remembered how I used to love to do that to Dad's short brown hair when he was alive.

"I miss you, Daddy," I said. My voice cracked. "I miss you so much."

Crickets chirped in the pasture several feet away, and in that sound and the whisper of the soft autumn drizzle and the gentle sigh of the wind between the graves, I imagined I could hear my father's reply. . . .

He missed me, too. A lot.

"I'm sorry I haven't been to see you lately," I said. "It's just that . . . I don't think you're down *there*, you know? Buried under all this dirt and grass. I like to imagine you're looking down on me, watching out for me all the time from a much better place than this."

I peered heavenward, toward the infinite black dome of night above me. When thunder rumbled again, closer this time, I could feel it in my knees like a faint seismic tremor in the earth.

"I know I've probably disappointed you," I went on. "I know I haven't done the right thing. I should have. I know it could have all been over that next morning, after the Apple Gala, if I'd just taken Dan's advice. But I messed up, Daddy. I was so, so scared. I messed up bad . . . and I'm sorry."

I peered down at my trembling hands.

"It's going to end," I said. "Tonight. Isn't it?"

Far off, in the distance, I could hear the blare of a train whistle. I wished I could jump aboard that train, and it would take me far away.

And that's when I heard it.

As if on cue.

Something closer than the train.

The sound of a car engine. Nearby. Tires on wet pavement.

A vehicle, pulling into the church parking lot.

My heart skipped a beat. I hit the cold, wet ground.

I lay like that, prone atop my father's grave, for what felt like hours before I dared turn my head to look back toward the lot.

Goose bumps broke out all over my body when I saw it. My heart leapt into my throat.

"N-n-no," I whispered.

It sat at the very bottom of the hill. Long, sleek, flesh-colored.

KILLER, read the sloppy red writing across both doors on the driver's side.

It didn't move. It just sat there, its low idle sounding like the sated purr of a very large, well-fed feline.

I clenched my teeth, let out a little whimper.

"Kyle!" Sheriff Baker called out to me.

I gasped.

His voice echoed among the tombstones, seemed to come from everywhere at once.

God, how I wished I could sink down into the soft, muddy earth to join my father six feet below. I felt naked. Vulnerable.

"Kyle!" Sheriff Baker shouted again from the bottom of the hill. "You out there, son?"

Please, God, I prayed, *Please don't let him get me. . . .*

From the patrol car's open window, I could hear the birdlike squawk of his radio. The voice of a female dispatcher. "Ten-Four," she said, and something like "will take care of it."

"Come on now, son," Baker called again. His voice boomed across the hillside like the thunder overhead, and for a second or two I was quite sure he had already climbed out of his car to walk up the hillside toward me.

"It's been a long day. I ain't in the mood to play hide n' seek!"

God, please . . . just make him go away. . . .

"Come on out. Nobody's gonna hurt you. We can talk about this."

I shook my head where I lay. *No way, man. No WAY . . .*

Suddenly the bright white glow of a searchlight split the night from his driver-side window. Or maybe one of those long, ultra-powerful flashlights cops carry. I couldn't be sure.

I pissed my pants.

That blinding white light swept across the cemetery slowly, from one side to the other. Three times. To the right, toward the woods, then back to the left. Right. Left. Back and forth. Each time it passed over me I could not only see the beam a few feet above my head—tearing open the night, parting the darkness like a soft black curtain—I could almost feel its evil heat as well. Radiating like an alien invader's atomic death-ray from some cheesy B-movie Dan and I had laughed at long and loud back when things were good. I closed my eyes, felt so conspicuous clinging to my father's grave like that. The hill seemed so much steeper, as if it had begun to tilt toward the heavens and any second I would go sliding off, screaming, until I landed with a *thump* right at Burt Baker's feet.

I wondered where I had left my bicycle. Was Burner sitting right out in the open? I couldn't remember. What if the sheriff spotted Burner lying in the grass somewhere in the middle of those first few graves at the foot of the hill?

Oh, God . . . oh, God . . .

Then it would all be over for me.

An ant crawled across my hand as I lay there, but I didn't dare move even to flick it off. My heart slammed in my chest as I waited for the terrible *click-whine* sound of Sheriff Baker's car door opening. I waited for the metallic *thunk* of him slamming it shut behind him, of change jingling in his pockets and his leather gun belt squeaking and his shoes making gentle *whisk-whisk* noises in the wet grass as he headed for the grave of his lover's late husband. Coming closer.

But it never came.

A minute later I heard him cough once.

His radio squawked again.

He mumbled something that sounded like "sooner than later."

And then he drove away.

I breathed again, though I did not stand for at least five minutes after Baker pulled off. I feared it might have been a trick.

At last I jumped to my feet, and I wasted no time in finding Burner where I had left him farther down the hillside.

I ran to my bicycle, climbed atop it.

Before we took off, however, I glanced back toward my father's grave one last time.

"I'll see you soon, Daddy," I said with a little sniffle.

Chapter Thirty-five

By the time I returned home, the rain had begun to fall with a fervor unlike anything I had seen for several weeks. Lightning illuminated Midnight every few seconds, filling the air with a lingering, electric ozone smell, and thunder crashed all around me as if some invisible war were being waged in the swirling black skies above my hometown.

The house was dark. Only Mom's station wagon sat in the driveway.

I wasn't surprised, of course. I had known he wouldn't be there. He was out looking for me. And he would keep looking for me, all over Midnight, until he found me.

The front door was unlocked. I entered the house as quietly as possible, but every sound I made as I eased the door shut behind me seemed louder than the constant barrage of thunder and rain roaring against the roof and outside walls.

I ran one hand through my dripping wet hair, bent to remove my tennis shoes. After setting my shoes against the wall to the left of the doorway, I pulled off my soggy white socks. They looked like limp, lifeless things as I threw them into my shoes, like the carcasses of something that had once lived and breathed but had been drained of everything by the violent storm outside.

"Kyle?" Mom called out to me from the darkness as I tiptoed across the living room. "Is that you?"

My heart skipped a beat.

"It's me," I said. "Mom? Where are you?"

"In here," I heard her say, from the kitchen.

"Oh." I frowned. "Why are you sitting in the dar—"

But when I rounded the corner and entered the kitchen, I knew.

Mom sat at the kitchen table, a single red candle centered before her. Its flame quivered slightly as it burned, basking the room with its mellow orange glow. Judging from the single drip of wax trailing down its length, the power had not been out for very long. She had propped the candle up in a slim vase to keep it from falling over. Another candle, this one short and fat and green (NOEL, read the logo on its side, the letters shaped like holly leaves and berries), sat in a saucer atop the refrigerator behind her.

Mom wore a thin blue nightgown. Her long brown hair fell to her shoulders, and droplets of sweat glistened on her forehead. She did not move. Her hands were on the table before her, palms down. Next to her right hand sat a box of matches and a wrinkled piece of yellow paper. Her face looked almost unreal—like something sculpted out of flesh-colored plastic—in the candle's flickering light.

I shuddered when she offered me a sad little smile. But her eyes were not smiling. Her eyes were not happy at all.

"I've been worried sick about you, Kyle," she said.

I bit my lip, sat down at the table across from her. "Is everything . . . um . . . okay?"

"It's been raining cats and dogs out there."

"Tell me about it," I said.

"Where the hell have you been?"

"Why do you care?" I couldn't help it. I had to get one good dig in, just to let her know that I knew:"You had your company. . . ."

"Oh, stop it, Kyle," Mom said. "Jealousy does not become you."

"Whatever."

The rain batted at the windows. The candlelight flickered. Lightning flashed beyond the window over the sink.

When my mother said nothing for several minutes, I cleared my throat, said, "So when did he leave?"

She gave a loud, exaggerated sigh. "He's been gone for a while, son. Jesus Christ, I wish you would quit acting like he's some sort of monster. He cares a lot about me, you know."

"Sure," I said.

"You can't expect me to be alone forever."

"I don't."

"We're very good for one another."

"Right."

I ran my hands through my dripping wet hair again, watched a small puddle collect on the table before me, and fought back tears. I wished I could just leave again.

"So where did you go?" Mom asked me.

I looked back up at her. She didn't seem to be talking to me, though. She seemed to be staring through me, at a place on the wall behind me.

I couldn't think of a lie. So I told her the truth: "Dad's grave."

"At ten o'clock at night?"

"Yes."

"Why?"

I shrugged.

"I just don't think you should be running around town at all hours of the night, Kyle. That's all I'm saying. It's dangerous."

"Maybe," I replied, thinking, *You don't know what dangerous is, Mom*.

"Let me know before you go doing that again, would you?"

"Sure," I said. "If you're not . . . preoccupied."

"Don't be a smart-aleck. You're not too big for me to bust your bottom."

I rolled my eyes. She hadn't said it with much conviction. And the mood I was in, I almost wanted to tempt her. *Just you try it, lady. . . .*

"I only fuss because I love you, Kyle. Because I worry about you."

"Mm-hmm."

"I worry about you and Dan both. All the time. Sometimes I think I might go crazy, worrying about you boys."

She gave a little shrug then, as if deciding it wasn't worth the trouble trying to convince me of something I steadfastly refused to believe. She stood. Shoulders slumped, she moved to the cabinet beside the refrigerator, and returned to her place at the dining room table with an empty glass and an unopened bottle of Wild Turkey.

She sat down again, across from me.

Suddenly my mother's body began to hitch with violent sobs. For several long and very awkward minutes she hid her face, and at first I thought she might be having a seizure.

"Mom?" I said. "Are you . . . are you okay?"

I almost expected her to tell me something had happened to Dan.

"Mom?"

Her hands came away from her face at last, and in the candlelight her tears glistened on her cheeks like a dozen slimy snail-trails.

She looked horrible. So worn out. Old and tired.

"Mom, what is it? What's happened? Are you okay?"

"No, Kyle," she said finally, her voice thick with tears and snot. "I'm not okay. I'm not okay at all."

My brow furrowed. I said nothing, just waited to see if she might explain further.

"It's all gone downhill so fast, since that night of the Apple Gala. My God. Everything's just been building up and building up . . . I can't keep it inside anymore. . . ."

"The Apple Gala?" My jaw dropped. My heart began to race. "Wh-what are you talking about, Mom?"

"Everything. It's just turned so *bad* since that night. Everything. It wasn't supposed to, but it did. If I'd only known . . . I never would have . . ."

Again I asked her: "M-mom . . . please . . . what are you talking about?"

"There's some things I have to tell you, Kyle. Some things I've . . . d-d-done . . . that I'm not very proud of."

"I don't understand," I said, my voice so weak and uneven I barely even heard it myself.

"I can't go on like this. I have to tell someone. And who better than my youngest son . . . my dear, precious Kyle."

Her hands reached out to me, but then dropped to the table as if she no longer had the energy to go all the way with her gesture. Her empty glass rattled upon the table. The candle wobbled back and forth. She started crying again, her thick, wet sobs echoing off the kitchen sink, off the refrigerator behind her, off the scuffed tile floor.

And then she began to let it all flow out of her, as if she knew this was her last chance to confess all of her sins, lest she keep them inside forever. . . .

"It actually goes back even further than the Apple Gala," she told me, though her glassy-eyed gaze seemed to go right through me once again. "I mean, that's when it all started, but it technically began long before that. The little slut's death was just the turning point. When the shit really started hitting the fan. But all of it was set into motion . . . oh, it goes way back to early summer, I guess. May or June, at least, right around the time your brother graduated. . . ."

"What—" I started.

"Back when he was with *her*."

"You're not making any sense, Mom," I said, urging her to continue, although I did not want to hear any more—I could go the rest of my life without hearing another godawful word of this, if my suspicions were correct as to where it might be leading—but I *had* to. I had to know what she was getting at even if it killed me. "Tell me what you did . . . what did you—"

"Shhh," said Mom, holding a long skinny finger to her lips. It trembled in front of her mouth like a dying branch in a cold winter wind, but her gesture was nonetheless sincere. "Listen, Kyle. Just be quiet for a minute and listen. Please."

"Okay," I said.

"I've done a bad thing," said my mother. "It's something I'm going to have to live with for the rest of my life."

"Mom—"

"Shh," she said again. She winced, as if my hoarse whisper caused her head to throb.

I began to gnaw at my nails as she told her
story. . . .

"You know how I've always told you that everything I do, I do it for you and Dan? I've always meant
that, Kyle. I always will. But you see, darling, mothers don't always make the right decisions. We do our
best, but we are far from perfect."

I nodded, not understanding at all, but pretending
I did so she would continue.

"It's been like one great big row of dominoes," she
said. "One falls, it hits the next, on and on and you
can't stop it . . . Jesus . . . no matter how hard you try,
you cannot stop it."

"Stop *what*, Mom?" I said. "Please tell me. . . ."

"I'm talking about this whole godforsaken mess,"
she said. "With the Rourke girl. And Dan. And now
Deputy Mike and this Calvin Mooney fellow . . . I
never meant for it to go this far. . . ."

The temperature of the room seemed to rise thirty
or forty degrees. I could feel the heat radiating from
that single candle, could feel its warmth upon my
cheeks like the hottest fires of hell, and I wanted to
run out into the midnight rain and let it soak me
with its cleansing flood. I did not want to hear any
more.

But I had to.

"Dan was involved," I said, under my breath. A tear
ran down my cheek. "Oh, God. I knew it."

Mom gave me another sad little smile. I never
knew whether she heard me. She still had not
opened her Wild Turkey, but she kept glancing down
at it every few seconds while she spoke as if the bottle held the answers to all her problems.

"There used to be a time," Mom said, and her
voice came out gruff, from somewhere down in her
chest. She coughed gently, then started over, speak-

ing slowly and carefully, as if she only had one chance to get this right. "There used to be a time . . . when a girl got pregnant before she was married . . . she was considered a slut. Having a child 'out of wedlock,' they called it. A girl got herself in a predicament like that, she was the talk of the whole town. They called her all kinds of filthy names. She was a whore. An 'easy lay.' Good girls just didn't *do* things like that. . . ."

She took a deep breath, said, "I should know. I was Midnight's own Hester Prynne, at least for a little while. And your brother was my Pearl."

I could not comprehend Mom's analogy at the time. Though I understood what she meant all the same. My eyes grew wide.

She laughed, a sick wet sound that sent a chill down my spine. "Yes. It's true. Do the math sometime, Kyle. Your father and I, we were young . . . stupid. . . ."

Mom seemed to be lost in her own thoughts for a minute. Tears gathered in the corners of her eyes, but she wiped them away with the back of one hand.

"I'll never forget the look on your father's face when we decided to tell my parents. Your Grandpa Ballard, he was as old-fashioned as they come. Always said that any guy who didn't respect me, he'd be waiting for him with a shotgun. And I believed him. Your daddy was as white as a sheet that day we offered to fix dinner for them. I guess they should have known we were buttering them up for something. They just had no clue we were about to tell them they were gonna be grandparents before they were forty."

Mom sniffled a bit, glanced out the window over the sink. The rain batted at the glass like something malevolent. Thunder shook the house, and I could feel it in the ground beneath my feet.

She said, "Your dad offered to do the dirty work, but I couldn't let him. They were *my* parents, after all. And God, he was so scared." Again with her sick little laugh. I shuddered. "Halfway through dinner—I'll never forget, Daddy had just asked me to pass the green beans and your father nearly tripped over himself getting them for him—I brought it up. Out of the blue. Because I knew if I didn't, I might never get up the nerve. 'Mommy, Daddy,' I said, as nonchalant as you please. 'I'm pregnant.'

"You should have seen your father's face. He was just as surprised as my parents at first, I think. And then Daddy looked at him. Just turned . . . real slow . . . and raised his eyebrows, as if to say, 'Oh, really, now?' Boy, did your father look like he wanted to cry. Like he would have rather been on the other side of the world than standing over Daddy with that bowl of green beans in his hands. He looked like a lost, scared little boy. But then he just nodded. Said, 'It's true.' And practically ran back to his chair.

"Your grandpa took it better than we thought he would. Oh, he wasn't happy. Not at all. While Mama looked on and never said a word the whole time, he calmly asked, 'Well, I reckon you're gonna marry her, ain'tcha, Emmett?' Daddy was always so Southern. Sometimes you could barely understand what he was saying even if you'd grown up under the same roof as him all your life. Your father didn't hesitate when Daddy asked him that. He just nodded and nodded and kept on nodding like a damn fool. I had to kick him under the table to get him to stop."

I swallowed a lump in my throat, tried to imagine my mother as a very scared, very pregnant teenager.

It wasn't easy. I tried to imagine my father as anything but the strong, fearless military hero I had known. And that was even harder.

Mom stared off toward the rain again, sighed wistfully.

"Today it's as easy as getting an abortion," she said. "Just scrape that baby out of you, and no one's the wiser. Not like it used to be."

I squirmed in my seat as she rambled on.

"How could he have been so stupid?" Mom exclaimed. "That's what I wanna know! I always thought your brother had such a good head on his shoulders. He was so smart. Not like all the other teenagers in this town, who only think about smoking pot and screwing up at Storch's Rim any chance they get."

I blushed.

"Christ, did he prove me wrong."

"What happened?" I said. "Tell me."

"He had it all, your big brother. And he still does. But he almost didn't. The basketball scholarship. Julie. The fool almost lost everything, Kyle. You know, I always gave Danny a hard time about that girl Julie, but it's only 'cause I love him. I don't suppose she was so bad, when it came right down to it. She did seem to care about your brother, didn't she? I guess I just couldn't get used to Dan showing another woman besides me all of his attention. But the thing with kids these days, Kyle . . . and remember I told you this, because it won't be too many years till you start sniffing around the opposite sex . . . they don't know what love is. They can't. They think they do. But it's just their hormones talking."

"Hmm," I said.

"Danny had it all. But he screwed it up. For all I know he might have married Julie one day—they may still, although I think this college thing will probably put a crimp in that, just you wait and see—but that never would have been if Cassandra Belle Rourke had fucked it all up. If I'd *let* her fuck it up for Danny."

I licked my too-dry lips, began to gnaw at my fingernails again as she went on.

"That's all it takes, Kyle. One teeny tiny mistake. And everything you have can go down the drain like *that.*"

She snapped her fingers, and the sound seemed very loud in our small kitchen. I flinched.

Mom scowled down at the table then, as if she could see Cassie Belle Rourke right in front of her and wanted to slap the dead girl silly. Her hands balled into tight white fists, and her voice grew a bit louder as she explained. . . .

"Cassie Rourke's little crush on your brother started two or three years ago. Remember—when he worked the concession stand at the skating rink? She used to hang out there a lot from what I hear, and she got this . . . this *thing* for Danny that wouldn't go away no matter what. Even then she was way too young for him. She would have been around your age, I guess. Dan was fifteen. But it didn't matter to her. She kept on and on, always bugging him. Always calling, asking for him. Dan was always so polite, told her he had a girlfriend, but I could tell he liked it. Deep down inside. He liked the attention. I told her she didn't have any business calling here for him, but she wouldn't listen. Little sluts like her never do. She started sending him these dirty little love letters, every other week or so. Dan thinks I didn't know, but

I did. I knew all along. Don't ever forget, Kyle—no matter what you get yourself into—that it's not easy keeping secrets from the person who does your laundry day in and out."

"Um . . . okay," I said.

"I can't fault Dan for being a typical man. He can't help he's got two balls between his legs. That's the way God made him. But I just hope and pray he learned his lesson after this little scare."

I said nothing. Just waited for her to continue. Thunder rumbled overhead like the horrible truth of this whole situation crashing down upon me.

"Always remember how much trouble your penis can get you into, son," Mom said. "You'll do that for your mother, won't you?"

I cleared my throat, looked away into the darkness of our living room. Blushed again. "Umm . . . y-yeah. S-sure."

"Good. Good boy. My precious Kyle . . ."

Finally, Mom opened her bottle of Wild Turkey. She poured about three fingers of it into the glass before her, set it back down. She didn't drink from it, though. Not yet.

Beside Mom's bottle I again noticed that piece of yellow paper sitting on the table in front of her, beneath the matches she had used to light the candles. My curiosity got the best of me.

"Mom?" I said. "What's that?"

"Oh. This?"

She slid it across the table to me. The candlelight twitched and shifted on the walls like a living coat of paint. Our shadows danced around us.

My eyes grew wide when I saw what was on that piece of paper. My lips worked soundlessly as I tried my damnedest to make sense of it all. . . .

In one trembling hand I held the results of a pregnancy test, as given by Dr. Jim R. Falconer across town. The date at the top read 7/12/77. The patient was one Cassandra Belle Rourke, 15. She had tested positive, and at the time of the diagnosis was about five weeks into her first trimester.

In bold blue ink, someone had written SEE! across the bottom of the page, in all capital letters. The word had been underlined several times, so hard the pen had nearly torn through the paper.

"I found that in his pants," Mom said.

She studied her amber glass of whiskey for several long, awkward seconds. Licked her lips. Finally, she gave a little shrug, raised her eyebrows and drank deeply. Loudly.

"Dan screwed up, Kyle. He screwed up bad. He gave in to that little tramp, he cheated on Julie, and he let his penis do his thinking for him. He slept with Cassie Rourke, at some point—I don't know when, but of course a mother can't keep dibs on her boys twenty-four hours a day, can she, not when she has to pay the bills and put food on the table, too—and you see what happened.

"What Dan didn't realize is that this slut held his entire life in the palms of her frigging hands. Because . . . not only would he lose everything he had worked so hard to achieve, if word got out about their dirty little tryst . . . your brother could have also gone to prison."

"P-prison?"

"She was only fifteen. Dan is a legal adult now. What he did . . . it was statutory rape."

"Oh, God," I said.

"Didn't matter how bad she wanted it. Didn't matter that the little tramp had been begging for it for years. Dan would have gone to prison. He would have lost everything."

Mom took another sip from her glass, then slammed her glass back down on the table. Some of the whiskey splashed onto her hand, but she didn't seem to notice.

"I couldn't let that happen, you understand."

A single tear trickled down my cheek and dripped onto the table. For the umpteenth time, I said, "Oh, God . . ."

"He screwed up, yes. He did something that was very stupid. But you've got to understand where I was coming from, Kyle. It was up to me to see to it that my first-born son's perfect life wasn't flushed down the toilet because of one persistent little bitch who had basically seduced him. Who had been chasing him since she was twelve years old, for God's sake."

I didn't know what to say. I just stared at the table-top, numb.

"That's why I set Cassie Rourke up with the sheriff's son," Mom said. "I knew I had no choice."

"What?" I looked up at her. "What do you mean? How—"

"The sheriff and I . . . you know we've been seeing one another for the past few months."

"Uh . . . yeah," I said, wondering if her love for alcohol had killed every last bit of her memory.

Her gaze averted from mine, went to the candle between us. She twirled a curl of her long brown hair around one finger as she explained, "Well, one night . . . we . . . we had a bit too much to drink. Burt and I."

You? Too much to drink? I was tempted to say. But I didn't.

"He took me to see a movie. *Annie Hall*. We stopped in at Lou's Tavern for a few drinks on the way home. We didn't plan to stay long. I told him I had to get home to my boys. But Burt's really good friends with the owner, Lou Raintree. We eventually lost track of the time, and the sheriff just talked Lou into letting us close up shop. We could stay as long as we wanted, and all our drinks were on the house. Before I knew it, it was two or three in the morning, and the night still seemed so young."

"Okay," I said, though it came out a disgusted grunt more than anything.

"We shared a lot of secrets that night. I've never been able to just talk with a man, like I can talk to Burt, you know? I learned about his wife, Connie, how she had been in the hospital for almost two years with ovarian cancer. She died the same day Kennedy was killed in Dallas, apparently. Now, Burt said, all he had was his boy. Henry. I sure could relate to that. I felt so sorry for him, Kyle . . . he went through a lot, back when all that happened . . . it almost reminded me of those first few years after your father died, and all the shit we went through. . . ."

I just sat there, not allowing my expression to give away how I felt about Burt Baker at all. Or how it compared to my own situation.

Mom said, "He also told me about how Henry had gotten himself into some trouble with the law a few years back, when Burt was sheriff in Gastonia."

"Deputy—" I started to correct her, but then I shut up.

"Seems Henry messed around with some girl back in the day. Burt told me his son was very 'high-strung,' that he liked to get a little rough during . . . er . . . in the sack, so to speak. Sometimes . . . sometimes he hit them. The girls he went out with. Burt said he'd always wanted to get help for his son, but with his career he was always too busy. He thought Henry was all better now, anyway. It'd been years since one of his 'episodes' . . . and even the last one he wasn't really sure what happened, if anything did happen at all, 'cause the girl recanted her story before it even got to court. . . ."

Mom stared through me.

I stared back at her.

"Still, I thought, there had to be a way."

I slowly began to shake my head, and I did not stop until after she was done. . . .

"I thought about that a lot, Kyle, during those sleepless nights when I laid there staring into the darkness wondering how Dan was gonna get himself out of this mess. I thought about what Burt had told me about his son, and I knew that an answer to your brother's problems lay somewhere in the things Henry Baker had done before he moved to Midnight. The solution was there . . . so close . . . but I couldn't quite put the pieces of the puzzle together. . . ."

"What did you do, Mom?" I whispered. "What did you *do* . . . ?"

"First and foremost, I'll have you know that I *did not* hold a gun to his head," she said, frowning. As if I had already accused her of doing something like that. "I was the catalyst. That's all. I hooked them up. I didn't make that boy do anything."

"Tell me," I said. I had a hard time looking at my mother for the next few minutes. She made me sick. Though she seemed remorseful of the things she had done, there was something about the way she spoke as her story met its terrible conclusion that seemed defiant, cold, as if she dared me to question the love she felt for her sons, or the unimaginable lengths she would go to protect us.

"That little slut had the nerve to come up and introduce herself to me one day in the Big Pig Grocery. As if I couldn't wait to make her acquaintance. I was standing in the meat department, I remember. I'd been thinking about asking Julie over for a cookout, believe it or not. Thought we could all get together and talk and pretend everything was gonna be okay. But then I saw *her*. Cassie Belle Rourke. She had the nerve to walk up to me in her tight little blue-jean shorts and ask me in this voice that was so sweet it made me want to puke, 'You're Dan Mackey's mother, aren't you?'

"I should have denied it. Should have told the bitch I didn't know Dan Mackey from Little Richard. But before I even thought about it, I was smiling at her, saying, 'Yes, sweetheart, and you are?' all the time wishing I could claw her eyes out. And it hit me, just like that. All of the pieces suddenly clicked into place. I realized this was Dan's only chance. By the time I got up to the front counter, and saw Henry Baker standing there bagging groceries the next aisle over—this was when he first started working as a bagboy at the Big Pig—the plan was already formulated in my brain. The possibilities of what could be, knowing Henry's history with young women.

"That's why I introduced them. Oh, I did such a wonderful job of it, Kyle, the way I took her hand and put it in his. I could tell there was something between them even then. I saw Henry's eyes glance over her perky little breasts—she wasn't wearing a bra that day, I remember—and he obviously liked what he saw. As for her . . . well, Henry's not a bad-looking boy by any means, you know, even if he does have those nervous twitches every now and then. I could tell the way they looked at each other, there was something there. I had done my part. Now

I just had to sit back. Wait. And hope that if she couldn't have Dan, she would throw herself onto the next best thing."

"Oh, God," I wept. "Mother . . ."

"Six days later, Cassie Belle Rourke was dead."

"That's so . . . *awful*. . . ."

"I never meant for her to die. I just thought maybe . . . maybe he would . . . cause her to miscarry or something . . . that's all. . . ."

"Jesus, Mom!" I cried.

"I have to live with this for the rest of my life," she said.

"Yes. You do."

"Is that punishment enough, you think?"

I said nothing. I didn't know *what* to say.

Mom buried her face in her hands again. But if she had begun to cry anew, her sobs were soft and soundless.

"I think I'm going to quit drinking," she said when she was done, even as she raised her glass of Wild Turkey to her lips.

"Really?" I said.

"Yes. Really."

She set her glass back down on the table. It glistened almost prettily in the candlelight.

"I'm going to try, anyway."

"Good."

"I'm tired of living like this."

Again she took a drink. But this time from the bottle. I suppose she meant she would try to stop *eventually*. Tomorrow, maybe. Or the day after that.

"Do you hate me, Kyle?" she said. "Please . . . tell me you don't hate me. . . ."

"I don't hate you, Mom," I said.

I got up to leave the room.

"I just . . ."

"What?" Desperation burned in my mother's eyes. She wiped at her mouth with the back of one shaky hand as I pushed in my chair and shuffled into the darkness of the hallway, toward my bedroom.

Again I said, "I don't hate you."

And I left it at that.

Chapter Thirty-six

I don't remember actually going to bed that night. I shouldn't have been able to fall asleep in the first place, I suppose—after everything that had happened during the last few hours—but eventually fatigue must have outweighed even my fear. I could not fight it any more. I soon drifted off on top of my covers to the sound of the storm outside, and might have slept for days had my slumber not been interrupted a few hours later. . . .

Somewhere in the middle of a dream about Mom, Dan, a braless Cassie Rourke, and a screeching baby with a dead blue face lying in the meat department of a pitch-black grocery store, I was awakened by a terrible stinging sensation about my cheeks. Like needles sliding in and out of my flesh, or an angry swarm of bees stinging my jaws, over and over.

I came to slowly, realized someone was slapping me awake. Rough hands gripped my shoulders, shaking me back and forth in my bed.

"Wake up. God damn you, wake up."

I knew that voice.

Oh, Jesus.

All the blood seemed to rush out of my head once my eyes adjusted to the deep blue-black darkness of the room, when I saw who stood over my bed.

"Wake the fuck up," said Sheriff Burt Baker.

Lightning flashed in the window behind him.

He had come for me at last, a massive black shape in the night.

"Hey! What are you—" I started, trying to sit up.

His humongous hand slammed over my mouth. It was rough and work-callused. It scratched at my lips like steel wool, smelled of sweat and leather and—faintly—beer. It pinned me to the bed like a thousand-pound weight.

With his other hand, he held up a fat brown finger.

"Shut up," he said, in a voice just above a whisper. "Don't speak."

"Mmm!" I cried, trying to call out for my mother, though I knew she could not help me. "Hnghh!"

He slapped me again.

"Did you hear what I just said? Make another sound and I will snap your fucking neck."

A single tear collected in one corner of my eye, trickled down my cheek onto his hand. At the same time, a drop of dirty rainwater dripped from the bill of his hat onto my forehead.

"Now you're gonna cry?" he taunted me. "Not so fuckin' brave anymore, are you, big man?"

Behind him, the clock on my nightstand read 1:11.

I stared at him, sure that my eyes were going to pop out of my head any second. His hand was like a vice around my cheeks . . . squeezing . . . squeezing. . . .

P-p-please, I tried to reason with him, but beneath his gigantic hand all that came out was: "Mm-smm-mmmmsh . . ."

He grinned at me, and his teeth were very white in the night.

"I think it's time you and I had a little talk, Kyle. Don't you?"

He took his hand off my mouth. Stepped back.

His khaki uniform was rumpled and wet. His badge was crooked. It caught a hint of soft blue glow from my Spider-Man nightlight across the room and seemed to wink at me.

"Not now, though," he said. "Not here."

His monstrous fist seemed to explode right in my face then.

Everything went black, and I felt as if I were falling into forever. . . .

Chapter Thirty-seven

Creedence Clearwater Revival. On the radio. "Someday Never Comes." Close, but muffled. As if through an old dirty sock. Accompanied by the off-key sound of someone singing along. Tentatively, though. As if he likes this song a lot, but doesn't quite know all the words.

It's a deep voice. A voice I know.

I groaned, sat up, but then let out a pained yelp when my forehead struck something hard and unyielding. Metal.

I lay in a fetal position. I couldn't move. I couldn't see. Everything was black. I inspected my surroundings blindly, with my palms and the tips of my fingers, and I could feel that same warm metal on all sides of me. Less than a foot or two away in all directions. It vibrated against my palms.

It was as if I had been buried alive in a throbbing tomb.

Then suddenly I realized where I was, from the gentle rocking motion of my steel prison.

I was trapped inside his trunk. In his patrol car.

My heart began to race. The air was thick, hot. Fuzzy, somehow. Like trying to breathe cotton. I whimpered softly. The tires hummed beneath me, hissing on the wet pavement below as if the vehicle traveled on a bed of writhing snakes. My left foot tingled painfully, pleading for circulation with a silent pins-and-needles scream. It had gone to sleep, but I did not have enough room to move around and try to wake it up. Something slammed against the right side of my head every few seconds—something that felt and smelled like a can of gas—and once I nearly bit my tongue in half, tasting blood, when we hit a pothole that must have been the size of a swimming pool.

I slammed my fists upward, into the lid of the trunk. Trying to bust free. But of course my efforts were futile. Before long I grew tired, breathless. My hands were numb, and the heat in my sweltering black prison seemed to double. Triple.

"Help me," I cried. My voice was hoarse. "P-p-please . . . s-somebody . . . help . . ."

Sweat dripped into my eyes. Into my mouth. Salty. Bitter. Blood trickled from my nose, onto my upper lip, where Baker had hit me. The entire bottom half of my face felt soft and swollen, like a rotten peach.

I tried my damnedest not to panic. It would do no good.

Long before we got there, I knew where he was taking me. I knew it as surely as I knew I would not live to see the morning sun.

We were going back to the place where it all had begun.

Back to the Snake River Woods.

Baker's patrol car jerked to a stop a few minutes after I came to. My heart raced as I waited for him to come for me. But he seemed to be taking his time about it. Toying with me. He gunned the engine once, let it die down, and then the vehicle reversed. Gravel crunched beneath its tires, ticked and clacked and popped against its undercarriage, echoing through my throbbing skull. Then we stopped again. Hard. I slammed so violently into the backside of a taillight I don't know to this day how my nose remained unbroken. That gas can beside my right ear thumped into my temple, and I felt some of the flammable liquid inside slosh onto the nape of my neck.

The smell of it filled the trunk. My nose. My mouth.

The radio grew quiet. The engine's rumbling ceased.

A few seconds later I heard his car door open. The vehicle wobbled slightly, and I felt myself rise an inch or so as he got out.

Thunder barked in the distance, like the long, gruff yawn of a dragon awakening from a century's sleep on the other side of Midnight. The rain drummed upon the car, over my head, like ghostly fingertips taunting me and my dilemma.

A key snicked into the lock before me then. It turned. So loud, right there in front of my face.

A *click*, and the trunk lid popped open at last.

Cold drizzle struck my face, filled my eyes. I blinked it away, recoiled when he smiled down at me.

"There you are," he said.

"Wh-what do you want?"

"Mr. Nosey himself. The bane of my existence."

"Please, Sheriff," I said, "whatever you're about to do . . ."

"It ends tonight, you little fucker. Hope you said your prayers before you went to bed."

He pulled me out of the trunk by my left arm before I had a chance to say another word.

And then he dragged me into the wet black bowels of the forest.

Toward the Old Shack and the Well.

Around us, the rain sighed through the treetops. Lightning flickered directly overhead, illuminating our way to what I had once called my Secret Place. A crack of thunder split the night, like the sound of a gargantuan tree falling somewhere nearby.

Baker seemed unfazed, however, by the storm's increasing fury. He had a job to do.

"What are you gonna do to me?" I asked him, but my voice was barely more than a pathetic whine.

"I haven't decided yet. But you'll know soon enough."

"Please . . ."

"It didn't have to be like this, Kyle," he said, his gun belt squeaking and change jingling in his pants as he walked. "Things could have been just fine, if you hadn't stuck your damn nose in my business. Peeking in that window. Talking to Mike . . . like I *know* you did . . . making me do something I wish I didn't have to do. That guy was my best friend. One helluva deputy. But you put me in a predicament, you backed me into a fucking corner, and there was only one way out. Then of course there was your little phone call. And let's not forget the paint. That took balls, I gotta admit. Rain's washed most of it off by now, but do you realize how hard it's gonna be to keep your little message from leaving a stain?"

"Please, Sheriff Baker—" I started.

"Where am I gonna take it? Who's gonna touch it up for me? Not like I can ride around in broad daylight with that . . . *word* on the side of my car."

He was practically dragging me along the ground, my feet sliding through the carpet of wet leaves and pine needles along the forest floor.

"Fuck this," he said after a few minutes. He let go of my arm, shoved me forward. "You're a big boy. You can walk."

"Please . . . look . . ."

He pulled his pistol from its holster, pointed it at me. It was huge. Black. Evil.

"Go."

I did as I was told. He didn't have to tell me which way. I knew where we were headed.

"What are you going to do to me?" I asked him.

"No questions. Just walk. You'll find out when we get there."

I wept softly as I staggered toward the heart of the forest. I wished I could be back home. In my bed. Safe.

Before long, I could see the Old Shack up ahead. A crooked black shape darker even than the infinite ebony night around it. It almost looked as if it had been waiting for us, crouched like a hungry predator in that grove in the center of the woods.

I expected it to spring for me any second.

I swallowed nervously, slowed my pace, but the sheriff shoved me forward again. Hard. His hand was like a blow from a sledgehammer between my shoulder blades. I slipped in the wet leaves, nearly fell, but caught myself just in time.

"Ya know, Sheriff," I said, desperately trying to buy myself some time as we approached the Old Shack, "even if you kill me, you won't get away with it. I wrote a note. About what you did to Cassie Rourke. How you lied about Calvin Mooney. I have it at home in a safe place. The whole town will know you're a murderer."

"Is that so?"

"Y-yeah," I said.

"Lemme tell you something," said Sheriff Baker. "This town will know what I *want* them to know, son. I rule this town."

"Bastard," I said, under my breath.

"Besides, who's to say when we're finished here that I don't go back, find the note, kill your mother, and torch the whole goddamn house?"

I gasped, stumbled, went down. My knees sank into the mud at the edge of the forest grove.

Baker laughed.

"Get up." He motioned with the gun.

I obeyed. But my knees were weak. And I wasn't so sure anymore, had the Old Shack not stood less than a hundred feet ahead of us, that I could continue any farther.

"Walk," Baker said again.

And I did.

He shoved me roughly inside the cabin when we came to it. I fell, and splinters from the shack's rotting wooden floor dug into my palms.

I turned, preparing to die, but then I could just barely see in the darkness that he had put away his gun.

He wiped his hands on his pants, pulled something long and black from his belt with a little snap. A flashlight. He turned it on, shined it around the shack for a minute in a clockwise motion. Dust motes danced in its bright white beam. The light lingered the longest in each corner of the room, as if witnesses to the sheriff's scheme might have been lurking there just below eye-level. Then he held it on me.

I winced. One hand came up in front of my face, shielding my eyes from the light.

"It's a shame it has to be like this," Baker said from behind that blinding corona. "I really like your mama."

Lightning flickered outside. Thunder boomed above the forest, and the shed's battered tin roof rattled as if it were trying to speak.

When he finally turned the flashlight off I scooted away from him as far as I could go until I slammed into the western wall of the Old Shack. I kept wishing Dan would arrive to save the day. My big brother, the super hero. That's how it always happened in the movies. At the last second.

But this was real life. This wasn't a movie.

My big brother never came.

"I can see myself marrying her someday, you know," said the sheriff. "I mean, I haven't said anything to her about it, and I don't wanna count my chickens before they're hatched, but the way things have been going so far, anything's possible."

"Where is she?" I asked him. "D-did you hurt her?"

"Of course not," he replied. "She's sleeping like a baby. Won't make a peep till mornin'."

I scowled at him.

"Darlene sure does like her hooch, doesn't she?" He chuckled, shook his head. "But I guess we all got our vices."

"It's not right," I shouted at him, suddenly wishing if he were going to do something to me he would just get it over with and quit stalling. "You killed Cassie Rourke, and you blamed Rooster! He's never hurt anyone. It's not fair. It's not fair!"

He raised his eyebrows. Shrugged. Made a clicking sound with his tongue. "There's no such thing as 'fair' in this world, son. It's not about who's right or who's wrong. Who's guilty and who's innocent. It's about who gets caught."

He turned to stare out one of the Old Shack's dirty yellow windows. The same window I had peered through the night I had seen him kill Cassie Belle Rourke. The one through which all this had started, when I had allowed my curiosity to get the best of me. I didn't dare take my eyes off of him for a second.

What came next? I wondered. *What was he waiting for?*

"Where's that damn Henry?" Baker mumbled to himself.

"Please don't do this," I said from my place in the corner of the shack farthest away from him. "P-please . . . I promise I won't tell—"

"Don't even start with that, Kyle," he said. So calmly. But he didn't turn around. "I think you know it's much too late for that now."

Once again, lightning lit up the night outside the Old Shack. Flickered five times fast. Died.

Burt Baker didn't move. He didn't even blink. He was a massive black silhouette looming over me as he stared out at the forest, a nightmare shape ten feet tall.

A crack of thunder, then. The loudest yet, like a violent rip in the fabric of night itself.

"Good," Baker said. "Here comes Henry now."

Indeed, I could hear the sound of someone walking through the forest. Leaves rustling, twigs snapping every few seconds beneath shoes. Maybe a tuneless whistle. Coming closer. Approaching the Old Shack.

"Jesus Christ. Could he make any more fucking noise?" The sheriff glanced back toward me, sighed. He seemed to be talking to himself, though, more than anything. "He's a good kid, you know. He really is. He's just made some bad decisions. A bit too impulsive. He doesn't think before he acts. And one of these days I'm afraid I'm not gonna be there to pull his skinny ass out of the fire."

I watched him, wondered if I should have made a run for it after all, while his back was turned. But I knew he would have caught me before I even made it to the door. He would have wrapped his giant arms around me, just like he had with Cassie Rourke, and he would . . . he would . . .

A cloud of utter hopelessness descended over me. I felt so cold. So alone.

"A good kid," Sheriff Baker said again. "But, so far, one stupid-as-hell adult."

He looked back at me, almost as if he expected me to agree. Or laugh.

I did neither. I just glared at him. Hating him.

"Oh, well," Burt Baker said when his son's skinny shape filled the doorway. "Whaddaya say we get this show on the road?"

He pulled out his flashlight again, shined it in Henry's face when his son's skinny shape at last filled the doorway.

"Whoa," Henry said, covering his eyes. "Hi, Dad."

Henry waited till his father had put away his flashlight before he stepped inside the shack with us. He glanced down at me, gave me a barely noticeable look of distaste, then quickly looked back toward the sheriff. His hair was wet, sticking up here and there in stiff black spikes. In one hand he held a bottle of Coca-Cola. He had changed clothes since the last time I had seen him, but there was still some dirt in his hair from our encounter up at Storch's Rim. Raindrops beaded the sleeves of his leather jacket as if he had bathed in a sea of precious jewels, and under it he wore a faded black Styx T-shirt.

"Took your time gettin' here, didn't you?" his father said.

"Sorry."

"Trying to wake the whole town, were you?"

Henry shook his head, ran one hand through his dripping wet hair, and glanced my way again. He took a sip of his Coke.

He said, "So what are we gonna do?"

"We're gonna take care of business, Henry," replied the sheriff. "That's what we're gonna do."

"Oh. Okay."

"Think you can handle it?"

"It depends on what you mean."

"I think you know what I mean."

"Oh."

Baker stepped toward his son. "You got any better ideas?"

"Well . . . n-no. Not really."

"You ain't gonna pussy out on me, are you?"

"No, Dad."

Henry looked sick. The sheriff stared at him long and hard. Overhead, the rain struck the Old Shack's tin roof with a sound like gunshots from a small-caliber pistol. *Plip. Plap. Pop.*

"Listen to me, son. This is our only option. I don't like it either, but it's got to be done."

"I know, Dad, b-but—"

"You wanna spend the rest of your life in prison?"

"What?"

"You heard me. They'd really like you in prison, you know. I'll bet you'd make some nigger a real nice bitch."

Henry was repulsed. "Jesus, Dad . . ."

"And do you know what they would do to an officer of the *law* in a place like that?"

Henry shuddered, as if he could imagine what they might do but he didn't wish to dwell on it. His head jerked upward three times fast.

332

"I wouldn't last a fucking day."

Henry started chewing at his nails. His eyes never left the Old Shack's dusty wooden floor.

"You see now, right? You see this has got to be done?"

"I . . . I guess," Henry said.

I started to cry again. "Please . . ."

"He needs to just disappear, I think," said the sheriff, his brow furrowed in deep thought. "That'd be the easiest way. . . ."

My eyes went wide. Henry's, too. I knew what he was going to say, somehow, a second before he said it.

"Let's take him to the well."

"The . . . the well?"

"Think about it. Thing's gotta be two hundred feet deep, at least. It could be years before they find the little bastard's body. . . ."

I made a high-pitched whimpering noise.

"When they do find him, one day, it'll look like an accident. That's all. Kid was foolin' around where he shouldn't have been playin', fell in and broke his neck. Fuckin' shame. Case closed."

Henry stared at the Old Shack's dusty wooden floor. His head jerked upward twice. Then again. He winced. Stood still.

"Yeah. I think this'll work," Burt Baker went on. "Of course, I'll have to console Darlene. She already lost her husband a few years back. Won't be easy burying her youngest son, I'm sure."

They both looked down at me then. I cowered against the Old Shack's far wall.

The sheriff sighed.

"Enough bullshittin'," he said, stepping toward me. "Let's do this."

* * *

I remember, as they hauled me out to the Well that night, how I kept trying to will the lightning to strike them, to roast them alive.

But I knew it would not happen.

The rain started coming down harder than ever as Burt Baker dragged me to the Well. It felt like needles lashing my face and sounded like the roar of a phantom lion in the trees around us.

"Please don't do this," I cried. "Please . . ."

"I want you to stay quiet," said Sheriff Baker.

At last we stood above that deep, dark hole in the ground. The sound of the storm swirled about within the Well like a ghostly voice calling out to me from the depths of the earth, crooning some forlorn midnight song.

Henry finished off his Coke, tossed the bottle over his shoulder, and it thumped up against the Old Shack.

"What the fuck are you doing?" the sheriff asked his son.

"What?"

"Are you really that *stupid*, Henry? We don't want anybody to know we've been here."

Henry looked hurt. "Oh. Yeah."

"Don't just stand there. Pick it up!"

Henry rolled his eyes, did as he was told. He stared at the bottle as if it were his own severed hand as he rejoined us by the Well. He looked pale.

The rain pelted down upon us like hail.

The sheriff took a deep breath. "Okay. Remember. This is for the best."

"I know." Henry's voice cracked as he said it. His left hand clenched and unclenched several times until he shoved it into his pocket self-consciously.

Sheriff Baker turned back to me.

"I'm sorry, son," he said. He resembled a father

about to discipline a misbehaved toddler, his face cast in a sad *this-is-gonna-hurt-me-more-than-it-hurts-you* expression. The rain dripped off his hat like a miniature waterfall, trickled down his chubby, pock-marked cheeks like a flood of tears. I could smell his sweat, stronger than ever. "You were just in the wrong place at the wrong time. You understand that, don't you?"

I said nothing. Just glared at him, and waited for what was to come.

"I'll take good care of your mama. I promise. All she needs is a good strong man, and she'll make it through this. Her and Dan both will learn to love me just like they loved your father. I know they will."

"Go to hell," I said.

And then I hawked up the fattest, greenest, prize-winning loogie in the history of fat green loogies . . . and I spat that sucker right in Burt Baker's ugly brown face.

My slimy gift to him was instantly gone, washed away by the rain into the leaves at our feet, but it had received the desired effect. Baker's gentle tone turned into a mask of unbridled rage.

His enormous hands went around my throat. And began to squeeze . . .

"Why, you little piece of shit . . ."

I fought for air. Tried to pry his hands away. But his arms were like stone. His fingers were like steel.

"Little fucker . . ."

Henry took a tentative step forward, reached out to his father. "Dad, wait—"

"Shut up, Henry," Baker said. His teeth were bared, his nostrils flared. His breaths burst in and out of him, explosive, like steam against my forehead. "This is it. *This is it!*"

Explosions of color flashed before my eyes. The

night grew darker. Blacker. The rain seemed to turn orange and white, like scalding hot embers falling from the heavens.

I felt my life ebbing away.

"Daddy, no!" Henry shouted.

Baker continued to squeeze. I grabbed a handful of his shirt, heard something rip, and his badge clattered down into the Well.

"Dad! No! Stop!"

Suddenly Henry Baker was between us. His hands were on his father's shoulders, pushing the sheriff off me.

The sheriff growled, tried to squeeze even harder, but finally let go of me.

He stumbled back, slid in the mud. Caught himself. Looked surprised, as if he'd just been shot.

I collapsed against the jagged rock walls of the Well, breathed again. Sweet, delicious oxygen. My chest rose and fell, rose and fell. I rubbed at my raw, red throat. Coughing. Wheezing. I could still feel the phantom sensation of his hands choking the life out of me . . . squeezing . . . crushing my windpipe. . . .

Burt Baker glared at his son. For those next few minutes, at least, it was as if he had forgotten about me entirely.

"Why, you unappreciative little prick."

"N-no, Daddy, it's not that . . . I just . . . I don't know if this is right. . . ."

"Don't know if it's *right?*"

"He's . . . h-he's j-just a kid. . . ."

"Everything I do," the sheriff said, "everything I've always done . . . has been for you. *You*, Henry! I put my career—my *life*—on the line for you, boy. How dare you fucking disrespect me like this."

"N-no," Henry said. "I didn't mean to . . . Daddy, look—"

"You shut your fuckin' mouth. You're the one who got us into this mess. Now I have to fuckin' deal with it."

"I just . . . I'm so confused . . . I don't know if I want to go on like this anymore . . . maybe we should just—"

"Maybe we should what? Turn ourselves in? We've been through this already, Henry! They all think Mooney killed that girl. You wanna jerk the rug out from under the whole town, see them turn on us like they turned on that nigger?"

"I don't know!" Henry cried, clenching and unclenching his fists again and again and again. "I . . . I'm confused, Dad. I don't know *what* I want anymore. B-But I don't . . . I d-don't think I want this. He's just a k-kid."

"Well, you don't have a fucking choice," the sheriff shouted. His voice echoed through the forest grove. Spittle flew from his mouth into the rain. "I was there for you when you had nowhere else to turn. When you let that fuckin' stumpy-ass dick of yours get you in trouble again. I made everything okay for you. Now you're gonna question my decisions? You're gonna walk away from me when I need you the most?"

"Maybe we were wrong," said Henry. "Maybe I should have just . . . taken my punishment like a man. First Mike, then the nigger. Now a little *kid?* It was never supposed to go this far, Dad."

"This isn't the time or place for second thoughts."

"M-maybe it's not too late to m-make it all right, Dad. Now. For once."

"Get over here."

"No," Henry said.

"What did you just say to me?"

"No, Dad. I can't do this."

Sheriff Burt Baker's bellow filled the night, echoed

337

through the grove like the voice of Satan himself:"By God, boy, you will do as I say or I'll throw you down in that goddamn well with him!"

Henry shook his head, started biting at his nails again.

"Fuck you, then. Pussy. I always knew you were a whiny little faggot. I'm doing this. You just stay the fuck out of my way."

The sheriff lumbered toward me. His boots made soft farting noises in the mud.

He pushed Henry aside.

"Come here, you."

I gasped, scrambled away from him. Putting the Well between us.

"Kyle." He snarled at me, unsnapped his holster and went for his gun. "Don't make me have to tell you twice. . . ."

And that's when Henry slammed his Coca-Cola bottle, hard, across the right side of his father's skull.

It didn't break. Just made a sound like someone hitting an old hollow tree with a baseball bat.

"Ungbakgh?" said Sheriff Baker, and he fell face-first into the mud and wet leaves beside the Well.

"I'm sorry, Daddy!" Henry bawled over the sounds of the wind and the rain.

Then he said the same thing to me:"I'm sorry."

I could only stare at him, speechless.

"I never meant for all this to happen," Henry said. His long black hair hung in his eyes, and he trembled all over like a man in the throes of hypothermia. "I want t-to get help. I want to make everything r-right."

I said nothing, just stared at the prone form of Sheriff Burt Baker before me.

"B-but he would never let me."

I rubbed at my throat again, nodded slowly, understanding so much more than he could ever know.

"Go home," Henry said. "Get out of here—"

I do not know how I did not see him getting up. But he did. Suddenly Burt Baker was on his feet—staggering, wobbling like a man who has had too much to drink, but on his feet nonetheless. The side of his head was bleeding. He lunged for his son, growling like a wild animal, his enormous brown hands hooked into claws. . . .

"You fucking piece of shit!" the sheriff roared. Thunder boomed in the sky overhead, and the sounds commingled like an explosion in the deep, dark heart of Midnight. "After everything I did for you! You turn on me!"

He fell upon Henry, and his hands gripped the young man's skinny throat.

"I'll . . . *kill* . . . you. . . ."

"Please—" Henry fought for air. "Dad-deee . . . nuh-ooo . . ."

His eyes pleaded with me.

I pounced upon that Coca-Cola bottle on the ground.

Picked it up.

Swung it at the sheriff, as hard as I could.

It bounced off his jaw, spun away into the darkness like a skinny green bird felled by a hunter's bullet. Landed with a soft *rustle-thud* in a bed of dead leaves somewhere off to my right.

The sheriff let go of Henry, turned to me.

"Oh, no," I said.

Sheriff Baker said, "You . . ."

And Henry rushed his father from behind.

The urgency in Henry's eyes told me what I needed to do. This was our only chance. As Henry shoved his father up against the shiny rock walls of the Well, trying to tip him over, I grabbed a handful of the sheriff's crotch. Burt Baker howled like a wolf, fighting us with every ounce of strength he had left. His fist collided with my left temple—once, twice, like a freight train. I heard a crunch as he punched his son in the face, and bright red blood began to stream from Henry's nose like rusty water from an ancient faucet. Somehow the sheriff's hand made it down to his holster. He got out his gun, but dropped it. And finally he lost his balance. He floundered, waving his arms like a big kid trying to teach us smaller children how to make snow angels, as the top half of his body teetered precariously over the edge. His hand slid down the sleeve of Henry's wet leather jacket with a short, audible squeak as he made one last grasp for something—anything—to hold on to. And then . . .

"Sweet Jesus," said the sheriff.

Headfirst he went, into the Well.

His girlish scream seemed to last forever as he plunged to what might have been the very center of the earth.

The sound he made when he hit the bottom reminded me of a sack full of wet clothes colliding into a brick wall.

"Jesus," Henry said. "Oh, Jesus, what have I done . . . ?"

I watched him stumble to a patch of mud halfway between the Well and the Old Shack. He threw up. Wiped his mouth with the back of one hand. Threw up again.

I peered down into the Well, my heartbeat slowly returning to normal, but I could see nothing in there but the deepest, most impenetrable blackness I had ever known.

I rubbed at my throat, wondered if I would feel

Burt Baker's grip there forever. If I would have ugly, purple, hand-shaped bruises around my neck for the rest of my life.

I realized it had finally stopped raining, though I still imagined I could hear the roar of the storm inside my head after everything that had happened.

"I'm sorry." Henry said, behind me.

I turned to him. Froze when I saw his father's gun in his hand.

"Henry, no—"

"Don't worry," he said. "It's not for you."

He brought it up, pointed it at his own temple.

I gnashed my teeth, looked away toward town.

There was a sound like a muscle car backfiring behind me, and Henry Baker slumped to the cold wet ground in my peripheral vision.

I stood there, not moving, for a very long time.

I could still hear the echo of the gunshot, reverberating against the Blue Ridge Mountains on the other side of Midnight. Like distant explosions every few seconds.

And then I heard *him*. Down in the Well.

I gasped.

"Help me," Burt Baker called out, his voice swirling 'round and 'round down in there, echoing up from the subterranean depths of the Well like the pleas of a hundred phantoms all sharing his deep Southern accent. "Please . . . s-somebody . . . get me the fuck out of here. . . ."

My heart skipped a beat. Maybe even two or three.

I couldn't believe it.

He was still alive.

"Hey!" Sheriff Burt Baker called out, his voice so distant and unreal. "Somebody . . . anybody . . . please! I think my legs are broken!"

Slowly, then, I began to walk toward home, search-

341

ing inside myself for the sense of closure that I knew should have come by now but probably never would.

The night smelled of earthworms and pine trees. Somewhere in the distance, perhaps as far as several counties away, lightning glowed and dimmed sporadically, like dying fluorescents. Thunder rumbled in the east. But it was a harmless, pitiful sound. So far away.

"Help me!" Baker's voice grew fainter down in the Well. "Please . . . my legs are broken . . . can anybody hear me? Oh, God, somebody, please, for Chrissake fuckin' *help me!*"

I shivered as I walked. My teeth chattered like castanets.

But not because of the cold.

August 20

Chapter Thirty-eight

POLK COUNTY SHERIFF ARRESTED FOR MURDER
STATE POLICE: MAY FACE ADDITIONAL CHARGES

Early Monday morning State Police Captain Andrew Maher arrested Polk County Sheriff Burt L. Baker for the murder of 16-year-old Cassandra Belle Rourke, whose body was found floating in Midnight's Snake River on August 6.

Captain Maher also speculated that Baker could face additional murder charges by the end of the week, though he declined to comment further.

While acting as sheriff of Polk County, Baker arrested Calvin Tremaine Mooney, for the murder of Cassandra "Cassie" Rourke. Mooney was killed several days later by a vigilante gang after escaping from the sheriff's custody. An investigation into that murder is also pending.

According to Captain Maher, there "is no doubt" that Baker will face indictment for his alleged crime, as there is one eyewitness—an unidentified Polk County minor—who has agreed to testify when the case goes to trial.

Fred "Tex" Irvine has agreed to act as temporary sheriff at Mayor Hiram Bentley's request until further notice. Irvine was Sheriff of Polk County from 1937 until 1975.

Epilogue

Hardly a day goes by when I don't reminisce on the things that happened in Midnight, North Carolina, during those two dark, wet weeks in 1977. Especially when the thunder rumbles outside my modest home, and the rain lashes at my windows like the memories of those times batting at the corners of my mind.

I still think about Cassandra Belle Rourke.

I think about Deputy Mike Linder. And Calvin Mooney, the man we all called "Rooster."

And, of course, I think about my unborn niece or nephew. The baby who died inside Cassie Rourke that night in the Snake River Woods. I mourn for a life no one knew existed save for the dead girl, my mother, my brother, and me.

I think about Burt Baker, too. I think about him a lot.

For a while Baker was my own personal boogey-man. The khaki-clad monster in my closet. The devil in my dreams.

347

I am glad to say, however, that he did stop visiting my nightmares. Eventually.

On December 12, 1977, at approximately three o' clock in the afternoon, a jury of five men and seven women found former Polk County Sheriff Burt Baker guilty on two counts of second-degree murder and one count of aggravated assault on a minor. The trial lasted nearly eight weeks, but in the case of *The State of North Carolina v. Burt Leroy Baker* the jury deliberated all of twenty minutes before making its decision.

According to those in the know, it was the testimony of one twelve-year-old boy that proved Burt Baker guilty beyond all reasonable doubt.

That'd be me.

For his crimes, Baker was sentenced to forty-seven years in prison.

He barely served a third of that, however.

On New Year's Day, 1993, about six months before his first parole hearing, Burt Baker was killed in a fight with another inmate. A man twice his size, from what I heard. Baker's neck was broken in the scuffle, as the story went, and he died instantly.

In some twisted, vindictive way, I suppose I should have been elated when I learned of my old enemy's demise—it could certainly be argued that he got what was coming to him, albeit a decade and a half too late. But when I heard the news I only felt a dull sort of hollowness inside. A numb sense of tardy resolution that depressed me more than anything. It did not matter by then anyway. . . .

Cassie Rourke was still dead, even after her murderer was gone. As was her unborn baby.

Deputy Mike Linder did not magically rise from the grave the second his old friend ceased to exist.

As for Calvin Mooney, he still lies buried in a weedy, unmarked plot somewhere in the old black cemetery out near Jefferson Circle.

Speaking of the man we called Rooster, I should mention what happened to the person who took his life in a misguided attempt at vigilante justice. Several days after Burt Baker's arrest, Cassie Rourke's father confessed that *he* had been the one who shot Calvin Mooney on the night of August 19. When several eyewitnesses came forward to corroborate his story (not through any moral obligation, mind you, but to protect their own sorry skins—said eyewitnesses had been part of the very redneck mob that prowled the streets of Midnight along with Mr. Rourke, searching for Calvin Mooney with mouths full of tobacco, rotgut whiskey, and an endless repertoire of racial slurs), Cassie Rourke's father was charged with murder. Ultimately he pled guilty to voluntary manslaughter, received a sentence of four years in prison, but served only eleven months for his crime.

Shortly after Clinton Rourke's release from the Polk County Correctional Facility in the fall of '78, his wife Bonnie left him for another man. At least, that's the story I got from my hometown's eager gossipmongers. Supposedly Rourke owns a construction company somewhere in West Virginia now, and he has also since remarried.

Brian Rourke, Cassie's little brother, still lives in Midnight. In fact, he teaches sixth-grade Remedial English at Midnight Middle School, and is a soccer coach at the local 4-H camp.

My big brother Dan and I eventually grew apart, as siblings will do as time passes. I never thought that could happen—would have cried for hours on end when I was young if I'd thought such a thing was possible—but I should have known it was inevitable. By the time Dan began his third year at FSU, and I started high school, I had long ago accepted the fact that we would never share the things we had once shared.

We were both different people. We had been for quite some time. We were traveling our separate ways. And there was no going back.

When I was twenty years old and a sophomore in college myself, Dan moved to Seattle, where he got a job working for Microsoft. He played a little basketball in college, as everyone had expected, but he never had much of a desire to take it to the professional level. By the time he graduated, he was sick of it. Wanted to expand his mind, he said, because athletes cannot stay young and athletic forever.

I don't fault him for it. Dan is currently bringing home somewhere in the vicinity of a hundred thousand dollars a year, and that's after taxes. He married a beautiful Hawaiian lady named Renee about ten years ago, and they have one son, Daniel Emmett Mackey III. I would say my brother has done well for himself, even if he chose not to go on and play for the Lakers or the Bulls.

Dan and I still speak, but only once or twice a year. In fact, it's his turn to call now. Has been for the last two or three months, but I've heard nothing out of him.

I'm not too worried about it, though. Dan will call. He always does.

Our mother died in the winter of '94. She was fifty-three years old. I knew it had been a long time coming. When it happened I was surprised only by the fact that she lasted as long as she did. The drinking, of course, was what killed her. It got worse than ever after the truth came out about Sheriff Baker and the way he had betrayed our town. Mom stayed in a perpetual drunken stupor for the next three or four years, and I guess her liver finally couldn't take any more. We watched her go downhill fast, until she gave in and just slipped away.

She's buried beside my father now, in the cemetery behind Trinity First Baptist.

Less than a hundred feet from the grandchild she never wanted.

As for me?

I left Midnight for a little while. As soon as I could, in fact. Three months after I graduated from Gerald R. Stokely High School, I wasted no time at all in packing my bags and—much to Mom's chagrin—I went away to the University of North Carolina for four years with dreams of some day working in journalism.

As soon as I graduated from college, though, I came back.

Why?

Call it an epiphany, if you will. An awakening. At some point as I ventured out of childhood and into the vast, wide realm of manhood I realized it was not Midnight that had changed. It was not my hometown that had shown me so many dark things, so many evil ways of the world.

I loved Midnight. I always had.

One person had ruined that place for me. A man who had sworn to protect and serve the citizens of his community. A man who had betrayed all our trust.

He was the virus. *He* was responsible for tainting my hometown, for causing me to hate it for damn near a decade.

Midnight, I decided, was where I wanted to be. I would run from it no longer.

Shortly after my twenty-fifth birthday, following a campaign that was considered to be more one-sided by the citizens of Midnight than any they had ever seen, I was elected Sheriff of Polk County. The youngest sheriff, in fact, in our fair county's history.

Sometimes I have a hard time believing it myself. But it's true. I honestly cannot cite any single, specific reason why I chose to fill the shoes of the man I once hated with every fiber of my being. Perhaps I wished to assure the citizens of Polk County— even those who had not thought about what happened in years, or were too young to remember Burt Baker's scandalous term in the first place—that such a thing could never happen again. That the respected position of their protector-of-the-peace had *not* been tarnished forever.

Perhaps I wanted to assure myself of that.

It seems to be working so far.

As for the Old Shack, six years ago I went back to that grove in the middle of the Snake River Woods, to that dreary little corner of the world I had once called my Secret Place. I went back not by choice, however. Not because I wanted to. I certainly did not go there to appease any burning desire for nostalgia or to bask in the warm recollections of boyhood wonder.

I revisited my Secret Place, for the first time in twenty years, because it was my job.

Seems a group of white trash entrepreneurs were running a part-time meth lab out there, using the Old Shack as a place to cook up their stash without any worry of ever being caught. They used the Well to hide their merchandise between visits to the Old Shack, keeping their Schedule II goods in small steel boxes they could raise and lower into the depths of the earth as needed upon long black cords with magnets on the end. Sure, it was clever, but practical ingenious is far from a valid cause for clemency. After staking the place out for several weeks, my deputy—a young man by the name of Roy Schifford, whose grandmother had been the meanest old crone ever to walk the aisles of the Midnight Public Library—busted the place and arrested six gentlemen who are now serving time in the very prison where Burt Baker resided until his death in '93.

Two weeks after they were convicted, with the help of a demolition company owned by a distant cousin, I had the Old Shack torn to the ground.

The Well, too. After it was destroyed it was filled in with gravel and several truckloads of thick red clay, to prevent anyone from stumbling into that deep black hole in the forest floor.

I used the mossy gray rocks that once formed the exterior walls of the Well to build my fiancée a fancy flowerbed.

It felt good, doing that. As if I have to tell you. Some might call it catharsis.

I can't believe I almost forgot to mention Burner!

Yes, he's still around, believe it or not. Six months ago I had my old blue bicycle fully restored over at Darnell's Bike Shop on Tenth Street. It wasn't cheap, but I didn't mind. It was worth every penny just to see Burner back in all his glory.

I gave the new and improved Burner—or "Version 2.0," as I like to call him—to my oldest son for his seventh birthday.

My, how the kid beamed. I don't know who was happier, little Calvin or me.

Then again, maybe I do.

* * *

I don't think I ever want to leave Midnight, insane as it sounds.

Maybe one day I will. Because nothing ever stays the same. Things change. People change. My wife, Charlene, is living proof of that.

We never know where the roads of life will take us. We just find out when we get there.

For now, despite everything that happened in Midnight when I was a boy, I believe I am exactly where I want to be.

I have come home. I am content.

Even if the midnight rain never seems to cease, even to this day.

JOEL ROSS
EYE FOR AN EYE

Suzanne "Scorch" Amerce was an honor student before her sister was murdered by a female street gang. Scorch hit the streets on a rampage that almost annihilated the gang, but it got her arrested and sent away. That was eight years ago. Now Scorch has escaped. The leader of the gang is still alive and Scorch wants to change that.

The one man who might be able to find Scorch and stop her bloodthirsty hunt is Eric, her prison therapist. Will he be able to stand by and let Scorch exact her deadly vengeance? Or will he risk his life to side with the detective who needs so badly to bring Scorch back in? Either way, lives hang in the balance. And Eric knows he has to decide soon. . . .

ABDUCTED

BRIAN PINKERTON

Just a second. That was all it took. In that second Anita Sherwood sees the face of the young boy in the window of the bus as it stops at the curb—and she knows it is her son. The son who had been kidnapped two years before. The son who had never been found and who had been declared legally dead.

But now her son is alive. Anita knows it in her heart. She is certain that the boy is her son, but how can she get anyone to believe her? She'd given the police leads before that ended up going nowhere, so they're not exactly eager to waste much time on another dead end on a dead case. It's going to be up to Anita, and she'll stop at nothing to get her son back.

THE CRIMINALIST

WILLIAM RELLING JR.

Detective Rachel Siegel is a twelve-year veteran of the San Patricio Sheriff's Department. But she's never seen anything like the handiwork of the Pied Piper, the vicious serial killer who's been terrifying that part of California for months. Because she's the best at what she does, it's now her job to catch this maniac—but she has very personal reasons, too, for wanting him stopped

Kenneth Bennett works for the Department of Neuropsychiatry at St. Louis's Washington University. There's something special about the Pied Piper case that draws Bennett almost against his will to the west coast. He has no choice but to help Siegel in her frantic search—even if it gets both of them killed in the process.

- -

DOUGLAS CLEGG

THE HOUR BEFORE DARK

When Nemo Raglan's father is murdered in one of the most vicious killings of recent years, Nemo must return to the New England island he thought he had escaped for good, Burnley Island. But this murder was no crime of human ferocity. What butchered Nemo's father may in fact be something far more terrifying—something Nemo and his younger brother and sister have known since they were children.

As Nemo unravels the mysteries of his past and a terrible night of his childhood, he witnesses something unimaginable... and sees the true face of evil ... while Burnley Island comes to know the unspeakable horror that grows in the darkness.

Dorchester Publishing Co., Inc.
P.O. Box 6640
Wayne, PA 19087-8640

_____5142-7
$6.99 US/$8.99 CAN

Please add $2.50 for shipping and handling for the first book and $.75 for each additional book. NY and PA residents, add appropriate sales tax. No cash, stamps, or CODs. Canadian orders require $2.00 for shipping and handling and must be paid in U.S. dollars. Prices and availability subject to change. **Payment must accompany all orders.**

Name: _____

Address: _____

City: _____ State:_____ Zip: _____

E-mail: _____

I have enclosed $_____ in payment for the checked book(s).

For more information on these books, check out our website at www.dorchesterpub.com.
_____ *Please send me a free catalog.*